Barbara Tifft Blakey

The Angel of Second Street

Enduring Hope

Book One

Print ISBN 979-8-89151-112-5
Adobe Digital Edition (.epub) 979-8-89151-113-2

All scripture quotations, unless otherwise noted, are taken from the King James Version of the Bible.

This book is a work of fiction. Names, characters, places, and incidents are either products of the author's imagination or used fictitiously. Any similarity to actual people, organizations, and/or events is purely coincidental.

Published by Barbour Publishing, Inc., 1810 Barbour Drive, Uhrichsville, Ohio 44683, www.barbourbooks.com

Our mission is to inspire the world with the life-changing message of the Bible.

Printed in the United States of America.

Praise for *The Angel of Second Street*

It's love at first sight for Ida Dempsey and Blaine Prescott, who share a deep faith and a desire to help others. But nothing is easy for this couple as they face challenge after challenge in pursuing a future together in their home town of Eureka, nestled between the Redwoods and the Pacific. Barbara Tifft Blakey deftly weaves historical events, a family secret, and forbidden love, tying all the threads together in a delightful story of faith, love, and grace. *The Angel of Second Street* is a must for fans of historical fiction!

–Leslie Gould, bestselling author of *The Shop Down the Lane*

The Angel of Second Street is a well written book, filled with diverse characters that were likeable and sympathetic to the reader. The plot was believable and drew me in from page one. The setting was painted so vividly I could picture the Victorian homes, smell the saltwater, and hear the clanging of the streetcars. There were more than a few shocking plot twists that kept me turning pages well into the night, but Ms. Blakey skillfully tied everything together and crafted a satisfying and happy ending.

–Debby Lee, 2024 Selah Awards nominee,
author of *Beneath a Peaceful Moon, Heart of Endurance,*
and *Tailed Sweethearts* from the *Sew in Love* collection

The Angel of Second Street exposes the darker side of Chinese immigration in Eureka, California, in the mid 1800s. Ida Dempsey's one desire to serve God takes her to Second Street where the "working women" make their homes. Blakey tells a tale that is both raw and sweet. The love story between Ida and Blaine is woven through the fabric of the conventions expected of a young woman in that era. But Ida's desire to please the Lord causes her to press against the expectations of society to be a wife and mother to the exclusion of all else. This book accurately tells how the Chinese population in Eureka was forcibly expelled from the city. It shows how prejudice can influence decisions with lasting consequences.

–Jane Daly, author of the *Broken* series and *Where is my Sister*

In The Angel of Second Street, Barbara Tifft Blakey takes readers on a journey to the streets of Eureka in the mid-1800s, where a delightful protagonist fights to share the gospel with Chinese immigrants and ladies of the night. Single and carefree, Ida dismisses the censure of others while exhibiting the love of Jesus as she plays with children, tosses a stick to a dog, and tries to help the workers of Second Street. Blaine, who prayed to God for the right woman to love, encourages her missions while grappling to navigate tensions at home and in business. The author weaves an engaging fictional story around factual history that nobody should forget.

–Julie McDonald Zander, person historian, newspaper columnist, and author of *The Reluctant Pioneer*

DEDICATION

For my firstborn child, Terry Lee Blakey Jr.,
who joined the angels September 8, 2024.

CHAPTER 1

Saturday, July 19, 1884, Eureka, California

Ida Dempsey pinned her bonnet on and skipped down the staircase, eager to enjoy the church picnic among the redwoods. It was a perfect sunny day for such an outing. She bobbed into the kitchen where Qui Shau prepared food for the hamper.

"Come on, Qui," Ida's older cousin, Wallace, begged. "Just one piece." He eyed the three-layer chocolate cake then winked at Ida. "Shouldn't someone taste it to make sure it's up to snuff?"

Qui slapped his hand. "No, you wait." As her lips drew thin, a twinkle remained in her eyes. She pointed toward the door. "Go! You get out my kitchen."

Wallace grabbed a cookie. "Thanks, Qui." The door banged shut behind him.

"He trouble." The cook put a shiny metal lid over the cake and fastened it to the plate.

"Yes, he is," Ida agreed. "But we love him all the same."

"Who do we love?" Aunt Ruth bustled into the kitchen, pulling on her gloves.

"Wallace. He was pestering Qui for sweets." Ida kissed her aunt on the cheek. "I'm excited about the picnic. Are we ready to go?"

"Your uncle hasn't returned yet. He had some business this morning but promised he'd be back early." Aunt Ruth peeked into the hamper. "Qui, I believe you've outdone yourself."

Ida breathed in the aroma of fried chicken, baked beans, freshly made yeast rolls, and, of course, the chocolate cake. A sudden inspiration hit her. "Aunt Ruth, Qui should come too. We can squish together in the carriage.

She made this bounty—why shouldn't she enjoy it with us?"

"Oh, missy, no." Eyes wide, Qui threw up her hands. "I have plenty work here."

"Nonsense." Ida turned to her aunt. "Tell her she's to come with us."

Aunt Ruth shook her head. "Dear, sweet Ida, I don't know where these notions of yours come from." She linked her arm with Ida's. "I think I hear your uncle Harvey."

When they stepped outside, Wallace already sat in the front seat of the surrey, grinning broadly. "Father said I could drive."

"After you assist your mother and cousin into the carriage." Ida's uncle removed an ornate watch from his vest pocket, flipped open the cover, frowned, and replaced it. "I've got to be back for a meeting this afternoon, so we will have to depart promptly at three o'clock."

"Oh, Uncle Harvey, that's so early." Ida pursed her lips into a little pout. "We'll be the first to leave."

"And the last to arrive if we don't get started." Wallace jumped down and helped his mother into the carriage.

Uncle Harvey guided Ida to her seat. "I'm sorry, dear girl, it can't be helped. If it distresses you, you may remain home."

Shame warmed Ida's neck and face. "I'm sorry. Your business is important, and I don't mean to be selfish."

"Apology accepted." Uncle Harvey took the hamper and cake carrier from Qui, who was waiting near the door. He placed them on the floor of the surrey, then sat next to his son.

Wallace chucked to the horses. "Walk on."

"Yes, Father, I'll be there." Blaine Prescott handed his mother into the brougham coach. "I've a few things to do, but I'll arrive before the croquet game begins."

"See that you do." Mr. Prescott closed the coach door.

Mrs. Prescott addressed Blaine through the carriage window. "We are eager for you to meet important people. It is imperative you make a good impression."

"You mean important people in the form of eligible young ladies, I assume?"

His father leaned forward, making eye contact with Blaine. "I didn't send you to Santa Clara University so you could fritter away your life. Now that you've graduated, it's time you married."

Blaine dropped his gaze to the ground, then looked back up. "I do understand, Father, and I'm willing. I hope you understand I won't be pressured into a match that doesn't suit me." Showing his parents proper deference and maintaining his own self-respect was a difficult dance.

His father scowled and chucked to the horses to walk on.

Blaine watched the carriage leave, then turned back to the house.

Pratt, their butler, closed the door behind him. "May I take your coat, sir?"

"Thank you, no, I'm leaving in a moment." Blaine paused, chewing his bottom lip as he thought. Pratt had served his family as long as he could remember, one of the few constants in a household that changed cooks and housemaids and grooms almost as often as the storms that blew in from the Pacific Ocean. Blaine knew him to be an extraordinary man, a person of integrity and wisdom. At the moment, he coveted an advisor, someone other than his father. "Pratt, might I impose on your good judgment?"

"I am at your service, sir."

"I'm attending a picnic at which there will be a number of eligible young women."

"Yes, sir."

"I've chosen not to arrive with my parents—to come on my own—so I might have a few moments to observe without drawing anyone's attention."

"Very good, sir."

"My parents are eager for me to meet certain daughters and their fathers."

"And you are not, sir?"

"Actually, I've been praying that God would direct my steps to find the right young lady. One of His choosing. I am quite willing to fall in love."

"Excellent. And how may I assist you?"

"I'm averse to choosing anyone based solely on my father's approval." Blaine paced the width of the foyer. "You know the families, Pratt. Is there a special young woman I should take note of? One that would please my father—and myself?"

Pratt's eyebrows shot up. "Excuse me, sir. Just so I don't misunderstand, you are asking my advice regarding a potential wife?"

Blaine stopped pacing and faced the butler. "I know it seems odd, actually quite odd, but yes."

"I assure you the young women in your parents' circle of friends appear virtuous and accomplished. I know nothing ill of any of them." The butler turned as if to leave the foyer, then stopped as Blaine continued.

"Yes, Pratt, yes. Virtuous and accomplished are important. But I don't want an ordinary life. My father intends I join him in the family business, and I will." Blaine walked to the window and looked at the blue sky, painted here and there with wispy clouds. "I want to serve my God faithfully and boldly. I'll do that as a businessman, but it can't be limited to that. I want to make a difference in Eureka, in all of Humboldt County, maybe all of California." He turned from the window. "And I want a wife driven by the same desires."

"I see, sir. You want me to recommend a lady of class who is also a woman of strong faith."

"Yes, yes, Pratt."

"I'm sorry, sir, no one comes to mind. I suggest you continue to pray for God's guidance and trust He will lead you."

"You are right, of course." Blaine extended his hand. "Thank you, Pratt."

The butler hesitated before grasping the proffered hand to shake.

Blaine noticed his confusion. "I'm not that keen on distinction between classes. I appreciate your friendship as I might any man's."

"Yes, sir. However, your father wouldn't approve of such familiarity."

"Hmmm. There is that."

Mounted on Prince, Blaine joined the masses heading toward the redwoods. It appeared all of Eureka intended to take part in the picnic sponsored by the community's churches. As the path clogged with carriages, he chose trails too narrow for the buggies.

The air smelled musty—a combination of damp earth and ferns with a hint of decaying cedar. Towering trees blocked much of the sunlight. Shade-loving ferns lined the path, and mushrooms adorned fallen logs. Blaine eased Prince from a canter to a slow lope as he succumbed to the forest's spell. Surely God Himself inhabited this place.

As he neared the picnic site, children's shouts and laughter fused with adult voices disturbed the serene quiet. Tantalizing food aromas mingled together and overpowered the forest smells. Blaine's stomach growled. What were the odds he could snag a chicken leg before the dinner bell?

He tied Prince with the other horses and meandered toward the laden tables. Soon he'd make his presence known to his parents, or at least to his father, but for the moment he enjoyed the anonymity. He'd attended boarding schools in San Francisco for his early education, coming home only for holidays and the summer break. Then the past four years he'd stayed at the university except for brief visits at Christmas. Summers had been spent in San Francisco, learning bookkeeping from his father's friend. He knew almost no one, and, as he'd told Pratt, he preferred to gain a few first impressions before being paraded about as one of the town's eligible bachelors.

A group of children played ring-around-the-rosy between him and the tables. A young woman played with the children as if she were one of them; her laughter mingled with theirs in an expression of sheer delight. It seemed not to matter that her bonnet sat askew or that most of the other young ladies preferred croquet to rambunctious childish games.

Did she not see the critical glances thrown her way by the others? Could she not perceive they whispered about her? Perhaps she didn't care. She was beautiful, as were the women scorning her, but she possessed another quality. Confidence without snobbery. Her whole being spoke innocence and purity.

"Is she the one, heavenly Father?" Blaine scoffed at himself. To think the first woman he saw would be the one he sought bordered on ridiculous.

Suddenly she looked away from the children and their game, and her gaze met his. He couldn't divert his eyes from her face, as if some force held him captive. In a twinkling, her smile wrapped itself around his heart.

CHAPTER 2

Ida dropped the little girl's hand she held. The silly song died on her lips. Who was this bold young man daring to stare at her as if he could gobble her up? Well, if he thought he could intimidate her, he was mistaken. She'd play with the children if she wanted to, and if he or anyone else didn't like it, they could take their scornful stares and jump in the river.

Although, on second thought, his gaze appeared anything but scornful. Some might describe him as handsome, with penetrating steel-blue eyes, a strong, square jaw, and thick dark curly hair—if one liked that sort of thing. Which Ida suddenly realized she did.

A little one tugged on her arm, and she rejoined the circle, her skirts swaying as she skipped with the group of youngsters. She sang with them, "We all fall down," and tumbled onto the grass in a manner most undignified. Her behavior didn't frighten the stranger away, as she thought it might. He approached, removing his hat.

"Most impressive." He extended his hand to help her rise.

For the briefest moment, Ida ignored the proffered hand, but his unpretentious smile won her over. "Thank you." Once on her feet, she adjusted her bonnet. "Impressive, you say. May I ask what you most enjoyed? The singing? The dancing? The tumbling?"

"I must confess, none of the above." He nodded toward a small cluster of young ladies glowering in their direction. "I'm astounded you are alive, considering the daggers being hurled your way."

Ida glanced at the onlookers, then met the stranger's eyes. "I hadn't noticed." She lifted her chin slightly. "That's a lie. I did notice. It inspired me to sing a bit louder and fall a bit less gracefully." She giggled at the lively children dancing around her.

"More, more," they cried.

Ida patted the head of the child nearest her. "Not now. I'll join you again later."

"Oh, don't let me interrupt your fun." The stranger's eyes sparkled.

"Will you join us in 'London Bridge'?" Ida's inner being laughed. If he joined in the fun, if he dared to brave the censure of the lovely young ladies scowling at her, she'd declare herself in love forever.

"I believe introductions are in order, first."

"Oh dear." Ida feigned a pout. "I perceive you are a gentleman, and on the odd chance that you entertain any doubts, I am most definitely a lady. Therefore, we must have a third party introduce us. Do you know little Benny? He might do the trick if we don't mind his lisp and tell him exactly what to say."

How she enjoyed this unexpected pleasure. She found herself wishing all the others would go away so she might get to know this intriguing man by herself.

Then again, what would be the fun in that?

From the corner of her eye, she saw Mrs. Prescott approach. Before the woman drew near, Ida lowered her voice so only the stranger could hear. "Don't look behind you. She knows I've seen her, but it's not too late for you. Run! You can still escape. Go, quickly!"

Despite the warning, the stranger turned. "Hello, Mother."

His mother was pinched-faced Mrs. Prescott? And she had encouraged him to run as if a cougar were about to pounce. Great. Her face flushed. She couldn't look at him.

"Where have you been? I've looked everywhere. People are waiting to meet you."

"Yes, Mother, you are right. Let's not delay the introductions. Will you begin with this lovely young lady?"

The cheeks of the "lovely young lady" showed the color of a California poppy. Blaine struggled not to laugh aloud. Her warning to escape would be great fodder to tease her with later when they were alone. He'd make sure they had time alone.

Mrs. Prescott looked Ida up and down, pointedly scowling at a grass stain near the hem of her frock. "Yes, of course. This is Miss Ida Dempsey. Her uncle, Mr. Harvey Dempsey, owns a sawmill. Mrs. Ruth Dempsey, her aunt, is a member of my Wednesday afternoon whist club."

Mrs. Prescott's gaze roamed over the picnic site. "Ida, may I present my son, Mr. Blaine Prescott. He is newly returned after graduating college. Now, if you'll excuse us, I have *important* people waiting to meet him." She hooked her elbow around Blaine's arm.

Like a redwood rooted firmly in the ground, Blaine did not move. He would honor his parents and meet Eureka's socialites—in a little while. Right now, he intended to get better acquainted with Miss Ida Dempsey. "Yes, Mother. In a minute or two." He hoped she'd strut off, but she pursed her lips and kept her arm linked through his.

She obviously disapproved of Ida. He'd have to ask Pratt if he knew anything objectionable about the young lady. Until then, he was quite ready to be infatuated with the unassuming beauty at his side. "So Miss Dempsey is your name, and you live with your aunt and uncle?"

Ida's face had returned to its normal color. "Yes, I've lived with them all my life. And we aren't so formal here as in San Francisco or on the East Coast. Please call me Ida."

"Ida it is—of course, you must call me Blaine." He wanted her to say it. He wanted to hear his name on her lips.

She turned to his mother. "Mrs. Prescott, your front garden is especially beautiful this year. When I walked past yesterday, I thought it looked as enchanting as a fairyland."

"I'll give your compliments to my gardener."

A bit of silence followed, and then Ida again addressed his mother. "I've not made it to the picnic tables yet. I heard a rumor you brought your famous rhubarb-strawberry pie. I think it's everyone's favorite."

"I'll give your compliments to my cook."

Why wouldn't his mother even look at Miss Dempsey? Her rudeness aggrieved Blaine like an itchy mosquito bite. It might be better if he got the other introductions over with now. He could come back to Miss Dempsey—Ida—all the sooner, hopefully alone.

Before he could excuse himself, Ida gestured to a group of young men. "Oh, there's my cousin. I have a message for him from Uncle Harvey. It was nice to meet you, Blaine. Nice to see you again, Mrs. Prescott."

And she was gone. Running across the grass like a mythological nymph. He watched her even as his mother tugged him toward a group of young ladies, all holding lacy parasols and wearing frilly dresses sans grass stains.

"Wallace," Ida called, grateful she had an excuse to flee from the disagreeable Mrs. Prescott.

Ironic that the contrary woman was the mother of Blaine, such an amicable young man. Perhaps at home, away from society, Mrs. Prescott had a sweeter, gentler nature more like Ida's Aunt Ruth. For Blaine's sake, she hoped so.

"What do you want?" Wallace jarred her thoughts.

"Uncle Harvey asked me to remind you that we must be in the carriage at three o'clock, or he'll leave without us."

"I know, I know." Wallace turned away, calling over his shoulder, "If I'm not there, don't worry. I'll find a way home." He skulked off in the direction of his friends.

Ida watched him go, then spun around to see her best friend, Mattie, heading her way. The two were as different as salt and pepper—Ida blond, blue-eyed, petite, and Mattie with raven locks, chocolate eyes, and long legs.

"I've been looking for you." Mattie hugged her. She nodded toward Wallace. "He doesn't look happy. Something wrong?"

Ida sighed. "I think it must be hard to be Wallace."

"Why?"

As the two sat on the sunny hillside, Ida fiddled with a blade of grass. "He's ordered around as though he were still an adolescent. His life has been planned for him since his birth. I don't think any options have ever been discussed."

"In my opinion, he still acts like an adolescent. If he wants to be treated like an adult, he should try acting like one. Why is joining his father at the sawmill distasteful to him? My brothers would jump at an opportunity like that faster than a fish after a water skipper."

"I don't know." Ida picked at the lace on her sleeve. "He's not ambitious, and he hasn't enough to do to keep out of trouble. I think he might be happier if he could make his own choices, if he had something to look forward to."

"In some ways, our lives—yours and mine—are all planned too." Mattie's gaze followed a puffy cloud drifting across the blue sky. "I mean, aren't we supposed to get married, keep house, and have babies?"

"Don't you want to?"

"Yes, I do." Mattie took her friend's hand. "Just not yet."

Ida agreed. Sort of. She wanted marriage and children, but she yearned for more. "Mattie, do you ever pray for a husband?"

"Yes, all the time. I mean, how else am I going to snag a rich one?"

"Oh, I don't care if he's rich or not."

"That's easy for you to say. You've never been poor."

"Mattie, as beautiful as you are, you'll have your pick of men, rich or otherwise."

"I wish I had your confidence." Mattie leaned back on her elbows.

"As much as I'd like a husband someday," said Ida, "I pray for something dearer to me than that."

"What?" Mattie spoke as if nothing could be more important than a husband.

"I want to serve God. I mean, making cakes for a charity sale or quilts for the missionary barrels is fine and good, but I want to talk about Jesus, share His love." Ida's eyes sought Mattie's. She wanted someone to understand. When she had shared her desire with Aunt Ruth, the good woman bristled as if Ida had insulted her. How would missionaries survive without those barrels?

God had opened the eyes of her heart, and everywhere Ida looked she saw hurting people. Even Mrs. Prescott. If one dug deeply enough, Ida believed a wound of some sort would be discovered. And she ached to help. Rich, poor, in between, all seemed burdened. Her soul sensed the hurts and urged her to respond.

She tried to explain. "Sometimes I think we are all of us in these little tippy boats, paddling with all our might upstream. We don't even know why we're paddling or where we're going. We wear ourselves out without knowing why."

"That's a happy thought." Mattie threw a fistful of grass at Ida.

"I mean, I want to make a difference to the paddlers. Maybe if they knew Jesus, they'd know if they're supposed to keep paddling or climb out of the boat. Maybe there wouldn't be so much unspoken desperation."

Mattie stood. "Everybody knows Jesus. At least everyone in Eureka."

She reached out her hand to help Ida rise. “Look, there’s that fellow you were talking to.”

Hand in hand, the two walked down the hill.

“So who is he?” Mattie wiggled her eyebrows in a sort of caterpillar dance. “Will you introduce me?”

CHAPTER 3

Blaine smiled as he neared Ida and her friend. He'd narrowly escaped sharing lunch with the lovely Miss—what was her name? It was undoubtedly rude not to remember; however, none of the half dozen or so ladies he'd been introduced to stood out from each other. Their names and faces jumbled together—not that it was their fault. They couldn't help not being Ida.

"I've been looking for you." He picked up his pace in her direction. "I hoped to ask you to have lunch with me." He nodded at the young lady accompanying Ida. "And your friend as well, of course." He didn't mean it. He hoped the friend would have other plans or feel like a third wheel and excuse herself. He'd like to improve his acquaintance with Ida, alone.

"This is my best friend, Miss Mathilda Reynolds. Mattie, may I introduce Blaine Prescott?"

Mattie curtsied as if in the presence of royalty. "I'm pleased to meet you. We'd love to join you for lunch. And you can call me Mattie." The young woman hooked her arm through his and pulled him toward the food. The gesture unnerved him until he realized it gave him unspoken permission to link his arm with Ida's as well. What was more natural-looking than a gentleman escorting two young ladies to the picnic tables?

He filled his plate with fried chicken, deviled eggs, corn on the cob, and a roll. He wouldn't eat it all, but the plate had to be full, or somebody's grandmother would pronounce him undernourished and add sauerkraut or chili to it—decidedly unromantic foods.

He led Ida and Meg—or was it Maggie? Millie?—to the edge of the meadow. Although not so secluded among the towering redwoods as to raise eyebrows, it wasn't in the center of activities either.

They sat in a circle on the grass, and Ida's friend began to talk. And talk. And talk. To him. Not to Ida also, specifically to him. Not asking questions so in answering he could direct the conversation to include Ida. She related one anecdote after another, to which he could only nod and smile. He noticed Ida's gaze wandering to the little ones playing another game, to the young adults playing croquet, to the picnic tables.

"Mattie," Ida finally interrupted, "you've barely touched your food, and I'm dying for a slice of Qui's chocolate cake. I'm going to be rude and not wait for you."

"Oh, that's okay." Mattie shrugged. "Get one for me too. I'll be right here." She smiled at Blaine.

"I'm ready for dessert too." Blaine sprang to his feet. "We'll be back shortly."

As soon as he reached beyond Mattie's hearing, he blurted, "Your friend? Does she ever stop talking? I mean ever?"

Ida laughed.

Good. He hadn't offended her.

"She talks like that when she's nervous. Really, when you are better acquainted with her, you'll discover she's a dear."

"I want to be better acquainted with *you*."

"Your mother would not approve."

"Miss Dempsey, my mother's opinion matters very much to me. I respect both of my parents, but they don't get to choose my friends. Maybe when I was ten. Not now."

"You want us to be friends?"

He wished he could decipher her smile better. Was she teasing him? "I'd like a chance to find out."

"Me too."

At her words, his pulse raced. "Do we have to go back? Can we take the cake and run?"

"Mr. Prescott, you astonish me. Such an idea." Ida wagged her finger at him, then sobered. "I thought you might be offended by the way I spoke of your mother. I'm sure she is wonderful in many respects and not one to be avoided, as I suggested."

"No apology needed. She can be an intimidating figure. I apologize for her rudeness."

Ida chose a slice of cake for herself and her friend. Blaine helped himself to a piece of their cook's pie, and then they sauntered back toward

Mattie. Finally alone with Ida, he could think of nothing to say. Here he strolled with this intriguing young woman beside him, and he was tongue-tied. To disguise his confusion, he took a bite of pie.

"What did you study at college?"

Oh! She was making small talk. Very nice of her. He should respond. Except what he wanted to talk about, what he wanted to know, were things that mattered, such as what were her beliefs? Did she know Jesus? He swallowed then answered, "I received a business degree, upon my father's urging."

"Not what you wanted?"

"The degree is fine. I hope to be an asset to my father's business, but that's not what's most important to me."

Ida noticed the stares following them and felt their disapproval. It didn't matter, except she didn't know why they censured her. When she played with the children or ate chicken with her fingers, she knew exactly why others looked askance at her, and accepted their judgment. How could walking with a gentleman at an outdoor gathering be considered scandalous or socially improper?

"Mr. Pres—Blaine—what is important to you?" She loved that he was not content to maintain a frivolous conversation, that something solid lay underneath the trifling.

Mattie was in view. She waved, then rose and headed toward them.

Blaine stopped walking. He spoke hurriedly. "It appears we are about to be interrupted. Will you join me for ice cream tomorrow after church? We can talk about life and what's important."

Such intensity in his eyes. A very serious man indeed. Mattie neared. Time to lighten up. "I'd be delighted. Should we ask Mattie to join us? She's particularly fond of ice cream."

"You wouldn't."

At Blaine's pleading expression, Ida suppressed a giggle.

"She wouldn't what?" Mattie accepted the plate of cake. "What wouldn't you do, Ida?"

Ida's gaze connected with his. Time stopped, as if the two of them were the only people in the world. Mattie's voice faded, and she heard it no more. His eyes bored into her heart, leaving her powerless to do anything except search his heart as well. The bond left her breathless.

"Hello! I asked a question." Mattie jolted Ida back to the present.

"I'm sorry, what did you say?"

Mattie's face pinched into a little pout. "I asked what you wouldn't do. Mr. Prescott said something and—oh, never mind."

Mr. Prescott? Who was Mr. Prescott? Of course, Blaine. What was wrong with her? She closed her eyes a moment to recenter herself. "I'm sorry, Mattie. I was distracted."

"I'll say. Can I speak with you a minute? Alone."

Blaine excused himself and headed toward the crowd playing croquet. When he strolled out of earshot, Mattie grasped Ida's arm and squeezed tightly. "What are you doing?"

Ida hesitated. Friends were honest with each other, so she couldn't pretend not to know what Mattie meant. How to respond without risking a rift between herself and her best friend? "You're hurting my arm."

Mattie released her grip. "Sorry."

"Do you like him so much already?" Ida's gaze followed Blaine as he strolled away.

"Well, of course I do. What's not to like?"

"I like him too." Ida drew in a deep breath. Could she add that she thought he liked her as well? That he had invited her for ice cream? That they had shared a moment that connected their hearts? She didn't want to hurt her best friend. The plain truth was Blaine showed interest in her, not Mattie. She could not say those words.

"No, you can't like him," Mattie protested. "You don't need a rich husband, and I do. You said getting married isn't that important to you. You know it is to me."

"For goodness' sake, Mattie. We are only seventeen. There's plenty of time to think about marriage. I said I like him, not that I'm marrying him." Ida's heart melted at the tears in Mattie's eyes. "I'm not going to fight you over a man we've only just met." She hugged her. "Remember, we're best friends."

Mattie sniffed. "Then I can have him? If you're not going to fight over him, I can have him?"

"He's not mine to give or keep." Ida held back the words swimming in her head. Blaine was not a possession to have! She bristled at the idea of Blaine—or any person—being spoken of as property. But she knew what Mattie meant. Her friend wanted her to step out of the picture.

Should she? Or was the real question, could she?

Distracted by the croquet game and the rhubarb-strawberry pie, Blaine took his eyes off Ida. When he looked back, she had disappeared. Mattie smiled and waved. Dare he go to her and ask her friend's whereabouts, or would he be trapped by the garrulous girl? It appeared he had no choice. Mattie strode toward him.

He felt like a mouse in a corner watching the kitchen cat approach. Unlike the mouse, he couldn't dart into a hole for safety. He pasted on a smile as Mattie joined him. "Ah, Miss—" What was her last name? This bordered on absurdity. He'd never had trouble with names before.

"Mattie. Remember, I said you could call me Mattie."

"Yes, of course. Forgive me. So—Mattie—where is Miss Dempsey?"

"She had to leave. How about a game of croquet? What luck. It looks like another round is just beginning. We can join in now."

Blaine endured the longest game of croquet in his life. Conversation was not required of him, as Mattie kept up a constant chatter. He had only to say, "Really?" or "Is that so?" now and then, freeing his attention to scan the area for Ida and to make one bad shot after another. For once, he was thankful to see his mother approach. Interrupting Mattie's monologue, he excused himself and joined her.

Leaving the croquet field allowed him to seek Ida in other places, albeit attached to his mother's arm. She stretched to hiss in his ear. "You've spent entirely too much time with that young woman. What are you thinking?"

"I completely agree, Mother. Thank you for rescuing me."

Apparently pleased with his answer, she slowed her pace and relaxed her hold on his arm.

"Mother, you've introduced me to a good many delightful young ladies. Why don't we sit, just you and I together, and enjoy a cup of tea?"

She beamed at him. "Thank you, Son. I'd enjoy that very much."

He escorted her to a small wrought iron table with two matching chairs. "I'll be right back."

His gaze roamed the picnic area, searching for a glimpse of Ida. She'd vanished like a gnome or fairy into the redwoods. Disappointed he hadn't spotted her, he nodded and smiled his way back to his mother, carrying two teacups and consoling himself that he'd see Miss Dempsey the next day. Except the date hadn't been settled. "After church" was a vague time, and he'd not specified a location. Dare he show up at her home to escort her? He hadn't asked permission to court her.

There'd been that moment, that incredible moment, when their eyes met and he felt she was the one, the only one ever, for him, but he'd not base a lifetime decision on a fleeting enchantment. He yearned to know her better before declaring his intentions to her family.

He sat next to his mother, determined to give her his full attention. It would make her happy and help him put Ida from his mind. He succeeded for barely minutes at a time.

CHAPTER 4

Ida sat beside her aunt on their usual pew, quietly waiting for services to begin as the organist softly played "Nearer my God to Thee." Diffused light pouring in through the stained-glass windows combined with scents of polished wood and burning candles, creating an ethereal ambience. She held a hymnbook in her lace-gloved hands, eager to join the choir in praise.

This coming together with others who loved the Lord gave her joy; however, the steepled church building was not her favorite place to worship. That happened outdoors—sometimes the seashore, sometimes the redwood forest—those settings allowed personal, intimate communion with her Lord.

Typically, she used this interlude with the organist playing hymns softly in the background to reflect on the past week, to prepare her heart and mind for worship. This time, her thoughts lingered on the previous day's picnic. What a day it had been! Frolicking with the children under beautiful blue skies, surrounded by the towering redwoods, eating outdoors from such a bounty of food, sharing conversation with Mattie, meeting Blaine Prescott—there'd never been a day like it!

Perhaps sometime this afternoon she'd see the interesting gentleman again—he'd spoken of ice cream after church. From a heart filled with gratitude, she lifted a prayer of thanksgiving heavenward.

At the organ's crescendo, the congregation rose and joined the choir singing "Rock of Ages," one of Ida's favorite hymns. A rich baritone coming from behind caught her attention—certainly not from any of the Zander family, the usual occupants of that pew. At the conclusion of the song, as Ida regained her seat, she quickly peeked behind her.

Blaine Prescott? She'd never seen him in church before. Considering he'd been away for many years, that didn't surprise her. Didn't his family attend somewhere else, though? What did the Zanders think of a stranger trespassing on their pew?

Ida chided herself for drifting thoughts when she should be focused on the scripture reading. Through much of the service, she fought to rein in her straying attention. Errant mental pictures continually drew her mind to the proposed ice cream engagement.

After the benediction, Ida fidgeted as the organist played the recessional. She was eager to speak with Blaine but held in check by rules of decorum. She sat, fussing with her necklace, until her aunt and uncle rose. Somberly they exited the sanctuary together, then cordially greeted Reverend Huntington on the steps before Ida was finally free to acknowledge the man who had occupied entirely too many of her thoughts for the past hour.

Mattie had him cornered on the sidewalk. As Ida made a beeline for them, Mrs. Bickel stopped her with questions about items for the missionary barrels. Mrs. Alexander joined the conversation, bringing in Mrs. Lee to discuss the next ladies' auxiliary meeting.

When Ida had a chance to glance in Blaine's direction again, he'd been joined by two more young women. Laughter erupted from the group.

How could she escape?

Mrs. Lee touched her arm. "Go along, dear. Join your friends." She nodded toward the group on the sidewalk.

Ida smiled her appreciation and lightly bounded to the group. No one made room for her in the growing circle, not even Mattie. Blaine caught her eye.

Did he just wink at her?

Some men might be flattered by all the female attention. Blaine was not one of them. He had thought to attend services at Ida's church to secure their ice cream date. He hadn't planned on encountering a host of young ladies newly met at the picnic. Shouldn't he remember at least one of their names?

Well, actually, he did remember one.

"Mr. Prescott." A young woman blocking Ida from the circle addressed him. "Mother and Father would love for you to join us for lunch today.

Shall I tell them we'll see you at two?"

"Thank you, that is very kind. However, I have a previous engagement." Blaine backed out of the group. He had no desire to mislead any of the young ladies surrounding him—and the sooner he squelched all this interest in him, the better. He didn't *know* Ida was the one for him, but certainly none of the others were.

Blaine reached his hand toward Ida. "Are you ready, Miss Dempsey?"

An audible gasp sounded from several in the group. Ida's face reddened, and her eyes cast downward. Had he been too bold? This was not going as planned. Why did he think he could show up in a public place and not draw attention?

Mattie stepped forward. "I don't believe Ida is feeling well, Mr. Prescott. But I'd be happy to join you."

How to graciously escape this pickle? *Help me, Ida!*

She lifted her eyes, squared her shoulders, and turned toward her best friend. "Actually, Mattie, I'm quite well." She faced Blaine. "I need to inform Aunt Ruth of our plans."

"I'll accompany you." He offered her his arm, eager to flee the growing discord.

Ida's trembling hand surprised him. His first impression had been a young lady comfortable with herself and her choices. She'd certainly braved the scornful looks thrown while she played with the children at the picnic. Maybe she preferred children to him?

It took only minutes to find her aunt, and then the two of them strolled away. He felt the prying eyes of every meddlesome busybody following them, so he turned at the first corner available to exit out of sight.

Ida began to giggle. The giggles exploded into outright laughter. She stopped walking, placed one hand on her stomach, and with the other covered her mouth. Her eyes watered as they met his. She stuttered, "I'm sorry." The laughs continued to erupt.

He found himself joining her—not quite as boisterously, but without a reason why. "Do you need a drink of water?"

She nodded, made an obvious attempt to suppress more giggles, and failed.

Blaine led her to Wells Drug Store on the corner of Third and F Street. By the time they entered the building, the woman on his arm had composed herself. "What was that about?" he whispered. He really didn't know. Or understand. But he wanted to.

Ida drew in a deep breath. "You must think me very silly."

"I think you very interesting." Blaine grinned broadly as he seated her at a table then stood in line behind a woman who had followed them inside.

Ida knew better than to stare, yet something about the woman—perhaps the excessive rouge and red lipstick—drew her attention.

The stranger requested something from the clerk, but he shrugged and shook his head. "No more credit. You'll have to pay before you can get any more medicine."

The woman's shoulders slumped. Blaine intervened. "How much do you need?" He pulled bills from his wallet and offered them to the woman.

How gallant was that! If the gesture was intended to impress Ida, it worked.

Backing away, the stranger refused Blaine's generosity. He handed the cash to the clerk. "See that she gets what she needs."

Ida continued watching, intrigued by the unfolding scene. Who was this amazing man? His actions touched her heart.

The clerk disappeared into the back room where pharmaceuticals were kept and returned momentarily with a small bundle wrapped with brown paper. He handed the package to the stranger.

"Thank you," she mumbled, her gaze never leaving the floor.

"You are most welcome. I'm about to order banana splits for myself and Miss Dempsey." Blaine gestured toward Ida. "Will you join us?"

The woman glanced at Ida, gaping. Then, wordlessly, she hurried from the store.

Blaine returned with a glass of water and the banana splits. He sat across from her. Why did he look at her like that? She feared perhaps something had smeared on her face or her hat sat askew. Well, so what?

"I believe you were going to explain your laughter." His eyes twinkled.

"You might as well know right off that I'm prone to laughter and rarely feel the need to suppress it."

"Duly noted."

"However, today was a little different."

"Continue." Blaine settled back in his chair.

"It started when I couldn't concentrate on the sermon as I should, then it took forever to exit the building. I saw you with Mattie, and the look on your face pleading for rescue. Then the ladies' auxiliary waylaid me. I couldn't join the group."

"Why couldn't you concentrate on the sermon? I thought it quite good."

"Reverend Huntington's lessons usually are." Ida dug into her ice cream. "I'm not always frivolous, although my aunt might have a different opinion." Meeting his gaze emboldened her speech. "Tongues will wag over your reply to Miss Sutterman."

"You mean when I begged off the lunch invitation and announced plans with you?"

"Exactly." Ida took another bite before she spoke the next words. "You see, Mattie has taken a shine to you, and she's more ready for courtship than I am." Living and speaking honestly was all Ida knew, although she suspected she violated some rule.

"Mattie is a fine young lady, I'm sure, but I'm not interested in her." Blaine met her honesty with his own.

She liked that. Sort of. Not the part about his lack of interest in Mattie. She admired that he spoke openly. She continued. "So in the span of a little time, I felt all these emotions—even a little smug about the looks on the others' faces when you reached for me, which I've already repented of—and it struck me as funny that all these feelings were inspired by. . .ice cream!" Ida paused. "Sometimes, once I begin laughing, I have a hard time stopping. Don't you agree that laughter just feels good?"

The man in front of her chuckled. "I don't know what to say."

"I have that effect on people sometimes." Ida shrugged. "So tell me what I missed in the sermon."

"I'd rather talk about you." Blaine leaned back in his chair. "What's important to you, Miss Ida Dempsey?"

CHAPTER 5

"Can we walk by the waterfront?" The rhythm of gentle waves lapping on the shore, the fresh breeze, and barking harbor seals often calmed Ida, and she wanted that soothing effect.

"Of course." Blaine scraped his ice cream dish. "But why? Do you not like my question?"

"Your question?"

"I asked what is important to you." He stood, donned his hat, and opened the drugstore door for Ida.

"Oh! Yes! Talking about important things." Ida strolled beside him toward the harbor. "You mean things other than my favorite color and whether or not I like chocolate?"

"Those could be important." Blaine arched his eyebrows.

Ida laughed, then sobered. "I'm not sure what to say. The importance of a belief or ambition needs context, don't you think? I mean, on one hand, the joy I get from being near the sea is one thing, but in comparison to, say, being a friend to Mattie, the importance of the water fades."

"Point taken." Blaine gripped her arm as they navigated a pebbly slope.

"So, specifically, what do you want to know? By the way, it's blue, and yes, very much."

Confusion flitted across her companion's face, and then he broke into a wide smile. "Favorite color and your opinion on chocolate."

Ida nodded. "Next question."

"Let's start with my curiosity, unless it's painful or awkward to answer. Why do you live with your aunt and uncle?"

"Not painful. I haven't many details. My parents died when I was a baby. I have no memory of them. My mother was Aunt Ruth's sister, and I don't know anything about my father. My aunt and uncle adopted me but never hid the truth from me. Aunt Ruth told me she didn't teach me to call her Mother out of respect for her sister." Ida paused, seeking the right words. "I don't feel like a destitute orphan. I can't imagine being loved more than I am."

"You don't wonder about your parents?"

"Not really. It pains Aunt Ruth to talk about her sister, and there's no chance I can meet them, so I'm content enough. My father might have been a rogue the way Aunt Ruth avoids saying anything about him, but I have a heavenly Father who adores me." She glanced at Blaine to see how he'd respond to her last comment.

His face remained passive. What was he thinking?

"Do you have plans for your life other than marriage and children? Will you attend college? Nowadays many women do, although Mother asserts it makes them unfit for domestic life." He bit his lip. "I shouldn't have said that last part."

"It's all right. Your mother isn't the only one with that opinion." Ida drew in a deep breath in preparation for answering the most important question he could have asked. How he responded would determine their future together. If he so much as flinched or wrinkled his brow, Mattie could have him.

She gazed boldly into his eyes. "I don't dream of attending college, although I think it a proper choice for women. I do have plans outside of family." She made no attempt to hide her enthusiasm. The words burst from her like a spring waterfall. "I want to make a difference in the world. Like my aunt and uncle have made a difference to me." Ida kept her gaze locked on his face as she gushed, her pulse quickening. "I want everyone to know we have a Father in heaven and a Savior interceding for us, that despite our shortcomings and failures, we are deeply loved."

Blaine lifted her from the ground and twirled her around, completely taking her off guard. "Thank you, heavenly Father!" His words were as unexpected as his movements. Joy plastered his face. He set her down, grasped her hand, and pulled her with him, racing along the pebbly beach.

Was he crazy?

She'd hoped he'd take her seriously, but what was this? Out of breath from the unexpected trek to the edge of the water, Ida gasped, "Are you all right?"

"Never been better." He stopped out of reach of the waves and cupped her face in his hands. "I prayed for you."

What did he mean? She backed away, confused.

"I've frightened you." Blaine sighed.

"No, I just need a moment." To collect her thoughts. They stood silently, looking over the water. Seagulls squawked overhead, clamoring as a ship drew into port. The gentle breeze carried with it the smells of salt water, kelp, and wet driftwood.

She'd shared boldly and unashamedly with this man—basically a stranger—her heart's yearning, and he'd gone berserk. "What do you mean, you prayed for me?"

"On my way to the picnic yesterday, I asked God to show me the woman He'd chosen to be my wife, someone who loves Jesus as much as I do. I saw you first."

His answer shocked her as much as his actions. Usually, Ida admired honesty and openness from others. She embraced the traits for herself. But a wife? Not yet! It was one thing to discuss the future with Mattie—that was just talk. Something to look forward to, not to actually pursue at the moment.

She barely knew this person, and he knew very little about her. Maybe God had predestined their union, but she remained far from convinced. What had she told Blaine? She wanted to make a difference by sharing Jesus with the world.

Was that enough to build a lasting relationship on?

Maybe. Well, if he liked chocolate too.

"Say something." Within seconds, dismay replaced Blaine's joy. He'd come on too strong. He should have contained himself. In retrospect, his actions shocked him as well. What had come over him? He wasn't a twirling, happy-go-lucky sort!

Ida fidgeted with the strings on her bonnet. "So you prayed God would reveal His choice for you, you saw me first, and just now you liked what I said about Jesus?"

Blaine cleared the frog lodged in his throat. "Something like that. I don't want to rush ahead. I'm not trying to push you into anything."

"Good, because maybe you prayed for me, but I've not prayed for you."

Ida tilted her head, squinting against the sun. "I will. I mean, I'll ask my Father what He thinks about all of this."

"Fair enough." Blaine reached for her hand, and she allowed him to take it without meeting his gaze. He wished he could start over.

Sailors disembarked the ship and tied it to its moorings. Seagulls fought with each other over food thrown overboard by two men, probably the ship's cooks. Ida pointed and laughed as one bird stole a chunk of something from another. It took off and landed on a piling, downing the chunk in one gulp.

As more food floated on the waters, the birds went crazy, their squawks and cries resounding through the harbor.

Blaine watched, thinking a life lesson probably existed in the scene before them, but he was content to just enjoy the entertainment the scavengers provided, a welcome distraction from the past few minutes of misguided words and actions.

Having had their fill, several birds soared into the air, crossing overhead. Blaine's reflexes were no match for the white droppings that landed on his hat brim.

"Goodness!" Ida ducked and covered her bonnet with her arms as more birds flew their way.

"I'll take this as a signal to leave." Grasping Ida's hand, Blaine sprinted up the coarse, sandy incline to the street running the length of the bay. The gulls settled on rooftops and pilings nearby.

As they paused on the corner of E Street and Second, Ida looked right and left, a bit of rebellion rising. The area drew her with its aura of mystery created by taboos on children and decent women traversing portions of Second Street. Could this be where the painted woman from the drugstore resided?

"Blaine, have you ever visited this part of town?"

"I should say not!"

His shocked reaction didn't disappoint. She'd anticipated he might be insulted by such a question and asked anyway. He'd jarred her by the waterfront. Now it was her turn to jolt him, because an idea had formed that she couldn't shake, nor did she want to.

"Remember when Jesus told the Pharisees that He'd come for the sinners, not the righteous?"

Blaine nodded. "Yes. They criticized Him for eating with tax collectors and sinners." He turned to face her. "Oh no, Ida. I know what you're thinking, and it's a bad idea. Like you, I want to make a difference in the world. I want to serve God, but I wouldn't know what to say to these people."

"Not you, Blaine. Me."

CHAPTER 6

Aunt Ruth met her at the door as if she'd been waiting for her arrival. "Why didn't you ask the young Mr. Prescott to come inside?"

Ida removed her bonnet and outer wrap. "I did. He declined."

"When will you see him again?" Her aunt linked her arm with Ida's. "Come, tea is ready."

As much as Ida loved her aunt, she'd rather share her afternoon experience with Mattie. On second thought, that was a terrible idea. Talking to Mattie about Blaine would be like rubbing salt into a wound.

How much should she tell her aunt? Not in the habit of keeping secrets, what could Ida say that wouldn't put Blaine in a bad light? Being a romantic herself, Aunt Ruth might possibly understand his inappropriate mention of marriage. Uncle Harvey would not. He'd be mad as a wet hen to know Blaine hadn't asked permission to court her.

Was hiding her feelings and thoughts a part of growing up? Part of maturing? Ida didn't like it.

Qui brought in a tray laden with cream cheese and cucumber sandwiches cut in small triangles and a yellow rose tea service. She set it on the lace-covered round table.

As her aunt poured tea, Ida pushed back the deep orange velvet drapes from one of the floor-to-ceiling windows overlooking the garden. A splash of sunlight created a swath of brightness, highlighting the large flower prints of green, gold, orange, and tan of the carpet. The Victorian-inspired parlor was one of Ida's favorite rooms, especially when a small coal fire glowed in the fireplace encased by ornately carved cherrywood. Summertime meant a break from rain but did not boast overly warm temperatures. The room required a degree of heat.

"Come and sit." Aunt Ruth gestured to the gold damask settee flanked by two armchairs upholstered in red velvet.

Ida turned from the window, still hesitant over how much of her time with Blaine she could reveal. Her aunt patted the cushion, a smile lighting her eyes. Ida bit into a sandwich as she joined her—she'd not be expected to talk with food in her mouth.

Aunt Ruth's love-filled gaze melted Ida's reluctance. "I hardly know where to begin."

"I want to hear everything from the start. How did you meet the Prescotts' son?"

Ida began at the picnic, telling how they met and his invitation for ice cream. She included Mattie's interest in Blaine. "I'm not sure what to do about that. She's my best friend."

"Let nature take its course and be gracious in conversations with her."

"You mean don't gush about my time with him to her."

Aunt Ruth laughed. "Do you feel like gushing, my dear?"

If she hadn't before, she did now. "He asked me what I wanted to do with my life, and when I told him, he didn't laugh at me or pooh-pooh it as too idealistic."

Aunt Ruth's eyebrows raised. "You told him about wanting to make a difference by ensuring everyone in the world knows Jesus."

Ida nodded.

"And he didn't run away?"

"No. He did frighten me—at first. I'm not still afraid."

"What happened?" Concern filled her aunt's eyes.

Ida related Blaine's twirling and his prayer.

"My goodness. That was bold." Aunt Ruth grasped Ida's hand. "How did you react? What did you say?"

"It's all right now. In fact, the more I think about it, the happier it makes me." Ida paused. "I am worried how Uncle Harvey will react if I tell him, though. Do you think he'll be upset?"

"Hmm. Possibly. Probably. While I don't recommend keeping secrets, there's no reason we have to mention anything at the moment. Let's give your Mr. Prescott time. I daresay he hadn't intended to speak plainly so soon and will request an audience with your uncle in the very near future."

"One more thing, but it's not about Blaine." Ida drew in a deep breath. "I am serious about wanting to make a difference in people's lives. You know that. Now I think I know how to begin."

Aunt Ruth sipped from her teacup. "You want to find a match for Mattie?"

"Oh, nothing like that. Blaine and I walked up E Street, and as we waited to cross Second, I realized there's an entire community that needs to know Jesus loves them."

Her aunt shook her head. "You don't mean to visit Second Street. I can't allow that. Your uncle will absolutely forbid it."

"Today at the drugstore, this woman came in, and everything about her indicated she was from that district—her clothing, her painted face. Blaine paid for medication she couldn't afford, but she needs something more than that. She needs Jesus. I want to find her and help."

Aunt Ruth's teacup rattled as she set it back on the saucer. She rose. "Consider the shame you would bring to our family if anyone saw you there. The answer is no, dear one. Absolutely not."

"Missed you this morning at church services." Blaine's mother bent to smell a rose in the garden as they walked together.

"I'm sorry, Mother. I should have said something. I took a notion to attend the Congregationalist assembly."

Her eyebrows rose. "Is that right? Any particular reason?"

Blaine laughed. "Yes, Mother, a very particular reason."

"Ah! Someone from the picnic?"

"Again, you are correct." Blaine linked his mother's arm in his as they strolled down the path lined with rhododendrons and hydrangeas. The scent of lilies wafted on the gentle breeze.

"Very good. Your father will be most pleased."

"I hope so." After the picnic, he'd taken Pratt aside to gain information about the Dempseys. He suspected there might be something questionable about the family based on his mother's rudeness to Ida. The butler had no knowledge of anything disreputable. While he claimed limited knowledge of Ida, Pratt confirmed that Mr. Dempsey was a respected businessman and well liked in Eureka's elite social circles.

"Are you going to keep me in suspense?" His mother sat on the stone bench under the spreading oak tree. "Perhaps I can guess." She raised her eyes as if seeking an answer from heaven. "Let me see. The Suttermans attend services there. Their daughter Stella is quite the beauty. Is she the one? Am I right?"

Blaine couldn't put a face to the name. Was she the young woman who invited him to lunch? He shrugged. It didn't matter. "Actually, Mother, not Stella. Ida Dempsey. You introduced me to her first at the picnic."

His mother stiffened. "How nice she made a good first impression. I can save you much time and frustration, Son. On improving the acquaintance, you'll be disillusioned. I know you'll not want to disappoint the girl, but it's better to nip her hopes in the bud."

"Quite the contrary, Mother. I spent a delightful hour with her after church today. She's unlike anyone I've ever met, and I'm determined to, as you say, improve the acquaintance."

He purposely met her eyes. "I intend to speak with Mr. Dempsey at his earliest convenience for permission to court her. I could extend an invitation for the family to dine with us while I'm there. Do you think this week or next best?"

Mrs. Prescott rose from the bench. Shadows from the tree darkened her features as a passing cloud obscured the sun. "That is not going to happen. I will not allow it."

CHAPTER 7

As the moon rose high and stars studded the night sky like so many diamonds, Ida spent extra time in prayer before extinguishing the oil lamp. She asked her heavenly Father about Blaine, and then, not waiting for an answer, she rushed ahead, presenting her plan for the soiled ladies of Second Street and asking God's blessing on it. She wished she could pray for each one by name, but He knew who they were. Soon she would as well.

Monday afternoon she sought Mattie. Her friend pouted and refused to go anywhere except the small garden in front of her cottage. She plopped on a redwood bench near a sweet-smelling honeysuckle bush. "I can't believe you left without me," she whined.

"Mattie, I am sorry. He caught me unprepared. I had no idea he'd be so bold in front of everyone. You'll laugh at this, though. While we watched a ship arrive, a group of seagulls flew overhead and left droppings on his hat. I almost fell over laughing."

Her friend grinned, then sighed. "It's no surprise he likes you best. Still, I thought I might have a chance if you'd step out of the picture."

Ida met Mattie's gaze. "He does like me. I anticipate he'll speak to Uncle Harvey about courtship in the near future." She omitted his mention of marriage.

Mattie rose and walked to the picket fence separating the yard from the dirt road. She looked over her shoulder at Ida. "Do you think he has a friend?"

Ida giggled and joined Mattie at the fence. "You mean a rich one?"

The two friends hugged.

"Can we talk about something else?" Ida asked, pulling back. "I have a plan, and I need your help."

"Sounds intriguing." Mattie returned to the bench. She picked a daisy and twirled it between her fingers.

"I've been talking forever about making a difference in people's lives."

"Yes, you want to tell the world about Jesus. You know women can't be preachers, right?"

"I'd never want to get up in front of an audience, but one-on-one, or in a small group of women, I could talk about Him. I'm ready to get started."

"You want to have a Jesus party and invite our friends? They already know, Ida. Everyone in Eureka knows. Don't we get enough religion in church on Sunday? I know I do." Mattie picked petals from the daisy. "He loves me, he loves me not."

"I don't want to have a party. The women I have in mind wouldn't come, so I have to go to them. Aunt Ruth has forbidden it. She believes I'll bring shame to the family if I'm seen. I don't want to upset her, so I want to go in disguise."

Mattie's eyebrows knit together. "Keep talking."

"I need to blend in on Second Street."

The daisy fell to the ground. "Second Street?" Mattie's lips curved upward. "Oooo."

"You'll keep it a secret? And help me?"

"If I can come too."

Ida considered her friend's response. Might two be better than one? Scripture said something about a cord of three. Well, why not? "Come with me to Wells Drug Store. We can get rouge and eye shadow and lipstick."

"What about clothing?" Mattie's smile grew. "What should we wear? Can we show cleavage?"

Ida blushed. She'd not completely thought through the disguise idea.

Wanting to avoid a confrontation with his father, Blaine evaded him most of the morning by working directly with laborers who unloaded cargo from the ship that had docked that morning. He inspected the crates and barrels, looking for damage, and directed the sailors where to put them. His father would likely be pleased with his efforts.

He assumed Mother had informed his father about their conversation in the garden. He wanted to speak with Mr. Dempsey about courting Ida before his father could forbid the relationship. The scandal resulting from reneging on a formal commitment could work in his favor, but he had an entire day to get through before Ida's father would be home from work and available to accept visitors.

Unless he went to the Dempsey's sawmill and addressed him there.

As the noon hour approached, he poked his head into the shipping office. "I've an errand, Father. I'll be back before one o'clock."

Without looking up from the ledgers spread out in front of him, his father nodded. "See that you are. We need to talk."

Mixed feelings battled within Blaine as he pedaled the bicycle he'd used through college toward the sawmill. If he didn't know with absolute certainty that God had chosen Ida for him, he'd heed his mother's wishes. He respected the wisdom of his father as well and hoped they'd make a great team working together. However, in this matter, he would forge ahead regardless of his parents' disapproval. They'd come around. After all, he had honored their wishes to find a wife. She came from a respectable family. They could have no serious objections about his choice.

His entire life he'd followed their plans for him. He suffered through the boarding school they chose, coming home only when bidden, doing well in his studies. He attended the university his father had selected, again dedicating himself to his studies in order not to disappoint anyone. He returned home as requested to join the family business and had honored his parents by looking for a woman of class and character. Aside from that, the decision had to be his—and God's.

Blaine waited, hat in hand, as the secretary announced him to Mr. Dempsey. Suddenly, doubts attacked. Was he being cocky? What if Ida's uncle didn't consider him worthy of her?

Had Ida told her uncle about his blunder in speaking of marriage so inappropriately? That would give Mr. Dempsey a reason to refuse. Blaine drew in a deep breath. God would go before him.

Mr. Dempsey stood as Blaine entered the dusty, cluttered room lit by an eight-paned window and several oil lamps. Muffled rumbling from the steam-powered sawmill made its way into the office. They exchanged pleasantries, and then Mr. Dempsey sat and gestured for Blaine to do the same. "What can I do for you, Mr. Prescott?"

Blaine remained standing, fidgeting with his hat. "I'll intrude on your time only a moment and get directly to the point. My mother introduced me to Miss Dempsey at the picnic Saturday, and I enjoyed the pleasure of her company after church yesterday. I'd like very much to call on her again with your blessing."

"She's only seventeen." Mr. Dempsey drummed his fingers on the polished maple desk.

"Yes, sir. I'm not interested in rushing into anything, only the chance to get to know her better."

"Have you spoken to her about this?"

Actually, he hadn't. He'd skipped courtship and gone straight to marriage. He met the man's gaze. "Yes, sir. She seemed favorable to the idea."

"I will grant you my blessing as long as we have an understanding. Her aunt and I are in no hurry to see Ida married. She is a sweet, naive girl, easily influenced. The courtship will of necessity be long. And I will speak with Ida to ensure this is her desire as well."

"Thank you, sir. I understand and agree there is no reason to rush."

"One more thing, Mr. Prescott." Mr. Dempsey rose from his chair. "At the slightest hint of impropriety regarding your behavior to my niece, instead of blessing, you will suffer under the severity of my displeasure."

"I understand. You have my word that I will treat your niece with the respect she deserves." Blaine entertained no doubts that Mr. Dempsey would carry out the unveiled threat. But he didn't need that motivation. He had God to answer to.

He whistled as he bicycled back to the Prescott and Son Shipping Company, negotiating the rutted dirt roads, until he rounded the corner and his workplace came into view. One more obstacle lay before him.

Blaine entered his father's office and closed the door. "I've returned from my errand with news I'd like to share." He determined to be on the offensive rather than wait for the expected disapproval. Sitting on a wooden chair, he met his father's gaze. "You will be pleased to know I've done as you requested and have been granted permission to court one of the young ladies Mother introduced me to at the picnic."

His father's eyebrows rose. "Is that right? Well, I hope you're prepared for a long-distance relationship. I'm sending you to San Francisco to oversee our interests there."

CHAPTER 8

"When did this become part of our plan?" Blaine rose from his chair, the tidy desk between him and his father. Less than a week ago, he'd arrived home, enthusiastic to begin employment with his father, eager to strengthen their relationship after so many years away at school. The goal of working alongside this man had motivated him to excel in his academics, to endure the long separations. "Friday last you spoke of my becoming more familiar with the accounts receivable side of our business."

"I decided that's best done in San Francisco, where a number of our shipping partners have their offices. I've made arrangements for you to stay with the Goldbergs."

He'd attended the university with Samuel Goldberg and had escorted his sister Abigail to one of the many balls last spring. He'd spent two summers in an apprenticeship-type role with Mr. Goldberg, learning the ins and outs of bookkeeping and accounting. "How long will I be gone?"

"As long as I need you there."

Not the answer he was looking for. "We don't have an office in San Francisco. Where exactly will I work? What will my duties be?" Confusion plagued Blaine's thoughts.

His father shuffled papers into a folder. "Mr. Goldberg has a spare desk in his office you'll be able to use. It's near the wharf where our ships dock. You'll oversee the loading and unloading of cargo, much as you did this morning."

Blaine stiffened, suddenly suspicious about the assignment. Although words of affection were rarely exchanged between himself and his father, he let his heart speak. "Father, please reconsider. I've looked forward to working with *you* for four long years. I covet the opportunity to learn from *you* firsthand. Let me put my education to use under your guidance."

The words hung in the air, completely missing their target. He had tried to make eye contact with his father as he spoke, but the man's attention remained on the ledger to his left as if Blaine had remained silent.

Only the scratchings of pen on rough paper broke the silence in the room. "Father, did you hear me?"

"Blaine, answer me this: Do you trust me?"

"Yes, of course."

"Do you believe I know what I'm doing?"

"Yes, sir."

"Then don't question my decisions."

Blaine had meant no disrespect, only to plead his case to remain in Eureka near his family. He'd want to remain even if he'd not met Ida. There'd been little meaning in his life thus far, residing away from home more than he'd been there. He wanted to put down roots, become part of the community, *live* in his home, not just *stay* in a dorm or rented room.

His father rose and focused his gaze on him. "Your ship leaves with the tide in the morning."

Blaine left the office, frustration replacing confusion. He didn't remember a time when joining his father at Prescott and Son wasn't his goal. He'd experienced life in San Francisco and didn't relish returning to the city.

Was this God's will for him? How could he know?

And if it wasn't God's will, what could he do?

"I'd like a word with you, Ida, in the library." Uncle Harvey pushed back his chair from the dinner table.

"Of course, Uncle." He'd glanced her way off and on throughout dinner. Ida couldn't determine his mood. Did he intend to admonish her for her plans to minister to the women on Second Street? Or had Blaine spoken to him and he wanted to inform her of his decision?

She tried to meet her aunt's gaze for a clue, but Wallace had his mother's attention. She sent a silent prayer heavenward and followed her uncle from the room.

In the library, Uncle Harvey bypassed his massive desk in front of the windows opening onto the veranda and sat in one of the upholstered armchairs facing the fireplace. The fire had been stoked and the chandelier lit, providing a warm, inviting atmosphere. Ida drew in the aroma of books mixed with the wood polish smells of linseed oil and beeswax before sitting across from Uncle Harvey. She folded her hands in her lap to keep them from fidgeting and waited, her heart thumping wildly.

"I had an interesting visit from Blaine Prescott today."

Immediate relief flooded Ida. She barely heard the rest of her uncle's speech—something to do with her youth and his expectations. Her mind and heart joined in anticipating this new chapter in her life. She wanted to run out and find Blaine. She pictured more walks on the beach, more interesting discussions, more opportunities to share experiences.

"I said, 'Do you understand?'" Uncle Harvey scowled.

Oh dear. Understand what? She didn't dare ask and risk ruining the joyous moment. "Yes, sir. I am eager to better my acquaintance with Mr. Prescott." Ida managed to sit still only because of her uncle's somber tone. Her thoughts continued, centered on Blaine. Would he call that evening? How she hoped so!

"I said you may go now." Uncle Harvey had risen from his chair.

"Oh, yes, of course." And although nothing in his posture invited a hug, Ida wrapped her arms around him and squeezed. "Thank you," she breathed into his vest.

He patted her back. "Yes, dear. Now that's enough."

She released her embrace and glanced into his face. He met her smile with slightly upturned lips and a nod. Ida tripped from the room, leaving the door open on her way out. If Mattie lived closer, she'd beg permission to visit. Such news must be shared!

No, she couldn't do that. What had her aunt cautioned? To be gracious in conversation with her best friend. She wouldn't be able to do that at the moment. Joyfully distracted, she bumped into Wallace, nearly losing her footing.

"I take it you're not in trouble." He steadied her. "That's not fair. Every time I'm called into the library, I get an earful."

"As it turns out, the man I met at the picnic has asked permission to court me, and Uncle agreed."

Wallace shrugged. "Glad it's you not me."

"You've just not met the right girl yet."

"Hard to do when I'm not looking."

Ida stared a moment at her cousin. "What are you seeking, Wallace? What do you want?"

He grasped her arm and led her down the hallway and out into the garden. As they strolled along, their steps grated against the white agates lining the walkway. Wallace sighed. "You're the only one who has ever asked me what *I* want."

Ida didn't know how to respond.

"Honestly, I don't know. I'm sick to death of talking about lumber. I don't care that prices and demand have fallen. Do you know how many times I've heard Father joke that the only good tree is a stump?" Wallace's lips formed a tight line as his brows knit together. "Sometimes I think I'll explode."

"Have you spoken to him?"

"What good would that do?"

Ida suspected her cousin was right. She grasped his hand and squeezed it, remembering what she'd said to Mattie at the Saturday picnic. It must be hard to be Wallace.

CHAPTER 9

Ida watched from the parlor window as the lamplighter climbed one post after another all along the street, a trail of luster dotting his path. If Blaine was coming, it had to be soon.

She played a sonata—poorly—on the piano.

She gathered her needlework in the drawing room and set it back down.

Picked up a book—didn't open it.

Her thoughts had gone from eager anticipation over a relationship with Blaine to anxiety regarding what exactly courtship entailed. She meant what she'd said to Mattie. She hoped to marry someday—just not yet.

Aunt Ruth joined her in the drawing room. "Do you think Blaine will call this evening?"

"I thought he would, but it's getting late." Ida paced in front of the fire. "What happens next? Not much, right? Because I'm in no hurry to—you know—um—well, I hardly know him."

Her aunt chuckled. "That's what courtship is about. An opportunity for two people to get better acquainted and decide whether they have a future together. The next step is for us to invite him and his family to dinner, then they will reciprocate."

"Oh my!" Ida's eyes widened. "Do we have to? Mrs. Prescott flusters me so."

"Dear one, she is Blaine's mother. You'll have to find a way to like her."

"Good thing we aren't rushing into anything." She returned to the window. A dark figure approached—her pulse raced. But when he neared the lamppost, she could see it wasn't Blaine.

The grandfather clock chimed nine o'clock. Too late for visitors. Disappointed, Ida plopped onto the settee. For hours she'd been both looking forward to Blaine's visit—and dreading it. She'd enjoyed every minute of her time with him so far. How might this formal courtship arrangement change things? Would there be an awkwardness not present before?

"I'm sure he'll call tomorrow." Aunt Ruth picked up her tatting. "Now, why don't you read aloud? Where did we leave off?"

Ida picked up *Pride and Prejudice* and began, " 'Chapter Thirty-Three. More than once did Elizabeth in her ramble within the park unexpectedly meet Mr. Darcy…' "

After breakfast the next morning, Ida pulled Wallace aside. "Will you walk with me to the docks?" She'd not spend another day waiting for an evening visit, wondering if he'd come. And she didn't want to seek him alone.

"Do you think you'll see your Mr. Prescott there?"

"I won't bother him in his office. I know two of his father's ships are in port, so maybe he'll be—I don't know—supervising or something outside."

"Sure, I'll go. It's interesting to see ships arrive and depart. The tide will be high in an hour or so. There's bound to be a lot of activity."

Even though the calendar declared it the middle of summer, a foggy chill hung in the air. Ida wrapped herself in her wool coat and scarf and strolled alongside Wallace. "Do you ever think of sailing away from here?"

"All the time, but I'd make a poor seaman."

"Why's that?"

"I get seasick."

They arrived at the dock to see it abustle with seamen preparing to set sail. Shouted commands competed with squawking seagulls. Ida's gaze flitted from one scene to another until she spotted Blaine walking up the gangplank. "There he is!"

Wallace shouted, "Mr. Prescott!" but the commotion around the ship drowned out his voice.

"It's all right." Ida tugged on her cousin's arm as he waved aggressively with the other. "The ship is untied from its moorings. It will be leaving momentarily, and we can meet him on the pier."

No sooner had Ida spoken than sailors drew in the gangplank and the ship began the slow process of moving away from the wharf. "I must have missed him. Wallace, did you see him disembark?"

"I saw the older Mr. Prescott, but your Blaine is not on the dock."

"Let's go closer."

As they rushed onto the pier, Mr. Prescott headed toward them. Surprise flitted across his face, and then his eyes hardened. "Good morning, Mr. Dempsey, Miss Dempsey." Tipping his hat, he strode past.

"Excuse me, sir," Ida called after him. "I hoped to see your son this morning."

"That won't be possible. He's headed to San Francisco." Mr. Prescott lifted his chin. "He'll be residing with the Goldbergs for the foreseeable future. Did he speak to you of that family? Perhaps not. They have a daughter, Abigail, with whom he's spent much time. I don't expect his return anytime soon."

Mouth agape, Ida watched Mr. Prescott strut away.

Blaine couldn't be gone. She lifted her skirts and raced down the dock as the vessel moved into the shipping channel. Was that him near the railing? She waved vigorously. "Blaine!" Most unladylike, she shouted loudly.

She waved both arms in the air and called out his name again. The person turned from the rail and, in a flash, disappeared. Had he seen her?

Wallace placed an arm around her shoulders. "Let's go home."

Ida didn't move until the ship disappeared, her heart beating double time. Why would he leave without explaining his absence, without saying goodbye? It made no sense that he'd go to the trouble of speaking with Uncle Harvey if he lacked sincerity.

And no, he'd never mentioned Abigail Goldberg. They'd talked about their future, very little about their past.

Nonetheless, her eyes hadn't deceived her. He'd been on that ship headed to San Francisco, without a single word of explanation.

What did it mean?

As the ship sailed past Indian Island, Blaine paced the deck. Little about this trip felt right. He'd left a message with Pratt, trusting he'd get it to Ida for him. He'd understand if she was upset he didn't deliver it himself. He had excuses, although upon review none of them held water. His father had kept him at the office providing details of the expected tasks until it grew too late for a visit yesterday. Why hadn't he insisted on cutting the session short, leaving time to call on Ida?

He had determined to see her in the morning. As he prepared to do so, his mother suffered a fainting spell. Concern over her health kept him by her side. After the doctor assured him she'd be fine, he purposed to find Ida, but too much time had elapsed. It vexed him that his sudden departure would undoubtedly cause Ida distress. It would certainly grieve him if she unexpectedly disappeared.

The idea hounded him that behind it all existed a ploy to keep him and Ida apart. As soon as the thought hit, shame followed. He'd always trusted his father. Part of their conversation the previous evening centered around the confidence his father placed in him to carry out this assignment with all its responsibility. He had praised Blaine for being such an asset to the company that he no longer had to make such trips himself.

Might his mother have influenced him? Unlikely. His father ruled their household. Blaine didn't believe his mother would prevail in any disagreement, nor would she wish him sent away after being home so short a time.

Why look for hidden motives or let unfounded doubts create a barrier between himself and his father? A lack of time and unforeseen circumstances prevented him from explaining the change in situation to Ida. As soon as the ship docked, he'd post a letter explaining more than he could in a short note.

All the self-talk did nothing to erase the nagging feeling that something wasn't right.

The conversation with Mr. Prescott as well as the vision of Blaine on board the ship repeated over and again through Ida's mind, producing an acute headache. After Wallace escorted her home, she retired to her room, closed the heavy drapes to block out the light, and snuggled into her bed. When Aunt Ruth entered to check on her, she considered feigning sleep to avoid discussing what she didn't understand, but deception didn't suit her.

"What's wrong, dear one?" Her aunt gently brushed the hair off Ida's forehead. "You are not prone to headaches, which tells me something has upset you."

"Could we talk later? I'd really like to just take a nap."

"Of course."

As soon as her aunt left the room, Ida slipped from the bed and knelt to pray. She didn't like to bother her heavenly Father with every little thing in her life, but this felt huge—too overwhelming to handle on her own. She asked for wisdom and His direction, for better understanding, and for Him to guide her steps.

Then she scooted back under the coverlet and slept. When she awoke, her headache had abated, and she knew her next step. She had no control over whatever was going on with Blaine.

The poor, misguided ladies on Second Street still needed help. She'd devote her energies in that direction.

CHAPTER 10

When Ida slipped down the stairs, the house appeared empty except for Qui in the kitchen.

"You are feeling better?" Qui's eyes showed her concern.

"I am."

Qui put a hard-boiled egg, cheese, and crackers on a plate. "Sit here and eat."

"I'm not hungry—and there's somewhere I need to go." Ida wanted to disappear before anyone returned home and asked questions. She started to leave the kitchen, when Qui called her back.

"Missy should rest. Take care of yourself. I'll make tea."

Did other servants speak with the same authority as Qui? Moira, the housekeeper, barely spoke at all. Ida's friendly overtures seemed to unsettle the woman. Aunt Ruth had suggested Ida leave her to do her work. The Chinese men who retrieved and delivered their laundry shared the same reticence.

Qui spoke her mind—not to Uncle Harvey, of course, which Ida thought showed wisdom on the cook's part. Uncle Harvey did not believe in interacting with "the lower classes" as he put it. Ida suspected he'd consider the women on Second Street above the Chinese servants in his own household.

Ida settled at the small kitchen table and nibbled on the crackers and cheese while she waited for the tea. "Qui, have you ever wondered about the women on Second Street?"

"None of my business." Her eyes narrowed, brow furrowed as she faced Ida. "None of missy's business."

"I'm thinking that if they knew Jesus, they'd change their ways." Ida reached for the teacup Qui handed her.

"I not know Jesus, and I not live on Second Street." Qui turned her back as if to say she'd speak no more on the topic.

Qui's words jarred Ida. How many years had the cook worked for the Dempsey family? Longer than Ida had been alive. How could she be a part of the household for decades and not know Jesus? Maybe what Qui meant was even before she knew Jesus, she'd never have resorted to prostitution. Definitely something to consider. At the moment, Ida had a more pressing errand. She finished her tea, said goodbye, and left.

Out of sight of the house, Ida donned her winter cape and pulled the hood over her head. It wasn't much, but it served as the best disguise she had at the moment. She hoped for Aunt Ruth's sake it would be enough to curtail wagging tongues.

She stopped first at Mattie's house. No one answered the door. Even though a twinge of guilt nagged her, she continued on. Mattie would be disappointed she didn't wait for her. Even so, Ida couldn't put off her mission. The women of Second Street—the "Second Street Souls"—needed her—needed someone to tell them about Jesus and His love for them.

She'd intended to go to Second Street, but disobeying Aunt Ruth weighed heavily on her conscience. Instead, she stopped at Wells Drug Store. Perhaps the woman Blaine helped would return there, and when she did, Ida would speak with her. She ordered a soda and waited at the same table she and Blaine had occupied—had it been only a few days ago? The window provided a view of the street. No one strolled the boardwalk. Few horses and fewer buggies traversed the rutted road. As the only drugstore in town, the business catered to all of Eureka's citizenry, including the women of Second Street. Ida reasoned one or more women from there would happen by. Or so she hoped.

She'd wait, although her strengths did not include sitting still. As she lingered, her mind wandered to Blaine—sailing away. Had he seen her and purposely turned his back?

If so, she didn't want to court him anyway. Maybe her heavenly Father was protecting her from a broken heart and she should be grateful for the turn of events. She had never been in love and couldn't call her feelings for Blaine "love." Did such a thing exist as being "in like"? If she never saw him again, would she easily forget the past magical two days?

Was her attraction to him based on his pursuit of her? If he hadn't captured her gaze and forced an introduction at the picnic, would she have noticed him? Perhaps she should dismiss Blaine Prescott as an interesting episode in her life and move on.

Sadness accompanied the idea. She liked him, wanted to spend time with him, would always wonder what could have been if it ended like this.

Ida sat long after she'd finished drinking her soda, starting every time the bell above the door tinkled. As she stared out the window, a male figure passed by whom she recognized—the Reverend Huntington. After he passed, an idea presented. If she shared her plan with him, might he have advice how she could proceed?

She darted out the door and hurried after him, calling out his name as he came into view at the next corner.

A moment of surprise crossed his face before he smiled and greeted her. "Miss Dempsey, how are you?"

After so much time just sitting and waiting, enthusiasm chased away formalities. The words poured from Ida like water cascading down a mountain. "I've been waiting in the drugstore for this woman to return because I want to tell her about Jesus. I don't know her name. I saw her on Sunday, and I think she needs Jesus, and the other women on Second Street as well. Of course, I can't just walk up and down that street, so I thought the drugstore wouldn't tarnish my reputation—such things matter to Aunt Ruth, and I don't want to disobey her, but I have to help these women. Don't you agree that if they knew the love of God, their lives would be so much better? Can you help me?"

"Whoa, there." Reverend Huntington rubbed his temples. "Come with me to my office. It may be a better place for such a conversation."

"Absolutely! Yes! Of course!" Ida nearly skipped alongside the esteemed man of God. Why hadn't she thought to confer with him first?

Upon entering the church, Ida controlled her enthusiasm. One did not bounce into a sanctuary, speak above a whisper, or smile too broadly.

Reverend Huntington led her to a small room filled with books. He gestured for her to take a worn leather chair, while he sat behind a tidy desk dominating the center of the space. He moved aside a Bible and folded his hands on the flat surface.

Ida perched on the edge of her seat, the last of her enthusiasm quelled by the effect of the somber room, suddenly unsure what to say.

"So, if I understand you correctly, you want to spread the gospel among those who need to hear it." The reverend smiled at her, a degree of condescension in his eyes.

"Yes, sir." Ida rarely let others' opinions affect her actions—except, of course, to obey her aunt and uncle. She held this man of God in high regard and wanted him to value her as well, to treat her aspirations with respect, not as an idealistic child acting on a whim.

Well, except she wasn't actually an adult. And some would charge her with being idealistic.

She straightened her back. "I believe God is calling me to act, and I'm willing. You have so much more experience with telling people about Jesus, do you have advice for where I should begin?"

For moments together, Reverend Huntington said nothing. He remained in his seat, hands folded, looking into Ida's eyes. She met his gaze, daring him to dismiss her. If he refused to help, she'd not waste either of their time.

"You are an exceptional young woman," he finally said. "An aspiring angel to Second Street."

"I don't want to talk about me. I want to know if you have advice as to how to proceed."

His eyebrows raised.

Perhaps she'd spoken too boldly.

Reverend Huntington unclasped his hands and stood. "My dear young lady, I admire your desire, but the women on Second Street would gobble you up and spit you out. You've no idea what their lives are like."

Ida rose from her seat, glaring. "I'm sure you are right, as I am right that they need Jesus."

"So do the Chinese in Chinatown." The reverend spoke sternly. "So do the sailors coming and going from our harbor, and the loggers laboring in our forests, the miners, and the bootleggers and the gamblers and saloon owners and the men who frequent Second Street. I daresay you're no more qualified to preach to them than you are the fallen women."

As tears welled, Ida dropped her brazen gaze. "Thank you for your time, Reverend. I'll see you Sunday." She headed for the door.

Reverend Huntington opened it for her. "I'm sorry if I seem harsh. You are a sweet girl with a good heart. Be patient. Our Lord will use you in the ways for which you are suited."

Ida nodded. "Yes, sir, I believe He will."

CHAPTER 11

Two days after setting sail, the ship pulled up to the dock in San Francisco. Blaine's college friend Samuel greeted him along with his sister, Abigail.

She immediately linked her arm with his and cheerfully accompanied him to the waiting carriage, chatting about summer plans for picnics, evenings at the theater, and dinner parties.

As they boarded the buggy, Blaine chose the seat opposite Abigail. "It all sounds grand. Unfortunately, you'll have to make excuses for me. I'm here to work and return to Eureka as quickly as possible. I won't be attending parties and picnics." Did his frustration show in his tone? Her intentions may have been good, but he wasn't in San Francisco for frivolities.

"Don't be such a stick-in-the-mud," Samuel chided. "What's Eureka got that San Francisco can't beat?"

"Ida Dempsey." Blaine reasoned openness and honesty might go a long way in avoiding any misconceptions. If by some chance his father and Mr. Goldberg had plans for him with Abigail, he'd dash any such ideas from the get-go. He'd not play the game.

Samuel's eyebrows rose. "I don't remember you mentioning anyone named Ida."

"I met her recently." Blaine purposefully met Abigail's gaze. "We are courting, so you understand, I'm eager to conduct my business here and return as soon as possible."

A slight pink flushed Abigail's cheeks. Her lips pursed as she turned toward the window.

"I noted a different impression from Father." Samuel shook his head. "He believes you are here permanently, or at least long term."

Immediately upon their arrival at the Goldbergs' residence, Abigail disappeared, which suited Blaine perfectly. Mrs. Goldberg greeted him warmly, informed him dinner would be at seven, and instructed the valet to show him to his room.

Blaine could have found it on his own. He'd spent two summers there. "How are you, William?"

"I am well, sir." William set Blaine's portmanteau on the bench at the foot of the bed, opened the golden brocade drapes flanking the two windows, and then exited.

Samuel had followed him up the stairs. "Do you need time to get settled, or would you prefer a jaunt around town before dinner?" He smiled broadly, eyebrows raised. "There are a few, shall we say, interesting neighborhoods we were not allowed to visit as students."

"Thanks, Sam. Maybe another time. I'll get settled now." Blaine closed the door squarely behind his friend's exit, almost catching his foot in the act. He wanted to be alone, to think and plan, and needed solitude to consider his sudden departure from Eureka in view of Sam's comments.

A cherrywood desk stood between the two windows. He took paper from the left-hand drawer. The first thing, the most important task, was to write a letter to Ida. He'd have written aboard the ship to post immediately upon disembarking if he'd had access to paper. Sailing on freighters lacked both privacy and basic amenities.

What should he tell her? How could he explain that he'd not made time to visit her before leaving? It irked him now that he'd left at all. If nothing else, he could have postponed this trip until the next ship sailed. That would have been a matter of days at most. He had no good excuse. His actions puzzled him. He sat, ink pen poised above the paper, unable to write more than "My Dearest Angel."

He could not begin with an excuse for his failure to call on her that he himself perceived as weak. How could he defend what he didn't understand?

An apology straight from his heart flowed from his pen. He wrote assurances of his earnest desire to better their relationship, assurances of his sincere regard for her, and a promise for a quick return. A knock on the door interrupted his thoughts. He ignored the disruption, hoping the visitor would go away. The knock sounded again, this time accompanied by the door opening.

Abigail!

Not whom he expected to see. First, because modest, virtuous women did not visit men in their private rooms. And second, because he'd made it clear his romantic interests lay elsewhere.

"We need to talk."

"Here? Now?" Blaine continued writing.

"Somewhere private." Urgency coated Abigail's words.

"The garden?"

"No. The trees there have big ears and the benches big mouths." Abigail reached her hand toward him. "I told Mother you asked me to walk with you to the bookstore to pick up a particular item you forgot."

Such an elaborate tale for something as simple as a private conversation—one he doubted he wanted to have. "Can it wait? I'm in the middle of a letter to Miss Dempsey, which I'd like to finish." He didn't have to offer an excuse, but in case Abigail had missed his point, he'd bring up Ida's name again.

"No, it cannot wait."

"Miss Goldberg, I've barely arrived, dinner will be served soon, and I don't understand the urgency." Blaine disliked being rude to anyone, but this young lady drove him to it. "If I've not made it clear, please allow me to do so now. My heart belongs to another, and I will not be dissuaded from her."

"Mr. Prescott, allow me to make myself clear. I've no interest in a romantic relationship with you, not now and not in the future. Now, may we please go?"

Abigail's arm linked with Blaine's as they exited the house and headed downhill toward the bay.

She wasted no time continuing her thoughts. "I saw the look on your face when my brother expressed his opinion regarding the length of your stay in San Francisco."

"I'm not remaining long," Blaine interrupted.

"I need you to."

"Look, Abigail, I've enjoyed the summers I've spent here, and we've had some good times. Please understand, this is not where my life is. Didn't you just say you didn't desire a deeper relationship with me?" Blaine appreciated honesty and openness, the type he experienced with Ida. Beating around the bush, secret agendas, veiled statements, annoyed him.

Abigail stopped walking and faced him. "Not everything is about romance." Her lips tightened in a thin line. She looked into the cloud-speckled sky, then met Blaine's gaze. "I take that back. This is about romance—not yours—mine. If you've surmised that our respective parents have plans for the two of us, you are correct. You've been brought here to squelch your attraction to someone they disapprove of—and to tempt me away from the man I'm in love with."

Blaine let her words sink in. "So why do you need me to stay?"

"Chester and I have made plans and need time to see them through. If you remain and my parents believe we are growing attached, it will be easier to carry out our scheme." Abigail clung to his arm. "Please. You have to do this for me."

"You're asking me to participate in deceiving your parents?"

"I don't think of it like that." Abigail released his arm as they strolled side by side along the busy street. "You are in the same position, Blaine. Surely you understand. I'd love for them to accept my choice; however, they refuse. Why should I be denied happiness based on their misconceptions? If I must resort to deception, as you call it, whose fault is it?"

"I hear what you are saying, nonetheless I strongly believe truth is the only way to proceed." Blaine would not—could not—engage in such subterfuge as she suggested.

"That's because you are male. We females don't have the same options. When a man stands up for what he believes or what he wants, he garners respect even from those who disagree with him. If a woman dares do the same, she's chastised and treated as an incorrigible child."

They continued in silence amid the bustle of the city. After a while, Blaine asked, "May I meet this Chester of yours?"

"Why? So you can decide if he's good enough for me?"

For someone asking for his help, she didn't make it easy. "If I'm going to compromise my values, I'd like to know the person I'm doing it for."

"So you'll help? You'll stay?" Abigail's eyes brightened, and her lips lost their rigid lines.

"I didn't say that."

"But you're thinking about it?"

"I'll ask for God's direction." Blaine had never brought such a dilemma before his Creator before. Scripture clearly stated that Satan is the father of lies and deception. Were there circumstances when God approved of duplicity? He sincerely doubted it.

They plodded back up the hill toward the Goldbergs' home. Before they reached the door, Abigail turned to him, a smile lighting her eyes. "Thank you, Blaine. I knew I could count on you."

He'd promised her nothing, committed himself to nothing except prayer. Her thanks was likely premature.

CHAPTER 12

Ida left the Congregationalist Church, skipping down the steps in a hurry to get away. What a waste of time that had been! Everyone in town respected Reverend Huntington, and she did too, even though he'd not provided the advice she sought. She should have realized such a man of God would be unable to help her. What could this righteous man possibly know about the residents of Second Street?

Those women still needed Jesus. Someone had to witness to them. "Gobble me up and spit me out!" She repeated his words aloud as if they were detestable on her tongue.

Would no one understand? Was this mission to the Second Street Souls hers alone? Ida suspected Mattie's desire to help sprang from the excitement of wearing a disguise and crossing lines marked as taboo more than from a hope to help the women.

Spurred by frustration, Ida put up the hood of her cloak, effectively hiding her face, and marched straight down the forbidden street. Her steps slowed as she neared Kitty Farris' Joy Emporium. The high-pitched laughter of a woman mixed with a husky male voice floated out the open door.

Ida's cheeks flushed. Perhaps the reverend was right after all. She cowered further into her hood and cape and increased her pace, keeping her eyes on the boardwalk. The laughter followed her until she reached the corner and turned down H Street toward the harbor. Familiar cries of seagulls and the barks of seals chased away the shame covering her like a blanket. Pulling off the hood, she faced the wind and let the salty breeze ruffle her hair.

Why the sense of humiliation and ignominy? She'd done nothing wrong. Was this what the reverend meant when he indicated she was ill-equipped for the task?

She lingered on the shore, counting the waves rolling in, watching the seabirds dip and soar. Standing there brought back the vision of Blaine sailing away.

She turned from the water and plodded home. What a disaster of a day. Aunt Ruth would want to know how she spent her afternoon. Perhaps if she avoided everyone until dinner, she'd be spared giving an account of herself.

As Ida entered the foyer, her aunt descended the stairs, dashing her hope she'd escape notice.

"I'm so glad you are feeling better." Aunt Ruth waited on the last step as Ida removed her cape. "When Qui said you'd gone out, I worried a little. You were wise to bundle up, considering your health."

Ida met her aunt's smile with a shard of guilt. "I didn't mean to cause you worry."

Aunt Ruth gestured toward the parlor. "I can tell you, tongues wagged today at the auxiliary meeting." They entered the room and sat together on the settee. "Were you aware Blaine planned a trip to San Francisco? You haven't quarreled already, have you? Oh, by the way, the Prescotts' butler delivered a note for you."

A note from Blaine? Ida's pulse quickened. "No, we've not quarreled, and no, I didn't know he planned to go away. Where is the note?"

Her aunt pulled it from her pocket, an expectant look on her face.

Ida preferred to read it in the privacy of her room, away from her aunt's curiosity. Dare she excuse herself? She gently unsealed the envelope, struggling not to rip into it, taking her time, trying to think of a way to read Blaine's words alone.

Aunt Ruth lifted the envelope from her fingers. "I see you're nervous to discover what's inside. I'll read it for you."

Every cell within Ida's being cried out, "No, stop!" With much effort, her lips remained still.

"Oh my dear, you're as white as a ghost." Aunt Ruth pulled the paper from its sleeve and unfolded it. "Let's see if there's something here to ease your mind."

Blaine paced from the door to the windows in his room. Twice he'd opened the armoire with the intent of packing his clothing back into his portmanteau, and twice he'd closed the doors. He wanted to avoid doing anything rash, although the situation smelled of manipulation and deceit.

If he believed Abigail, his father had sent him to San Francisco to put distance between him and Ida. The accusation seemed far-fetched. There'd been no reprimand from his father regarding the relationship. All their discussions had been business related.

His mother disapproved of Ida—on what grounds he didn't understand. Even at that, she'd not want him sent away. She might make it difficult for him to see Ida and continue to treat the young lady rudely, but she couldn't be so against the relationship that she'd prefer Blaine's absence. Her fainting spell might have been a ploy to keep him from leaving at all.

So if his parents were not behind this subterfuge, it had to be the Goldbergs. Would his father send him to San Francisco at their request, unaware of ulterior motives? In a few aspects, the two companies complemented each other, often working together. Could his presence be more about dissuading Abigail from her beau than business based?

If so, he'd be no part of it.

Should he remain in San Francisco to help Abigail with her mysterious plans, or dismiss himself from the entire scheme and return home on the next available ship?

A compromise might be the wisest choice. He'd stay a day or two and see to the matters his father assigned him. Whether or not that would give Abigail time to carry out her plans, he didn't know but it appeared the best option. He'd be obeying his father's orders without undermining his own values against artifice.

When the bell sounded, Blaine entered the dining room, fully settled on his course of action. He'd sail back to Eureka in no more than two or three days, possibly beating the arrival of the letter he'd painstakingly written. Maybe he'd deliver it in person.

As the meal progressed, he noted Abigail's eyes often on him. She sent many smiles his way and directed most of her conversation to him. Probably a show for her parents to encourage their belief a romance existed between them.

The conversation began light and easy, with talk of San Francisco's growth and prosperity. It stayed politely mundane until Mr. Goldberg expressed his views about how great opportunities existed for hardworking men—if they could halt the influx of Chinese, scoundrels who stole American jobs. He supported the federal amendments passed barely two weeks previous further restraining Chinese immigration into the United States.

Blaine kept his views on the subject to himself.

Abigail changed the topic. "Father, you know they recently opened a new theater on O'Farrell Street—the Alcazar, I believe it is called. Might Blaine—I mean Mr. Prescott—and I attend a musical performance there, perhaps Saturday evening?"

"And open our family to scandal?" Mrs. Goldberg set down her fork forcibly. "I'm sure Mr. Prescott would object to such immoral entertainment. I'm shocked you'd even ask."

Abigail turned to her father. "The Alcazar isn't like that. Anyone who is anybody at all has attended a concert there."

Blaine wondered at her insistence. Was this part of her scheme to meet with Chester? He purposed to remain quiet until Mr. Goldberg addressed him directly. "Have you theaters in Eureka?"

"Yes, sir, we do."

"And are you in the habit of attending?" Goldberg's brow furrowed.

"No. If you recollect, sir, I've been home only about a week. Before that, as a student, I had no extra time."

"Of course. So, in general, your family and friends do not attend?"

He didn't know if his family frequented the theaters in Eureka. He guessed they'd consider the amusement as scandalous as Mrs. Goldberg did. A bit of rebellion rose within Blaine. If the entertainment wasn't of the burlesque nature or otherwise objectionable on moral grounds, then why shouldn't one attend?

He met Mr. Goldberg's gaze. "Speaking for myself, I'd enjoy an evening of classical music. With your permission, I'd be pleased to escort your daughter."

Abigail smiled smugly.

CHAPTER 13

Ida looked over her aunt's shoulder. Her pulse increased as her aunt cleared her throat and began to read.

"Your uncle received it from Pratt and forgot about it in his pocket. The important thing is we have it now." Her aunt cleared her throat and began to read.

Dearest Ida,

Circumstances beyond my control have prevented me from coming to you. By the time you receive this, I'll be on my way to San Francisco. I'll be back very soon.

Affectionately yours,
Blaine Prescott

Aunt Ruth dropped the note onto her lap. "It doesn't shed much light on his absence. I wonder what circumstances could prevent him from speaking with you before he left?" She handed the paper back to Ida. "And what does 'very soon' actually mean?"

"I don't know." Ida stared at the message, unable to glean anything from it other than he'd attempted to communicate his departure with her. Blaine's father had made it clear he'd be away for an extended time, but the note indicated otherwise. Would it be days? Weeks? Months? Any of those could be considered 'soon' compared to years or decades.

She refolded the paper, slipped it back into the envelope, and tucked it away in her pocket. Disappointment knocked on the door of her heart, but she refused to answer. She'd been content before meeting Blaine Prescott. She could be happy without him.

Except, in the confines of her room, when disappointment knocked again, she admitted a singular pain she'd never before experienced. She'd promised Blaine she'd pray about his courting her. As yet, she'd not seriously done that. She knelt on a pillow, raised her face, eyes fully open, and spoke the prayer aloud. "Heavenly Father, You are holy and righteous and just. You are worthy of my devotion and trust. See me through the blood of Jesus and claim me as your child."

Then, head bowed, eyes closed, and lips moving soundlessly, she asked her Father for wisdom and understanding and for the Holy Spirit to reveal His will for her, especially as it related to Blaine. As she knelt silently before her Lord, the poor woman from the drugstore came to mind. She interpreted it as a sign she should continue her mission.

Obviously, she had to make a better plan than waiting in a drugstore draped in a cape and hood.

At dinner, Ida forked a piece of salmon, moved it from one side of her plate to another, did the same with the green beans, and completely ignored the roasted potatoes. When Qui returned to remove the dishes and bring in dessert, Ida's plate resembled something a two-year-old had played with.

After excusing herself, she sought Qui in the kitchen. "Dinner was very good tonight."

Qui shook her head. "You made mess with plate, didn't eat."

"I had something on my mind." Ida picked up a dish towel and dried a plate.

"Missy, you put that down! You make trouble for Qui!" She grabbed the dish towel from Ida, scowling as if Ida had flung mashed potatoes on the wall. "Go play piano or something. I have work to do."

Ida plopped on a kitchen stool. "I have work too. I'm just not sure how to start."

"No start in Qui's kitchen. Shoo!"

Ida crossed her ankles and swung them back and forth. "I want to tell the good news of Jesus to the lost and hurting in Eureka. I'm not sure how to make it happen."

"Lost and hurting not in Qui's kitchen."

"Would you help me?" Ida rose from the stool and stood beside the cook at the sink full of soapy water.

"How help?"

"Will you let me practice on you?" The new idea pounced as if sent from God.

"How practice?" Qui vigorously scrubbed the bottom of a pot.

"You could question me about Jesus and see if my answers make sense."

Qui stopped scrubbing. "Yes, Qui do that. Qui have questions."

Aunt Ruth cleared her throat in the doorway.

How long had she been standing there?

"Ida, music might soothe your uncle's disgruntled mood. Will you come play, please?" Aunt Ruth gestured toward the door.

"Of course." Ida preferred to remain with Qui and respond to her questions, whatever they may be, but she couldn't refuse the request. As she exited the room, her aunt remained behind. "Are you coming?"

"Go ahead, I'll be along." The way Aunt Ruth held her lips signaled that she disapproved of something. Nothing improper had been said. Surely her aunt couldn't take exception to Ida answering Qui's questions about Jesus.

As she sat at the pianoforte, she addressed her uncle. "Is there a selection you'd prefer?"

"You decide." He kept his eyes on the newspaper in front of him.

Her fingers caressed the keys, producing a soul-stirring rendition of *Claire de Lune*. As she played, she lost herself in the melody. At the conclusion, her fingers hovered over the keys as if under a spell.

She'd not noticed her aunt's return, but she sat next to a lamp, looking serenely content as she embroidered a handkerchief. "That was beautiful."

"Thank you."

Did Blaine like music? She didn't know. Even though she had no desire to rush into a marriage, she yearned to discover more about his dreams, his likes and dislikes, his taste in music. Small talk frustrated her with others, but nothing seemed trivial regarding Blaine. When would she see him again?

"Will you play another for us?"

Her aunt's question brought Ida back to the present, back to wondering about the conversation in the kitchen. She could go ask Qui. "Might I be excused?"

"Yes, of course." Aunt Ruth glanced up from her needlework. "However, if you're planning to return to the kitchen, you should know Qui has gone home."

Was her aunt a mind reader? "I hoped to speak with her more."

"Dear one, that is not a good idea." Aunt Ruth's eyes remained fixed on her needlework. "In fact, I believe it would be wise for you in the future to avoid the kitchen."

"May I ask why?" Ida braced herself for a strong rebuke. Questioning authority was Wallace's lane, not hers. It was one thing to flout society's expectations at a picnic while playing with children, quite another to challenge her aunt over a direct command.

"You are old enough to understand there are differences between classes of people, yet you don't. It is part of your sweet nature, which I adore, so you must allow me to direct you." Her aunt's attention remained on her embroidery. "Qui is Chinese. When you run your own household, you must respect that difference."

Uncle Harvey looked up from his paper. "The Prescotts have certain standards. We won't have them believe we've not done right by you. You will obey your aunt."

Words of dissent like she'd never experienced before buzzed in Ida's mind.

She pursed her lips and stifled them.

CHAPTER 14

Ida rose from the pianoforte. "I'd like to go to my room now."

Emotional over her aunt and uncle's directive to avoid the kitchen, Ida snuggled into bed and reread Blaine's note several times in an attempt to erase the drawing room scene from her mind. She wouldn't dwell on Mr. Prescott's information that his son would be gone an extended time. The note said he'd be back soon. She'd little reason to doubt Mr. Prescott's words, but she had even less reason—actually none at all—to doubt Blaine's.

It rankled slightly that he'd be staying with the family of a young lady he'd spent time with in the past, but her annoyance fixed on Mr. Prescott. Why did he tell her that? An obtuse warning that his son was actually a cad?

She'd like to ask the man a few questions, such as did Blaine request to go to San Francisco? Whose idea was it? Who decided his departure time? She didn't need to know the answers to feel better about Blaine—she wanted to ask Mr. Prescott so he'd know she understood more than he gave her credit for. He couldn't so easily deceive her.

As she drifted to sleep, her thoughts turned to her and Blaine's walk along the shore and the conversation they'd had. If all he sought was a good time, he could easily have accepted Mattie's attention—not that Mattie would do anything impure or immoral, but her best friend displayed eagerness to spend time with him. Wouldn't a rogue take the path of least resistance?

She'd see him again soon. The earliest he could return would be a week—possibly by Sunday.

With her last thoughts remembering the feeling of his arms around her as they twirled on the shore, she drifted off. Before the sun broke over the horizon, she awoke, fully refreshed after a night of pleasant dreams.

Ida scuttled from her bed, eager to begin her day. Her aunt's directive could not be ignored. She'd steer clear of the kitchen. She did not, however, intend to avoid Qui. Tucking her Bible into her handbag, she slipped from the house and strode toward Chinatown.

She encountered Qui on G Street, barely a block from the Chinatown boundary.

"What you doing, missy!" Qui frowned. "Not safe for you here."

"Aunt Ruth says I have to stay out of the kitchen, but I have a plan and need to tell you."

"No, no, missy." Qui shook her head vigorously. "No plan. Mrs. Dempsey not like."

"Just listen to me for a moment." Ida placed her hand on the cook's arm. They paused on the corner of G Street and Fourth. "Answer me one question: Were you serious when you said you'd like to know more about Jesus?"

Without hesitation, Qui nodded.

"I have an idea how to make that happen without disobeying my aunt and without compromising your job. By tomorrow I'll have the details figured out."

"Not meet here." Qui wagged her finger at Ida. "Too dangerous."

"Fine. I'll meet you farther from your home, but not too close to mine. How about on the corner of H and Third?"

"I don't know. Now, we must go. Come!" Qui grasped Ida's hand and pulled her along the street.

A block from the Dempsey residence, Ida stopped. "You have to go ahead of me. We can't enter together."

"You go first."

"I've something else to see about." Ida darted away.

She hurried along the streets of the awakening town still shrouded in fog. She darted up the steps of the Congregationalist Church and entered the silent sanctuary. Spurred by the reverence due such a holy place, she eased her gait and tiptoed toward the closed door. Her rapid knock reverberated through the high-ceilinged room.

No one answered.

She had arrived too early.

Then she'd wait. She sat on the front pew.

She'd been inside many times, but only as far as their family bench, except the other day when the reverend escorted her to his office. Did God abide in this place now, or just on Sunday mornings? What a silly thought. God existed everywhere all the time.

Her aunt and uncle often referred to the building as the "house of God," so it wasn't the same as His being in the redwoods or at the seashore or even upstairs in her bedroom. The building's purpose was a place to worship—might His presence be stronger here? Did that mean her prayers would be more effective?

What if she prayed in front of the altar? Might that be more efficacious? She tiptoed slowly, softly, silently, to the ornately carved altar covered with a green brocade cloth. Was it sacrilegious to touch it? To stand behind it? What if she mounted the stairs to the pulpit where the reverend delivered his Sunday message? Might that be the holiest place of all—the place where he spoke the Word of God with power? She ventured up and stood behind it, looking out over the empty pews and imagining them full of worshippers. Such a different perspective from her view of the back of people's heads on Sunday morning! She envisioned faces attentive to the reverend's sermon, all eyes on him, listening intently.

She fingered the ponderous leather-bound Bible lying on the lectern. Then she opened it, wondering what passage it might randomly reveal. Psalm 58 spread before her. She read it aloud with passion as she imagined Reverend Huntington might do: "'Do ye indeed speak righteousness, O congregation? do ye judge uprightly, O ye sons of men? Yea, in heart ye work wickedness—'"

Loud clapping interrupted her speech.

"Well done, Miss Dempsey." Reverend Huntington smiled widely. "Should I fear for my job?"

Ida's face flushed. Stammering, she darted down the steps. "I'm so sorry! I—I don't know what to say!" She hadn't meant to get so carried away. Was her action forgivable? Women were not allowed to preach! But she didn't want to be a preacher, not from a pulpit anyway. "I'm sorry!"

Reverend Huntington patted her shoulder. "This can be our secret—as long as it doesn't become a pattern."

"Oh, no, sir, never!" Ida clutched her hands together to control their trembling. She glanced into his face. Mirth twitched his lips, and his eyes twinkled.

"Now, my dear, I assume your presence is for a different reason than auditioning for minister?"

"Yes, sir, quite." Ida drew in a deep breath. "I need your assistance."

"Something other than reaching the poor souls on Second Street?"

Ida nodded. "This is about the poor souls in Chinatown."

The reverend's eyebrows shot up. "You want to preach in Chinatown?"

"Not exactly." Ida explained her dilemma over obeying her aunt and responding to Qui's interest in Jesus. She omitted revealing her initial motivation was to practice on Qui to help prepare for teaching the "fallen" women. It didn't matter now that she understood Qui sincerely wanted to know about Jesus.

"So, what I am hoping is that we could meet here in one of the side rooms, and you would join us. I think that would honor my aunt's concerns. Could you make time to do that?"

All humor evaporated from Reverend Huntington's countenance. He folded his arms across his chest, pursed his lips, and furrowed his brow.

Ida straightened her back and raised her chin. She would not cower before this man, regardless of stern looks of disapproval. "If you won't help me, I'll take no more of your time." She started to step around him.

"I didn't say I wouldn't help."

Ida stopped. "So you will?"

"Your visit the other day robbed me of peace." The reverend took her elbow and guided her to his office. "I've been unable to stop thinking about it. The Holy Spirit directed me to consider the apostles Jesus called to follow Him. Fishermen, a tax collector, a zealot—none of them *qualified* to teach others. I was wrong to discredit you."

"Really?" Ida almost jumped up and down and clapped her hands, but one didn't express oneself exuberantly in the house of God. "I haven't given up on saving Second Street souls, not at all."

"I hadn't imagined you would."

"So, first, this is my idea for Qui. Twice a week she does our grocery shopping. If I help her, she'll get done faster, and with the time we save, we can come here and talk about Jesus. What do you think?"

"Will Qui come?"

Ida sighed. She didn't know if the cook would risk Aunt Ruth's displeasure, but people prayed to enlist the power of God for hard things. "I think I can persuade her."

"And what is your plan for 'Saving Second Street Souls'?"

"Maybe the less you know about that, the better."

Reverend Huntington hooted, then sobered. "Ida, I meant what I said about exposing yourself to the seedier side of town. Your zeal for the Lord is commendable, but I hate to see your innocence tarnished."

"You mean you're still afraid they will gobble me up and spit me out?"

He raised his eyebrows and blew out a breath.

Ida grinned. "Then we'll just have to pray I'm not on the menu."

Hurrying back home, Ida's spirits brimmed with hope. She had a plan to share Jesus with Qui. Now she needed to proceed with a scheme to find the poor woman from the drugstore.

A disguise still seemed the best option. Something that would let her blend in with the other women and hide her identity from potential gossips. She darted up the stairs to her room and rummaged through her wardrobe. She wanted something in red—a dress she could alter into a fashion suitable for Second Street. She'd purchase a flamboyant hat to hide her face, and her costume would be complete.

The next time she passed Kitty Farris' Joy Emporium, she'd be ready.

CHAPTER 15

On Friday, Blaine spent most of his hours toiling on his father's business interests. The tasks were not busywork, as he suspected they might be, but legitimate shipping-related duties, erasing his suspicions of his father's participation in the surreptitious scheme. Abigail had been wrong to accuse him. Ashamed he'd ever doubted, he devoted himself to the tasks, as if he could make up for such an erroneous allegation by hard work.

By Saturday, he'd completed his father's directions. As Mr. Goldberg entered his workspace, Blaine shuffled papers into a portfolio, preparatory to vacating the desk allotted to him.

"I've finished here." Blaine reached to shake hands with his father's friend. "Thank you for your hospitality. It looks as though I'll be sailing out tomorrow with the tide."

Mr. Goldberg ignored the polite gesture. "That's not the arrangement I've made with your father. You may have finished Prescott and Son business, but now I've accounts for you to attend. You may start on those Monday."

"Sir, I do not mean to contradict; however, I am eager to return to Eureka." Blaine forced an amicable tone. He wouldn't argue with this man, but he did not intend to remain past the sailing of the next ship headed north.

"Eager or not, your duties at the moment are here." Mr. Goldberg adjusted his wire-frame glasses. "I understand young college graduates think they know everything—my son, Samuel, certainly does—yet you've both much to learn. You will be wise to trust your father's and my guidance."

Blaine gathered his overcoat and portfolio. So he'd be wise to trust this man who apparently had no trouble devising schemes to manipulate his daughter? Likely Mr. Goldberg had a lot to teach him about business, but it would be a snowy day in July before he trusted this man with personal matters. And returning to Eureka couldn't be more personal.

The next morning, when Aunt Ruth tapped on the door, Ida hadn't yet found what she sought. Dresses, skirts, blouses, sweaters, and vests lay strewed over her bed and armchair.

"What are you doing, dear?" Her aunt's eyebrows arched. "Did Mrs. Zander ask for more clothing for the missionary barrels? Which garments are you donating? Oh, certainly not this blue one—it goes so nicely with your eyes. Here, let me help."

Ida had no problem parting with the pale yellow skirt or the high-collared white blouse that choked at the neck. Guilt plagued her that she received credit for generosity from her aunt when her motive had nothing to do with missionaries and their barrels. As a gesture of penance, she added her favorite straw hat with the pink ribbons. It felt more like a sacrifice, and one should sacrifice for missionaries.

"You know, I think I have a few frocks I could contribute." Aunt Ruth reached her hand toward Ida. "Come help me choose."

Aunt Ruth's closet dwarfed Ida's. Skirts lined one side, with blouses and vests hung above them. Day dresses hung against the opposing wall, with special-occasion frocks across the back. Shoes perched on cedar shelves below the hats and scarves. A pleasant aroma of lavender mingled with the cedar and, from somewhere, a hint of rose.

As if drawn by a magnet, Ida's attention was caught by a cherry-red dress. "I don't believe I've ever seen you wear this one."

"Red is not my best color." Aunt Ruth removed the velvet frock from its hanger and then shook her head. "I hardly think it's appropriate wear for missionaries."

"Probably not," Ida agreed. "Still, maybe it will raise someone's spirits. You know how having pretty things brightens our humor." She added it to her aunt's small pile of modest skirts and drab sweaters. Another pang of guilt attacked. Although her words reflected her true opinion, the red dress was not going to lift any missionary's mood. With a few alterations, it would be the perfect costume for Second Street. Now to find one for Mattie.

"I'll put these with mine and take them to Mrs. Zander after lunch." Ida took the garments to her room, hung the red dress in the back of her closet, and combined the others with her offerings. She surveyed the pile critically and added another skirt, blouse, and cardigan. The gesture did nothing to assuage her sense of wrong. Emptying her closet wouldn't be sufficient to erase her conscience's accusation of deceitful wrongdoing.

What would Blaine think? Based on fear for her, he disapproved of her plan for saving Second Street souls. What would he say about her deceptions? Did the end justify the means?

She sure hoped so.

As Blaine suspected, the outing to the theater was, in truth, an excuse for Abigail to meet Chester. Her beau waited for them a block away in an open carriage with seats for four. Samuel's appearance with a young female on his arm did surprise Blaine.

"You're not the only one who can dazzle the ladies," his friend whispered.

Blaine forced a smile at the comment. He didn't remember a time he'd tried to "dazzle" anyone. He assisted Abigail onto the front bench next to Chester and stood back as Samuel and his companion took the other seat.

Abigail switched her attention from Chester to Blaine. "We can squish together here. Come beside me."

"If it's all the same, I'll walk. Just point me in the right direction."

Samuel detailed the way to O'Farrell Street, then offered a caution. "If you decide to walk around the city, avoid the wharves. They're safe enough in the daytime but can get rowdy after dark."

"Should I wait for you outside the theater?" Blaine swatted at a fly buzzing around his head.

After an awkward pause, Abigail smiled sweetly then said, "We'll be along shortly. Don't wait for us."

Her response left no doubt the foursome had plans that didn't include any time at the Alcazar, which suited him fine. He'd rather not be involved with their schemes. Since he wouldn't lie for them, the less he knew, the better.

Only having Ida with him could have improved his stroll to the theater. He enjoyed the architecture of various buildings, the variety of people coming and going, the delicious aromas wafting from numerous eating establishments.

The Alcazar stood in the middle of the block, a tall adobe structure inviting pleasure seekers' admission. He stepped into the dirt lane to better appreciate the architecture. Patrons of the theater bumped into him as they made their way toward the arched entrance.

Did he want to attend the concert alone among so many couples?

Maybe he'd head to the docks instead and confirm his passage aboard the ship. That wouldn't take long, and then what would he do to pass the time? Returning to the Goldbergs' carried the risk of encountering the Mr. or Mrs., thus necessitating an explanation of Abigail's whereabouts. While he'd not participate openly in her deception, neither would he purposely expose her.

The concert remained a better choice. He strolled inside, awed by the theater's size and grandeur. As the performance began, he found his seat, slightly aware he might be the only one of the two thousand in attendance without a companion. The awkwardness vaporized as he lost himself in the music and heartily applauded at its conclusion.

Upon leaving the theater, he traversed crowded streets. The throngs diminished the farther uphill he trekked. To his relief, no one greeted him when he arrived at the Goldbergs', not even William or the butler. For a moment, he wondered at it—wouldn't someone be up to receive Abigail when she returned? Then thoughts of his own plans pushed other concerns aside. Once in his room, he reconsidered the wisdom of staying the night. Why risk confronting questions he'd prefer to avoid in the morning? Why take a chance on unexpected delays and miss the ship?

That Mr. Goldberg expected him to remain poked at Blaine's conscience. He had not continued the discussion from that afternoon, and his host likely assumed he'd stay. Was it cowardly to leave without announcing his departure? Perhaps, but why upset the household unnecessarily? He'd expressed his plans. That would have to do.

It took less than a quarter hour to finish gathering his things and exit the house, portfolio and baggage in hand. Fog climbed the hill from the bay with ghostlike fingers stretching through fences and shrubs. Closer to the water, the fog grew thicker until it obscured the ships and muffled the raucous shouts coming from saloons catering to sailors eager to let off steam after weeks aboard their ships.

The dense fog complicated finding the ship he sought. He paused to decipher a vessel's name, squinting to see the letters painted on the hull.

Someone shook him. His head pounded as if a horse galloped inside his brain. His clothing clung to him with dampness. He lay on something hard and splintery.

A voice penetrated into his consciousness. "Are you all right, mister?"

As he struggled to sit up, a wave of dizziness hindered his efforts. An early morning sun peeked through high clouds. Neither his portmanteau nor his portfolio were beside him on the dock.

And the ship had sailed.

CHAPTER 16

No choice remained to Blaine except a return to the Goldbergs' home. Dizziness prevented him from walking the distance, even with the assistance of the lad who had found him.

"I'll get help." The boy ran off, then returned with a couple of drunken sailors.

They half carried, half dragged him from the dock to the street. No carriages for hire were around at that early morning hour. Fortunately, one of the revelers had a buggy standing outside a rowdy saloon.

"I'll pay you to take me home." Did his words slur?

"Show me the money first."

Blaine dug into his pockets. Whoever took his portmanteau had taken his pocket watch and cash as well, not that he'd had much. "Mr. Goldberg will cover my expenses." At least that's what he hoped.

"Goldberg, you say?"

Blaine nodded.

"Get in."

Mr. Goldberg paid the sailor as Blaine's vision blurred and he slumped against the wall. He heard voices but couldn't understand the words.

William appeared and helped him up the stairs to his room, removed Blaine's torn and grimy overcoat, then brought in a pitcher and poured water into the porcelain basin. "Your head is bleeding. What happened?"

"I don't know." Blaine wanted to lie down and return to sleep—or unconsciousness—whichever would make the hammering in his head go away.

"I can't seem to find a change of clothes for you." William stood in front of the empty armoire.

"No, you won't find them. I packed everything into my bag." Blaine muttered the words with his eyes closed. He imagined the valet's reaction. It wouldn't take an educated legal mind to figure out he'd intended to leave. He'd been found on the dock where ships heading north moored, and he'd just confessed he'd had all his possessions with him.

"No problem, sir. I believe I can find something suitable."

A few minutes later, Blaine peeked through squinted eyes to verify he was alone. He wanted his overcoat, to see if the letter he'd written to Ida remained tucked in the inside pocket. The letter would mean nothing to anyone else, but he'd poured his heart into it with an intimacy not intended for others to read. He stood, wobbled as though crossing a creek on slippery rocks, and plopped back onto the chair. The letter would have to wait.

When the door opened again, he expected to hear William's voice, but Samuel spoke. "You're a sight!"

Blaine opened his eyes, felt the room spin, and shut them.

"I brought you one of my nightshirts." Samuel put the garment on Blaine's lap. "Can you put it on, or should I summon William?"

"I'll manage." In a minute. When the nausea passed. Why did his friend linger?

"So I thought I'd make sure we have our stories straight." Sam brought a straight-backed chair nearer to Blaine and sat. He lowered his voice to a whisper. "What have you told Father?"

"Nothing."

"Good. We'll have to explain your presence on the dock without Abigail or me. Why were you there? I warned you it could be rowdy."

Too many words! If Samuel didn't stop, Blaine's head would burst.

The door opened again. William? Blaine squinted through half-opened eyes. A pudgy elderly man with spectacles on the end of his nose swooped in, carrying a large black bag. Mr. Goldberg followed.

"I'm Dr. Sanders. Heard you got a knock on your head." The doctor shooed Samuel from the chair and set his bag on it. "Let's have a look." Probing fingers touched tender spots on the back of Blaine's head.

"No need for stitches, but I'll bandage this up. The bleeding has stopped." The doctor worked as he talked. "Bet you have a humdinger of a headache. I'll leave some laudanum to help with that."

When Blaine again woke, he lay on his side in bed, wearing a strange nightshirt. Light trickled through gaps in the heavy drapes. His parched throat begged for water. He sat up without dizziness but with an acute ache. His head felt swollen to the size of an August watermelon.

"Good to see you awake."

He recognized Abigail's voice in the dimly lit room. "Can I get you anything? More medicine maybe?"

Unable to utter intelligible speech with a tongue swollen to the size of a baseball, Blaine nodded his head—once. Pain attacked with the slight movement. "Water," he croaked.

Abigail handed him a glass. "I'm supposed to notify Father when you come around again."

Blaine downed the water, nearly choking himself, then attempted to hold the jarring coughs within. How long had he been asleep?

More importantly, how was he to get on board the next ship?

"You don't have to sit here as if I'm sick." Blaine squinted to see her better in the faint light.

"No, but it makes a good impression on my parents." Abigail parted the drapes slightly and peeked out. "It's a soggy day anyway. I've not much else to do."

"What have you told them?" Blaine wouldn't lie about the night's events, but it could be helpful to know what the Goldbergs believed happened.

"That we were separated in the crowd after the concert. We said we looked for you at various restaurants but never dreamed you'd go down to the wharves."

"They accepted it?"

"Hook, line, and sinker." Abigail stretched and yawned. "And don't judge me. I'm sure you've done your share of lying. With parents as strict as ours, we have no choice. They force it on us."

Although he'd not been guilty of an untruth, he admitted to himself that his actions reeked of deceit. He considered it cowardly not to have been forthcoming about his departure after Mr. Goldberg insisted he stay. Why hadn't he? He gave himself the excuse that he wanted to avoid a scene. But a man should walk with integrity, not skulk around like a criminal.

"I'm going to let Father know you are awake, unless you'd rather I not." She neared his bed. "I don't believe he's noticed the room is free of your possessions, but it won't take long before he or Mother does. What are you going to tell them about that?"

"The truth."

"What truth?" Abigail paced from his bedside to the window, wringing her hands. "You can't let them know about Chester. You can't."

"I don't intend to say anything about Chester or you or Samuel and the young lady accompanying him. It's none of my business, and I'm happy to leave it at that."

Abigail sighed her relief. "I'll tell Father you're awake." She exited the room, leaving the door ajar.

He'd prefer not to be in bed when Mr. Goldberg entered. As he stood, his head ached as if a vise grip tightened around it. Could he walk? He took a tentative step. No dizziness. No nausea. He'd like to retrieve Ida's letter from his overcoat pocket before someone decided to clean the garment and find it.

Slowly, as if trodding across a seashore littered with kelp, he put one foot in front of the other, taking his time. The bench held a clean nightshirt and handkerchief, but nothing of his. Just in case, he checked the armoire—perhaps someone tidying the room had hung up his overcoat.

Empty. Dare he hope that whoever took the coat would ignore the contents of his pocket, interested only in cleaning and mending the garment—for which he should be grateful?

He slumped into the nearest chair, fatigued by his efforts—not sleepy, but physically exhausted. At this rate, he'd require assistance to get to the ship tomorrow morning. He'd explain his intentions to Mr. Goldberg again and depend on the gentleman's support. If that didn't work, he'd ask William to send for a carriage.

Knuckles rapped on the door, and Mr. Goldberg entered.

"Good to see you sitting up." Mr. Goldberg shook his head. "You gave us quite a scare, young man."

"Gave myself one as well." Blaine attempted to rise. Wobbled.

"Don't get up. Dr. Sanders assures us a few days of rest, and you'll be as good as new."

"I believe I've recovered sufficiently to return home on tomorrow's tide." Blaine met his host's gaze.

"No need for that." Mr. Goldberg handed him a telegram. "I wired your father about the incident, and he sent back a reply. He sees no need for a change of plans. You are to remain here as initially arranged."

Blaine read the brief statement, leaving no doubt his father knew all along his stay in San Francisco was not the quick trip he'd been led to believe. Annoyance bordering on anger built within him. He hadn't sufficient energy to fight the feelings or let loose with his thoughts, but he spoke crisply. "I've completed the tasks my father assigned me. I see no reason to delay my departure."

"The tasks your father assigned? My dear man, you are here in my employ. It is not a matter of completing tasks. As soon as you are able, you'll begin in the accounting office."

"I'm not an accountant."

"No, you are not, but we are willing to train you." Mr. Goldberg's brow furrowed. "Surely your father explained to you the business agreement we made."

An agreement made without consulting him? Blaine bristled. He'd always done as his father bid. Always trusted his advice and direction without questioning. But he wasn't a little boy anymore. He couldn't—wouldn't—be manipulated into situations not of his choosing.

But that wasn't between himself and Mr. Goldberg.

It was a matter between himself and his father.

To be dealt with in person.

CHAPTER 17

Blaine debated how to answer Mr. Goldberg. The situation demanded tact, but he refused to pretend he had any intentions of remaining in San Francisco.

"Mr. Goldberg, I've no doubt there is much you can teach me, and I appreciate the opportunity to continue my education. However, I've misunderstood my role here and am unprepared to remain for an extended period of time."

Mrs. Goldberg burst into the room, waving a piece of paper. "You should have spoken to us first, Mr. Prescott! There are reasons for the rules of decorum. However, under the circumstances, you will be forgiven."

"What are you talking about?" Mr. Goldberg frowned.

"Read this, and all will be made clear." She held the paper out. "He's written in the most tender terms of his devotion to our dear Abigail."

Mr. Goldberg reached to take the note, but his wife drew it back. "So very sweet. Listen to his first line: 'My Dearest Angel—'"

Blaine leaped up, grasped the note, and jerked it from Mrs. Goldberg's fingers. "That was not meant for your eyes." Dizziness forced him to grip the bedpost for support.

"Of course not. The maid found it in your overcoat pocket, and I intercepted it. It's a good thing I did. Now you have opportunity to announce your intentions to Mr. Goldberg and proceed properly. Then you can deliver this in person to Abigail."

Blaine pocketed the note. "There has been a mistake."

"One you can rectify immediately." Mrs. Goldberg headed toward the door. "I'll leave you two alone." She smiled smugly. As the door closed behind her, she called out, "Abigail! Abigail! Come, my dear girl."

Honesty and truth demanded he not allow the misunderstanding to continue—how to proceed? It occurred to him that he'd not used Ida's name in the note, only effusive terms of endearment straight from his heart.

"Am I to understand you've written a declaration to my daughter without first consulting me?" Deep lines emphasized Mr. Goldberg's scowl. "Do you have so little respect for this family, for me, as the head of the house?" His voice rose. "What do you have to say for yourself?"

Closing his eyes against the spinning room, Blaine sank back into the chair. He swallowed a wave of nausea as sweat beaded on his forehead. Could he form the words required to answer? "I wrote the note to Miss Dempsey." Blaine pulled it from his pocket. "You can see for yourself, nowhere is your daughter's name indicated."

Scowling, Mr. Goldberg ignored the gesture. Blaine attempted to meet the man's glare with his own steady gaze, but the exertions of the morning hindered him. The doctor had been right about his needing rest. He closed his eyes.

When he regained consciousness, he was back in bed. This time no one sat in the shadows. A lamp on the nightstand revealed a glass of water alongside a packet of laudanum. What time was it? Tightly drawn drapes allowed no hint of day or night. He struggled to sit up, checked his pocket for the note, then reached for the water. The glass shook in his hand, spilling drops onto his nightshirt, but he didn't care. The note remained in place, and the water quenched his thirst.

He'd leave the medicine there, at least for now, as he wanted his head unmuddled. He needed a plan. Not a complicated one, and not one dependent on deceit, just a way to return to Eureka, to Ida.

No roads existed between the two communities. No railways. A few obscure Indian trails led over the mountains. Ships alone made the journey possible, but only possible for him if his condition improved.

Not knowing Ida's thoughts tore at him. Had Pratt delivered his message? What a paltry message it had been. The letter he'd intended to send soon after landing remained in his pocket.

How long before he saw her again?

Would she even be willing to see him?

After consuming the chicken soup brought to him, Blaine felt his energy improve, inspiring hope he'd be fit to travel soon, although too late to hope for that day.

Regardless, he could risk no more delays in sending his letter to Ida. He added a few lines of explanation for his continued absence, found an envelope in the desk drawer, and addressed it.

Who would post it for him? Mr. Goldberg? Unlikely. Mrs. Goldberg? No. He'd not let the missive fall into her hands again. Abigail? She owed him a favor, but could he trust her? He doubted it. That left either Sam or William.

It must be sent as soon as possible. Dressed only in a nightshirt, he couldn't very well leave his room to find either option. Perhaps a dressing gown had been left for him in the armoire.

What was this?

His portmanteau, scuffed and scratched, sat on the bottom shelf, stuffed with his clothing.

"Guess the thief didn't like your wardrobe."

Blaine turned at the sound of Sam's voice.

"You found it? What about the portfolio? Did you find it as well?"

Sam lit the lamp on the desk. "Both bags were near the docks, items strewed about." He sat on the desk chair.

"Probably didn't find my pocket watch or the cash?"

Sam shook his head.

Blaine began pulling clothing from the bag, searching for something suitable to wear. An onset of dizziness forced him to stop. He staggered to the bedside chair.

"Still a bit wobbly, eh?"

"I'll be fine in a minute."

"You sure stirred up the household." Sam rolled his eyes. "Father is beside himself over your lack of respect—he's talking of canceling business dealings with Prescott and Son, while Mother is ready to contact the papers and announce my sister's engagement to you. Lot of yelling going on downstairs."

"So your father has changed his mind about me as a future son-in-law, and your mother is ready to send out invitations."

"That about sums it up." Sam's eyebrows rose. "You poked a hornet's nest."

"I didn't mean to. I just wanted to get back to Eureka." Blaine paused. "I still do."

"Maybe I can help."

Blaine straightened in his chair. "Would you post the letter for me? Ida must be completely confused over my absence and lack of communication."

"Sure. I'll post the letter, but wouldn't you rather deliver it yourself?" Sam ruffled through the portmanteau, pulling out pants and a shirt.

"Do you have a plan?" Blaine accepted the clothing from his friend.

"Not much of one. After my parents retire for the night, I'll sneak you downstairs. Chester will be waiting with his carriage. We'll take you to one of your father's ships and see you safely on board."

"Why would you risk your parents' wrath over this? They aren't unhappy with *you*." This scheme put Sam in the middle. Why would he offer such a plan?

"They won't know I had anything to do with it." Sam headed for the door. "And isn't that what friends are for? To help one another? You'd do the same for me." He left, closing the door softly.

Blaine shut his eyes and rubbed his forehead. He could be in Eureka in two days—three tops.

So why wasn't he relieved?

Even with confused thinking, he acknowledged the scheme felt all wrong. Sneaking off? He'd tried that. It boomeranged on him, not just with the failure, but with the shame he felt. He would not steal away like a criminal. It had been a mistake to try. If a man lost integrity, what did he have left?

It took a half hour for Blaine to dress and repack his bag. Another half hour passed before he felt stable enough to lift it and the portfolio and leave his room.

The stairs were another matter entirely.

CHAPTER 18

Blaine waited at the top of the stairs. With a little luck someone—anyone—would come by and help him. As it was not past time for the family to retire, he hoped to find them in the drawing room together. He'd express his gratitude for their hospitality, explain the necessity of his returning to Eureka, and say goodbye. He'd ask the butler to call a carriage and be on his way. It was the honorable thing to do.

Although it was unlikely a vessel would get under way before the morning's tide, he'd make his way aboard and stay the night to be ready for an early departure. In some ways it would be better to wait at the Goldbergs' until morning; however, that carried the risk of missing the ship, and he wouldn't chance it. He patted his pocket with the envelope containing his letter to Ida. In two days or so, he'd be with her.

No one came. Not a servant, not a family member. With portfolio in one hand and gripping the staircase railing with the other, he left his bag at the top of the stairs and made his way down, pausing after each step. Sweat dripped from his temples. By the time he reached the bottom, he trembled breathlessly. Returning to the top would be impossible.

He rested until his breathing returned to normal and his shaking subsided. Then he straightened his shoulders and breathed a quick prayer before entering the drawing room. "Good evening, Mrs. Goldberg, Mr. Goldberg." He willed his voice to sound strong and hale.

"Oh, goodness!" Mrs. Goldberg rose. "Are you well enough to be up, my dear boy?"

"Yes, thank you. I'm quite well." Blaine dipped his head in her direction, then met the gaze of Mr. Goldberg. "I'd like to thank you for your generous hospitality. As I indicated previously, it is time for me to return to Eureka."

Mr. Goldberg's features hardened.

"You'll be back in a few days, though." Mrs. Goldberg glanced at Abigail, who had set aside the book she'd been reading, then smiled confidently. "I know you won't wish to be away long."

"On the contrary, I'm not sure when or if I'll be returning." Blaine cleared his throat. "I've commitments in Eureka that demand my attention."

"What could possibly be more important than your interests here?" Again Mrs. Goldberg glanced at Abigail then back at Blaine. "You surely don't mean to leave at this late hour."

"The man has his reasons." Mr. Goldberg spoke in an even tone, but with fire in his eyes. "Goodbye, Mr. Prescott."

"Again, thank you for your hospitality." Blaine left the room. Mrs. Goldberg's high-pitched protests could be heard through the closed door.

He met Sam in the foyer. "I've said my goodbyes, friend. I couldn't sneak away. Thank you for your willingness to help."

"You told Mother and Father you are leaving?"

"Yes. Tonight."

Sounds of quarreling reached from the drawing room into the outer area. Three voices shouted, none stopping to listen to the others.

"Like I said, you poked a hornet's nest." Sam patted Blaine's shoulder. "How can I help?"

"I left my portmanteau at the top of the stairs, and I need a carriage."

The gangplank was still lowered to the dock when Blaine arrived. Sam steadied him up the narrow ramp, carrying his bag and portfolio. "I've brought you some food as well. Not sure when the ship will sail, and you might need it." He handed Blaine a small package.

"Thank you. Tell Abigail I wish her and Chester the best." Blaine puffed out the words, straining to speak after the taxing hike to the ship's deck.

"She's unlikely to welcome any message from you."

"Sam, I have to go. I do wish her well, and you too."

His friend met his gaze. "I've no hard feelings—Abigail, on the other hand, will feel resentful. A resentful Abigail can be a dangerous woman."

Blaine shook his friend's hand. "Thanks for the warning, but I'll be far away. What harm can she do to me?"

On Sunday, Ida had no trouble listening to Reverend Huntington's sermon as she had the previous week with Blaine seated behind her. After their conversation in his office, she saw him in a different light, as an ally, not just a respected man of God—not quite a friend, because that would be irreverent.

Monday afternoon, she visited Mattie. "I've got something to show you." She opened the bag and revealed the red dress.

Mattie knelt beside her bed and pulled out a box. "You are going to love this." She lifted an emerald-green frock from the box.

Ida's eyes widened. "Where did you find it?" She fingered the silk dress.

"From the missionary barrels." Mattie held the bodice to herself and twirled. The skirt swished as if it were as light as gossamer.

"Mrs. Lee let you look through the barrels? What did you tell her?"

"Nothing. The barrels were right there in the church basement, and I figured that since our intention is to talk about Jesus, we are as much missionaries as the people in Africa." Mattie twirled again and giggled. "Missionaries with cleavage."

Ida gasped.

"Oh, don't act so shocked. This was your idea."

As both garments needed alterations, the two girls worked on their frocks together, cutting and stitching and making plans in Mattie's small garden. Because they often spent time together, Ida made no deceitful excuses to Aunt Ruth regarding her afternoon activities.

Meeting with Qui was another matter.

Ida avoided the kitchen, choosing to meet her a block from home as the cook prepared to grocery shop that Tuesday. "Qui, I'm so excited. You'll never guess the great plans I've made."

Qui increased her pace. "Missy going to get Qui in trouble."

"Not at all. I've got everything under control. Reverend Huntington will meet with us in his church on your shopping days—not today, next time. Aunt Ruth can't find fault with that."

Continuing her quick, choppy steps, Qui shook her head. "Cause too much trouble."

Ida hurried to keep pace with the cook's gait. "You said you wanted to learn about Jesus. Did you lie to me?"

The question hit its mark, as Ida hoped. Qui halted. Her eyes narrowed. "Qui never lie."

"I didn't think so." Ida gently placed her hand on the Chinese woman's arm. "You want to know about Jesus, and He wants you to know Him. Come once, and if you're still afraid, we'll figure out something else, all right?"

"Maybe. I shop now."

She'd pressured the cook enough. Ida let Qui go on alone, then headed toward Mattie's. The dresses were nearly finished. They needed only to try them on and make final adjustments.

Mattie waited for her in the front garden, the dresses stuffed into a valise. "Mother didn't work at the shop today as usual. Can we try them on at your house?"

"Of course."

Eagerness quickened their pace as they giggled together along the way. An empty house awaited them when they arrived, making it easy to scramble upstairs and into Ida's room without drawing unwanted attention.

"You go first." Ida pulled Mattie's gown from the valise.

The gown fit her friend snugly, emphasizing every curve.

"Oh my." Ida blushed. "Maybe the bare shoulders are too much?"

Mattie shimmied in front of the full-length mirror. "I like it." She lifted her chin, batted her eyelashes, and swayed her hips as she strutted around the room. "Ida, try on yours!"

Suddenly shy, Ida bit her lip. Would her frock show as much of her figure as Mattie's did? She slipped into the formfitting gown, avoiding the mirror as Mattie fastened the back buttons.

"You have to look, Ida."

The dress transformed her into how she imagined a mermaid might look: tight bodice, tight waist, tight through the hips, flaring from the knees down.

"I don't think I can walk."

"Try." Mattie took Ida's hand. "Just imagine our faces painted with rouge and blue eye shadow and red lipstick." She planted one of the ostrich-feathered hats they'd purchased on her head. "Our own mothers won't recognize us."

Ida strutted about the room, glancing in the mirror from the corner of her eye. The dress made her feel older, less innocent. How could that be? She'd not done anything impure her entire life. As she caught glimpses of herself, the Ida she knew disappeared, and this other creature—mature, experienced, worldly—took over. Could clothes do that? Change a person's identity just by wearing them?

She wanted out of the frock, back into her normal clothes.

Suddenly the door opened, and the housemaid entered, her arms full of folded clean clothes. Then, eyes wide, she dropped the bundle and ran out of the room screaming, "Mrs. Dempsey! Mrs. Dempsey! Intruders in Miss Ida's room!"

CHAPTER 19

"Moira, everything is all right, it's me!" Ida started to chase after the panicked housekeeper, then thought better of it. She turned to Mattie. "Hurry, hide the dresses!"

Mattie had already wriggled out of her frock. It lay in a heap on the floor as she scrambled to put her clothes back on. Ida followed suit. Footsteps pounded up the stairs. Wallace entered the room first, armed with his father's walking stick kept near the front door. "Who's here?" He turned in circles like a trapped wolf ready to attack and destroy.

"It's just us, Cousin." Ida struggled to fasten the buttons on her dress, the other gown at her feet.

Aunt Ruth's voice came from the hallway. "Wallace, who did you find? Are you all right?"

"No intruders here, Aunt Ruth, just Mattie and me." Ida kicked the disguise under her bed.

Wallace lowered his weapon as his mother entered the room.

"I don't understand." Aunt Ruth planted her hands on her hips. "Why did Moira panic?" She opened Ida's closet door and peered inside. "Is there someone else here? What frightened Moira so?"

Ida glanced at the floor. Her taboo garment lay half under the bed. "I don't think she expected anyone to be here and saw Mattie first."

Her friend jumped in. "We were trying on silly discarded clothes I found just for fun, and the housekeeper didn't knock or anything. She scared me more than I startled her." Mattie plopped one of the oversized feathered hats on her head and made a comical face.

Aunt Ruth looked from one girl to the other, shaking her head.

"It's comforting to know that if we were damsels in distress, a strong, brave man would rescue us." Mattie grinned at Wallace. "Armed with a most dangerous and deadly cane."

Wallace glowered and stomped from the room.

Ida wished Mattie hadn't teased her cousin, but she said nothing. What good would it do?

When again alone, Ida and Mattie sank side by side onto the Persian carpet in front of the fireplace. "Whew, that was close," Mattie breathed.

"Too close," Ida agreed. "We'll have to be more careful."

Mattie nodded. "When do we put Project Save Second Street Souls into action? Today? Why not today? We've everything we need."

"I've given it a lot of thought." Ida rose and gathered the items they'd collected for the project: makeup, hats, shoes, the gowns, and black lace parasols. "We can't go out at night. It has to be in the afternoon."

"Why not at night?" Mattie's lips formed a little pout.

"Because the women are, um, working at night." Heat flushed Ida's cheeks. "They sleep late, I'm assuming, so our best chance of encountering them is late afternoon or early evening."

"Have you considered where we can go to don our disguises?"

"Yes." Ida met Mattie's gaze. "Church."

"What!"

"The doors are never locked, and it's only a few blocks from Second Street." Ida shrugged. "Do you have a better idea?"

Since the ship delayed in port a full day before setting out early Tuesday morning, Blaine appreciated the food Sam had given him. He hid his compromised state from the crew—the captain especially might refuse him passage, even knowing he was the owner's son, if he suspected danger of a man falling overboard.

His headache persisted during the voyage, although not as debilitating as before. Dizziness remained the biggest problem. After the ship left port, he settled near a skiff used in shallow water to transport goods from ship to shore. It provided a degree of protection from the wind and, more importantly, eliminated the necessity of climbing up and down steep stairs. His condition rendered him unfit for such physical exertion.

He dozed on and off. As night fell, he descended the steps to his berth. He remained there in utter darkness, sleeping for he didn't know how long. Shouts from the crew woke him. Had he actually slept through most of the two-day voyage?

He'd not made a plan for disembarking with portfolio and luggage in tow. Even without those encumbrances, traversing the gangplank could be problematic.

At the first opportunity, he pulled aside a junior shipman and explained his dilemma. "After the ship is docked, when the gangplank is empty, come back and help me. There'll be compensation for your efforts."

The young sailor agreed and went about his duties. By the time he returned, the sun had set and the shipping office near the dock had closed. As they stepped off the wharf, Blaine addressed the young man. "Help me home, and I'll double the amount."

"Nah, my friends are already at the saloon."

"Help me home, or wait until tomorrow to receive compensation."

The sailor scowled. "Point the way."

At first he'd thought he'd head straight to Ida's, but the need to pay the sailor prohibited that. He didn't worry about obtaining the cash. His father wouldn't make a scene in front of an outsider. After that, he'd have to explain his presence. He viewed the pending conversation as a potential turning point in their relationship, a necessary one.

He wouldn't be welcomed with open arms. But he hoped once they had a chance to talk, he and his father, man-to-man, a new understanding would be gained and their bond strengthened to work together. If that couldn't happen?

It had to.

Blaine's steps faltered as the exertion brought on more dizziness. Having traveled almost a block ahead of him, the sailor turned back and handed him a stout stick. "Use this."

By the time they reached his home, sweat dampened his forehead and his breath came in short gasps. Pratt answered the door and immediately helped Blaine inside. "The sailor needs paid—generously." Blaine collapsed into a chair.

After Pratt saw the young man off, he addressed Blaine. "Your parents are at dinner, sir. Do you wish to join them?"

"Not yet."

"Would you prefer to wait here, sir, or might I help you to your room?"

"My room." He should have Pratt announce his arrival, but he needed to recover strength before facing his father.

Pratt returned with one of the servants, and together they took Blaine to his upstairs room. He sank into his favorite chair and closed his eyes. Finally home! Near Ida again. He'd eat, then call on her. Maybe he could do it before the confrontation with his father. "Pratt?"

"Yes, sir." The butler paused in front of the open door.

"Let's wait to announce my arrival."

"If you say so, sir."

Moments later, a knock at the door woke him, and a servant brought a tray filled with baked salmon, potatoes, green beans, and a steaming cup of tea. Nourished by the food, Blaine removed his soiled clothing and donned clean attire. The effort taxed him, requiring a few minutes to recover. The thought of seeing Ida helped.

How could he get to her without revealing his presence to his parents?

He'd been foolish to think he could. Foolish and selfish as well. A misunderstanding existed between himself and his father, one that a conversation would resolve. He owed the man respect. Wasn't it wiser to deal with it as soon as possible? Then, when he visited Ida, his attention would be all hers.

Pratt responded quickly to his ringing the bell.

"I'm sorry to bother you again. Will you help me back down the stairs? I want to let my parents know I've arrived."

"Of course, sir." Pratt hesitated. "Might it be better to explain you're wearied from the journey and have retired for the night?"

"Perhaps." Going back down also meant coming up again. How many trips could he make? Yet waiting to speak with his father until morning also meant waiting to see Ida. Nevertheless, the butler's suggestion held wisdom. So much exertion at the end of a long day might be more than he could handle. He wanted to see Ida to talk with her, not faint at her feet.

"Yes, tell them I've retired, but wait to announce my arrival until they've settled in the drawing room."

"Yes, sir." Pratt started to leave.

"One more thing. Since I'm not going to see Miss Dempsey until tomorrow, I'd like to send her a note. Will you come back for it and make sure she receives it tonight?"

"Of course."

Blaine slogged to his desk. He wrote a few lines and sealed the note inside an envelope. He'd wait to deliver in person the letter he'd written in

San Francisco, perhaps as they walked along the shore or picnicked again in the redwoods. He slumped into his chair again and closed his eyes.

For the first time in what felt like ages, he relaxed and let the peace of the room envelop him.

Until his door flew open and his mother burst in.

His father right behind her.

CHAPTER 20

"Blaine, my dear boy, your father just told me about that terrible incident in San Francisco!" His mother rushed to him and grabbed his hand. "Are you all right?"

Not a child to be fawned over, he reclaimed his hand by retrieving a handkerchief from his pocket. "The doctor said with a few days of rest I should be fine. I'm already much recovered."

"We'll have our own doctor check you over." She turned to Blaine's father. "Don't you agree we should have the opinion of someone we trust?" Not waiting for a reply, she resumed her attention on Blaine. "Are you hungry?" Again not pausing for a response, she pulled the cord for a servant to come.

"I've already eaten, Mother. Pratt made sure of that."

"Really? You've had time to dine and change your clothes?" Her brow furrowed as she cocked her head, scrutinizing him. "Why didn't you join us for dinner?"

"I wanted to. Truly, weariness from the journey prevented it."

His mother's eyes narrowed. "Pratt informed us you meant to retire for the night. I daresay your clothing indicates otherwise."

Ignoring his mother's comment, Blaine rose from his chair and extended his hand to his father. They shook. "I'm glad to be back home."

Without removing the pipe clenched between his teeth, his father spoke. "Yes, well, that's something we can discuss tomorrow, when you've rested."

Blaine noticed Pratt lingering in the doorway. "Thank you for responding to the bell. Mother didn't realize you already provided me with food, and regarding the other matter, I've decided to handle it myself."

"Very good, sir." Pratt nodded and left.

Puffing on his pipe, his father moved toward the door as his mother planted herself in one of the two chairs facing the empty fireplace. No embers glowed to add warmth to the room either in fact or atmosphere.

Blaine's father removed the pipe from his lips. "It's time to go, my dear."

"I want to know a few things first."

"Then ask your questions and leave the boy in peace." Blaine's father exited the room.

"Actually, Mother, now is not a good time. I'll answer all your questions tomorrow. Presently I'm eager to call on Miss Dempsey—perhaps you are aware I was unable to say a proper goodbye." He put on his overcoat. "I'm anxious to explain my absence and offer my promise it won't happen again."

"Don't make promises you can't keep."

Blaine stopped and caught his mother's gaze. She squared her shoulders and stared back, her jaw set defiantly. If he spoke and acted with confidence, not forgetting the respect due his parents, this critical moment could help establish his independence within his family.

"That is wise advice, Mother. A man's word is worth protecting." He put on his hat. "Pratt reported correctly that I planned to retire early; however, after eating and resting a few moments, I am revived." He stood in the doorway of his bedroom. "I look forward to seeing you again at breakfast."

He left her sitting in his room, red-faced and appearing ready to stage a fainting spell. "I am your mother," she shouted after him. "You will respect my wishes."

A twinge of guilt halted Blaine for a moment. He possessed great respect for his mother and didn't relish disappointing her, but now was not the time to show weakness. He made it down the stairs and out the door without an episode of dizziness. Buttoning his overcoat, he wished he'd brought along a walking stick with him.

As he passed the Congregationalist Church, two women, dressed shockingly provocatively, one in red, the other in green, dashed down the length of the building and through a back door, one he assumed led to the basement. Curious, he paused. Although none of his business, he wondered at the strangeness of it all.

Continuing on his way, he patted the letter in his pocket. Maybe, if the timing proved right, he'd give it to Ida this evening. If the quotation "Absence makes the heart grow fonder" was true, their reunion would be joyous.

Mr. Dempsey himself opened the door when Blaine knocked. "Come in, Mr. Prescott."

"Thank you, sir." Blaine entered the foyer. "Please forgive me for coming unannounced at this late hour. I am hoping to call on Miss Dempsey."

"Unfortunately, Ida is not home at present." Mr. Dempsey turned as his wife approached.

"Welcome, Mr. Prescott," she gushed. "Please do come in. Won't you join us in the drawing room?"

Blaine had no desire to sit in a drawing room and make small talk with Ida's aunt and uncle. As delightful as they may be, it was Ida he wanted to see, and if that wasn't possible, he should return home and make peace with his parents. "Mr. Dempsey has informed me Ida is not home. Would you please tell her I came by and will call again tomorrow?"

"Surely you have a few moments to spare." Mrs. Dempsey laid her hand on his arm. "Ida and Mattie are working on some sort of secret project together. She'll be home anytime now. She'll be disappointed to miss you."

"Thank you for your kind invitation." How to get out of this?

He'd simply be honest and stick to his guns. "I hadn't planned to remain long, as my mother is anxious for my return this evening. I look forward to calling tomorrow." He tipped his hat, nodded to Mr. Dempsey, and exited the house, leaving Mrs. Dempsey with her mouth agape.

He certainly had a penchant for upsetting mothers this evening.

Ida and Mattie slumped together in the dark basement beside crates filled with nativity scene items. Only the lamppost's gleam showing through the narrow basement windows kept the area from complete blackness. A somber mood replaced the excited hopefulness they'd experienced a few hours prior when they set out to begin Project Save Second Street Souls.

Finally, Mattie spoke. "That didn't go as expected."

"Can you believe that woman actually kicked us out?" Ida stood and struggled out of the "mermaid" red dress.

"What about that other one who threw our pamphlets in the street?"

Mattie joined Ida in removing her disguise to re-dress in their normal clothing. "I think she was jealous."

"Of what?" Ida folded the costume carefully and tucked it behind the manger used only in December.

"Of us." Mattie handed Ida her green dress. "You know—I mean, we aren't *droopy* anywhere."

"Mattie, what a thing to say!"

"Well, it's true. Some of those women are old. Probably in their forties or close to it. No wonder they wear so much makeup. They've got a lot to cover up."

"Seems to me they're covering up the wrong thing." Ida finished buttoning her blouse. "Did you see how far the slit in the redhead's dress went?"

"My goodness, not just hers. Did you notice the one with that veil?"

Ida blew out a breath. "Tonight did not go well, but I'm not giving up. If I learned anything this evening, it's these women really need Jesus. I knew that anyway. Seeing their lives up close makes it even more urgent."

With their disguises tucked away and their coats donned, the girls opened the basement door, checked right and left, and stole outside. Once in the open, they strolled together arm in arm without worrying anyone would discover them.

"Tomorrow we'll try the other side of the street and maybe begin a bit earlier." Ida lifted her gaze to heaven. "Tonight, I'll pray for more guidance."

They reached the corner where Ida's home and Mattie's stood in opposite directions.

"All right. Till tomorrow, then." Mattie waved goodbye.

Head down, Ida tromped toward her home. She didn't think ministering to the ladies would be easy. Neither did she fathom how difficult it would be to get their attention—the right kind of attention. Her idea of the costumes had been to blend in, to not make a "holier-than-thou" impression. It never occurred to her she'd be viewed as competition or forced to leave the premises. Deep in thought, she turned the corner onto her block, thankful the lampposts had been lit. Being outdoors alone after dark unnerved her.

"Ida?"

She looked up into the eyes of Blaine. "You're back! Oh, I knew you'd come soon!"

Why did he look at her like that?

"I called at your house as soon as I could." Blaine's brows furrowed.

"Is something wrong?"

"Not at all. I'm just not used to seeing you with—is that blue eye shadow? Your mother said you and Mattie were working on some sort of project together—"

"Oh!" Ida turned her back to Blaine. "We forgot about our faces!" She pulled a handkerchief from her reticule and began scrubbing her lips and cheeks.

"May I ask what type of project involves painted faces?" Blaine spoke lightheartedly. He'd not even try to guess what she and Mattie had been up to. Likely something surprising and wonderful at the same time. By the looks of her, maybe a clown act for children?

"It was part of our costume." Ida kept scrubbing.

"Look at me. Let me help."

When she faced him, he broke out laughing. Rather than wiping off the rouge and lipstick, she'd managed to streak it from chin to forehead. "I believe we'll need soap and water." Blaine continued laughing.

"I am so happy you are back! I have to get home. Will you call tomorrow?"

"Yes, of course. May I walk with you now?" Blaine could see Ida's house from where he stood.

"That's not a good idea. I can't let Aunt Ruth see me like this."

Ida sped off. He watched as she avoided the front entry, nearly tripped along the side of the house, and entered through the kitchen door.

Knowing Ida's penchant for openness and honesty, it made no sense she'd hide something as innocent as clown makeup from her aunt.

CHAPTER 21

Ida closed the door behind her softly, holding her breath. She waited for her eyes to adjust to the unlit kitchen, then tiptoed through the room. She bumped into the icebox, then the coal bucket, before making it to the door leading to the hallway. She scurried to the washroom. Once in the windowless room tucked under the stairs, she wished she'd grabbed a candle. In the utter blackness of the space, she leaned against the wall and waited for her breathing to return to normal.

Blaine was back! Not knowing when he'd arrive, she'd thrown herself into Project Save Second Street Souls and, of course, Qui. To say she'd forgotten him entirely would be untrue. Thoughts of him lingered in the back of her mind regardless of the worthy distractions before her.

Her heart had leaped at the sight of him. He'd said he'd been to call on her. How unfortunate she'd not been home! What a different evening that would have been from the one she'd just experienced.

Tomorrow he'd call again. She had so much to share with him, in private, of course. This skulking about didn't suit her in the least. She consoled herself that the greater good demanded it, and, most importantly, it was temporary. After she found the mysterious woman and had an opportunity to set up Bible studies for her and her friends, she could meet openly with them.

"Ida, is that you?" Aunt Ruth called from the other side of the door.

"Yes."

"Why ever did you come through the kitchen?"

"I needed to use the washroom." Ida grimaced. This telling of half-truths ate at her.

"Well, hurry. I've news you'll want to hear."

"Could you bring me a candle?"

Footsteps receded and moments later sounded nearer. Ida cracked open the door, poked her hand through, and grasped the candleholder. "I'll be right out."

"We'll be waiting in the drawing room." Aunt Ruth's footsteps again receded.

Water alone refused to remove the rouge and eye shadow. Her eyes stung and her cheeks burned against the lye soap, but at last every vestige of paint had been scrubbed away. Even in the flickering candlelight, the effects of scrubbing remained visible. Maybe if she kept her bonnet on and sat in shadow, Aunt Ruth wouldn't notice.

Drawing in a deep breath, Ida entered the parlor.

Aunt Ruth and Uncle Harvey occupied the armchairs near the fire.

"Here you are." Aunt Ruth beamed in her direction. "Tell her, Harvey, who came calling this evening."

Her uncle puffed on his pipe then set it aside. "Your Mr. Prescott has returned from his business trip. He appeared quite anxious to see you."

"I know! I bumped into him on my way home." Seeing the joy on her guardians' faces over such good news broke down the barrier in Ida that she had constructed to protect her secrets. She plopped onto her aunt's unoccupied footstool. "Literally, I bumped into him and didn't even know who it was until he said my name!"

"I think it's lovely he came calling as soon as he could." Aunt Ruth picked up her tatting. "I encouraged him to wait for you; however, he said something about his mother expecting him."

Overheated by her nearness to the fire and completely engaged in the conversation, Ida removed her coat and bonnet, letting them fall on the carpet beside her. "I know he'll call tomorrow, and then we'll understand why he whisked away to San Francisco without explanation. I didn't want to make too much out of it, but honestly, Aunt Ruth, it bothered me."

Uncle Harvey stood. "It appears I'm to be plagued with babbling female gossip. I hear the library calling." His pleasant countenance contradicted his terse tone.

"Dear girl, what happened to your face?" Aunt Ruth leaned forward. She lifted Ida's chin and studied her cheeks.

"I know, they're burning. I don't think lye soap is good for my skin."

"Of course not! Why ever did you put that on your cheeks?"

"Not just my cheeks, aunt, my lips and eyes are stinging too."

"Come with me." Aunt Ruth marched out of the room as if stomping on a trail of ants. She continued upstairs into her bedroom, Ida following close behind.

"Sit."

Ida perched on the stool at the dressing table. The cold cream her aunt spread on her face smelled of almonds and roses. The burning immediately eased.

"The next time you apply rouge and eye shadow, remove it with this, not soap." Aunt Ruth grimaced.

How did her aunt know? Ida cast down her eyes, remembering the scripture that warned "your sin will find you out."

"Are you upset with me?" Ida kept her gaze on the floor.

"I remember my sister and I experimented with such things in our youth." Aunt Ruth sighed. "You've never been secretive about anything before, and I hope this is not a new trend."

Lighthearted over his surprising encounter with Ida, Blaine made his way home without incident. Although he'd prefer going straight to his room, if his parents hadn't retired, then he would join them. Appearing to avoid his mother would upset her again.

Oil lamps burned low in the drawing room. Only a few embers remained of the coal fire. His mother reclined on the end of the green-and-gold silk brocade sofa, reading. Blaine sat at the other end and waited for her to acknowledge his presence.

She turned one page, then another, before looking up. "You've returned sooner than I expected."

"Yes, Miss Dempsey was not at home. I had no reason to tarry."

"At this hour? And the girl not home?" His mother tsk-tsked.

"Actually, I met her as I left." Blaine pushed down a flick of annoyance at his mother's tone. "I believe she and her friend Mattie were putting something together for children."

"Humph."

"Mother, may I speak plainly?"

"Don't you always?" She set her book on the mahogany table and fixed her gaze on him.

He met her eyes boldly. "I hope you will try to accept that I am attached to Ida Dempsey. She has captured my attention as no other young lady has. I've sought permission from her guardian to court her, and it would make me most happy if you would treat her with affection and respect."

"And it would make me most happy if you forgot entirely about her and chose someone closer to your station."

"Has she done something reproachable that you have such a hard opinion?"

His mother straightened her back as she kept her eyes locked on his. "I have the utmost respect for how her aunt and uncle have taken her in and given her every advantage; however, the truth is—as everyone in town knows—she was conceived out of wedlock." A shudder accompanied the last of her words.

Blaine dropped his gaze. That his mother would broach such a subject unsettled him. Such matters were not discussed in mixed company.

Was it even true? Did it matter?

Obviously, it did to his parents. He didn't care one iota. "She has been raised in a gentleman's home and brought up to be a chaste and moral young lady. It appears to me that should be what counts."

Bristling at his words, his mother's eyes hardened. "You do not know what blood flows in her veins, what defects might pass on to my grandchildren—to your children."

Silence followed. Nothing positive could come from further discussion.

"Good night, Mother." He lightly kissed her cheek and left the room.

Breakfast was a quiet affair. His mother didn't join them, and his father read the morning paper. After finishing his eggs, toast, and ham, Blaine nursed a second cup of coffee, black and strong, as he liked it. He'd spent a half hour praying in his room before breakfast. The session left him at ease—and determined to continue his relationship with Ida while finding a way to keep peace with his parents.

"Shall I meet you at the office this morning, Father, or do you have other plans?"

"That depends." His father put down the paper. "What did you mean by returning home before you were sent for?"

"I completed the tasks you assigned me." Blaine sipped his coffee. "Mr. Goldberg seemed of the opinion I was to work for him. As you and

I never discussed that plan, I determined I'd not delay my return, as my first obligation is to Prescott and Son."

A lengthy pause ensued. Blaine glanced at his father, gulped coffee, and waited for him to respond. More words pinged in his head. He forced himself to remain silent, not to give away the tension growing inside.

"You understood you were to remain until called for?"

"I understood I had tasks to complete, that you trusted me to do them well. I did. And, if you'll remember, before I departed for San Francisco, I explained my desire to work in Eureka with you." Blaine rose. "I am recovered sufficiently to assume my duties here. Should I plan to meet you at the office?"

His father thudded the refolded newspaper against the wooden table, rattling the china cup against its saucer. He stood. "I've a meeting first thing. We'll continue this conversation afterward."

CHAPTER 22

Ida awoke much later than usual. Troubled thoughts had plagued her dreams, preventing a restful sleep. She'd thought praying before she retired would soothe her distressed mind, but no peace replaced the disquietude. Her aunt's words—"you've never been secretive about anything before"—haunted her. She tried to dismiss them with thoughts of Blaine and his return. Not even that helped.

What did her heavenly Father want her to do?

Obviously, she'd continue with Project Save Second Street Souls as well as meet with Qui. Was anything more important than telling the lost about Jesus?

But also important were the scriptural directives to obey one's parents. In her case, didn't that mean her aunt and uncle?

Never before had she been forced to choose between two equally indispensable commands. She didn't know what to do except to proceed as planned. Reverend Huntington had encouraged her with the project and with Qui.

Still, he didn't know the extent of deceit she had succumbed to. What would he say if he saw her and Mattie in their disguises?

That could never be! She'd die of embarrassment and humiliation if any man she knew recognized her dressed like that. If any of the ladies from the auxiliary saw her, she'd never be able to face them again.

She and Mattie would be careful. Possibly, they'd only have to disguise themselves once or twice more. That's what she'd pray for.

Today was shopping day for Qui—which meant the first meeting with Reverend Huntington. The cook would want to leave after cleaning up from breakfast.

Ida hurried to dress, then skipped down the stairs. She found Uncle

Harvey still in the breakfast room, drinking coffee and reading the paper. The food and other dishes had been cleared away. Neither Aunt Ruth nor Wallace remained.

"Good morning, Uncle."

"You missed breakfast, Ida. Go to the kitchen and see if Qui saved something for you."

Eager to check with Qui, not just about food, but also their planned escapade, Ida bounced from the room, knowing her uncle's suggestion to go to the kitchen would override her aunt's objections.

Aunt Ruth stood at the counter, going over the grocery list with Qui. Ida stopped short.

"Good morning, dear." Her aunt tossed her a smile and continued checking the list. Apparently, visiting the kitchen was permissible as long as she didn't do it alone.

"I wondered if I might accompany Qui today." Ida snagged a biscuit from the bread bin. "I might slow her down, but isn't grocery shopping something I should know how to do?"

"That is a great idea." Aunt Ruth gazed at her proudly. "I'm happy to see you thinking ahead like this."

"I'll get my coat."

When Ida returned, Qui stood ready, a shopping basket held in the crook of her arm and Aunt Ruth beside her, coat buttoned and hat in hand. "I thought I'd come along too, just to oversee your learning."

Did Ida's dismay show on her face? The three left the house, Ida and her aunt taking the lead, and Qui following a few steps behind. They stopped first at the market stand for fresh fruits and vegetables.

"Look at these melons—we didn't put them on the list, nevertheless we've got to get some." Aunt Ruth picked one up.

Qui took it from her, put it back, and thumped one after another, listening with her head slightly cocked. "This one." She gave it to Ida to carry. "Take up too much room in basket. Will squash blackberries."

Neither the carrots nor the beets Aunt Ruth gathered received the cook's approval. Qui replaced them with those meeting her standards.

With the basket full, the trio headed back to the house. Ida had enjoyed the shopping, especially Qui's insistence on choosing the food—until she realized it had come at the expense of missing the meeting with Reverend Huntington. She pictured him shaking his finger at her, saying something like, "I told you she wouldn't come."

"A penny for your thoughts." Concern showed on Aunt Ruth's face.

"Oh, it's nothing." Ida thought of faking a smile to put her aunt at ease, then changed her mind. Were keeping secrets becoming a trend, as her aunt warned? That was not who she wanted to be. "Actually, it is something. I'd rather discuss it another time, if that's all right."

Every word was true. She'd love to discuss everything with her aunt, only not as they walked along the boardwalk loaded down with produce and meat.

In the future. Soon. Just not yet.

"I've changed my mind, Blaine." His father met him in the foyer. "I'd like you to accompany me to my meeting."

"Of course, Father." Blaine accepted his coat, his hat, and a walking stick from Pratt. How did the butler know he'd want a cane?

As they strode down the street, nodding to passersby on horseback and in buggies, Blaine asked, "With whom are we meeting?" Had something happened on the docks, possibly with the cargo?

"This is a meeting with other businessmen in the city regarding the current state of affairs. It is a secret gathering. I've chosen to include you because it's time you became a part of our community in a meaningful way."

Wasn't that one of the reasons Blaine yearned to remain in Eureka? To contribute to the welfare of the community.

His father continued. "I expect you to observe only. As a guest at this meeting, you will keep any comments to yourself. Can you do that?"

"I believe so, Father."

The meeting took place upstairs in Centennial Hall, not a very secret place in Blaine's opinion. Having been absent for so many years, he recognized few of the twenty or so attendees. Based on their clothing and manners, they appeared to be successful businessmen. He saw Mr. Dempsey and Mr. Kendall, a city councilman Blaine had spoken with at the picnic.

Before the meeting began, one of the men locked the door and another pulled the drapes over the windows. A man smartly dressed in a black three-piece suit stood at the head of a large table around which everyone sat, all grim-faced, some showing agitation by drumming fingers on the table or incessantly puffing on pipes. Blaine's father positioned himself near the head of the table while Blaine stood in the back, in a better position to observe. Tension permeated the room.

The black-suited man cleared his throat, and chatter throughout the space ceased. "I trust you are all aware of the urgency behind this meeting."

Nodded heads and grunts of assent responded.

"It has been two years since the Chinese Exclusion Act passed, and as you all know, it's done nothing to curtail the problem here in Eureka."

A lesser-dressed man from the far end of the table rose. "Curtail the problem? Things have gone from bad to worse. My lumber company can't compete with things as they are. We won't last another year at this rate."

A general outburst of agreement followed.

"Yes, gentlemen." The black-suited man pounded on the table. "And we can't depend on state officials to rectify issues this far from Sacramento, which means taking action into our own hands."

Another round of affirmation erupted. Blaine observed not a single attendee in disagreement. What issue had these influential men riled up?

Blaine's father stood. "Laws have been passed prohibiting landowners to lease or sell property to Chinese, but the squalor referred to as Chinatown is owned by John Vance and his associate, Casper Ricks." He pointed across the table at Vance. "What do you have to say for yourself?"

"You know as well as I do those laws were passed after the Chinese signed leases." Vance glanced around the table. "I'm in favor of removing them; however, our law-abiding sheriff won't back us. Ricks has tried."

"Our meeting today is not to point a finger of blame among ourselves but to discuss solutions to the Chinese problem and establish remedial steps." The black-suited man directed his comments first to Blaine's father, then scanned the room. "Suggestions?"

Comments flew from both sides of the table.

"Burn them out."

"Make it illegal to hire them. Without a way to make money, they'll leave on their own."

"Put them on an outbound ship."

"Heaven knows there's enough violence, opium dens, and prostitution in that filthy pagan community to warrant arresting every Chinaman there."

Blaine listened, confused and offended by the vehement hostility against the Chinese. Their household employed several Chinese servants, not to mention their cook and the men who did their laundry. He'd not visited Chinatown in years—he'd no reason to—could it be as bad as they claimed?

The meeting adjourned without agreement on how to handle the "problem," only a grim determination by all present that something had to be done—and done quickly.

On the way home, he asked his father, "Exactly what is it that the Chinese have done?"

"You've been away a long time." His father paused at the corner. "Follow me."

They strolled toward the block designated as Chinatown. As Blaine stood on the corner of E Street and Fourth, the stench of sewage, decaying fish, and other rotten food attacked his senses.

"They've built the boardwalk over open ditches into which they dump every sort of excrement and waste. Disease, even leprosy, is rampant."

"Shouldn't the city do something?" Blaine knew that in their neighborhood the city provided clean water and sewer. He thought it a citywide responsibility.

"No one says they have to live there." His father directed him away from the putrid effluvium. "They come in droves, and with them they bring violence and a complete disregard for our traditions, customs, and laws. Vance and Ricks have tried to make improvements, but the Chinese don't want them there."

Blaine listened as his father continued.

"The mayor says over two hundred Chinese live in that one block, and half are from rival Tongs. I've seen an armed gang carry their flag on one side of the street with their rivals brandishing their flag on the other side, shooting at one another. No telling how many dead, because Sheriff Brown lets them take care of their own matters. And I don't blame him. No point in risking his deputies' lives over whose flag survives."

As they walked on toward the wharf and the Prescott and Son office, Blaine wondered if there was more to the story. A part of him thought, so what if they keep to themselves, handle their own matters, and do their jobs? As long as they didn't attempt to force their traditions and beliefs on the white Eureka citizens, as long as no one got hurt outside that community, what did it really matter to the businessmen?

They were content enough to let sin reign on Second Street.

He wanted to ponder before asking his father more questions. He knew enough about business to understand that, when all was said and done, most disagreements of this sort boiled down to finances.

How were the Chinese hurting Prescott and Son's bottom line?

CHAPTER 23

All morning Blaine expected his father to summon him into his office to discuss his unbidden arrival from San Francisco. No such call came. He'd rather get it over with even if he had to broach the topic himself.

At noon, he entered his father's office and waited to be acknowledged. Moments passed before his father looked up from the ledger. "Do you want something?"

"This morning at breakfast, you indicated you had more to say about my early return home. Is now a good time?" Blaine sat in a straight-backed wooden chair in front of the massive desk.

"After considering the matter and noting how you behaved at the meeting, along with your insightful questions afterward, I'm of a mind to dismiss your insubordination."

Blaine ignored the offending word and focused on the positives in the message. "Thank you, Father." He continued, "I do have another question I'd like your thoughts on."

"Go ahead."

"How does the Chinese presence affect the economy in Eureka?"

Beaming a rare smile, his father set down his pen. "I see your university education has developed you into an astute young man."

Words of praise? From his father? He'd take it! Blaine leaned forward in his chair, eager to hear his father's response.

"The Chinese accept wages lower than other workers."

"Isn't that good for business owners?"

"Let me finish." His father cleared his throat. "In this period of a downturn in the economy, out-of-work loggers, railroad workers, and miners claim the Chinese are taking their jobs, which affects the whole county. The Chinese don't spend their wages in the community. They pay off the Tongs and send significant money back to China. Very little of it is circulated among Eureka's citizenry."

"What's a Tong?" It was the second time Blaine had heard the unfamiliar term.

"Basically, a gang. They began as groups working together, devoted to helping the Chinese settle in a community and acquire jobs. As can happen among such pagans, greed took over, and the groups fight with one another for power and control."

"Bringing violence to our city." Blaine rubbed his jaw. "One more question, if you will, Father."

"Go ahead."

"The people living in Chinatown mostly clean our houses, cook our meals, do our laundry. So how does that take jobs away from unemployed loggers and miners?"

His father picked up his pen again. "They run opium dens, prostitution houses, and illegal gambling establishments. They bring crime and poverty into the middle of our city. That's problem enough, wouldn't you say?"

While his father hadn't actually answered his question, he had a point. Opium dens. Rival gangs. Illegal gambling. None of it belonged in Eureka.

One more question begged to be asked—on an entirely different subject. Dare he risk fouling his father's good mood and broach the topic of Ida? He still didn't know his father's role—or lack thereof—in the plot to keep Abigail away from Chester and him away from Ida.

Did it matter now that his presence at home was no longer an issue?

As a ship drew up to the wharf, Blaine gestured toward the window. "I see we have cargo arriving. Should I oversee the unloading?"

At his father's nod, Blaine stood. "By the way, I wanted you to know that before I left for San Francisco, I received permission from Mr. Dempsey to court his niece. I told Mother and wish to share the good news with you as well."

His father frowned. "That is a subject for another time."

Not finding Reverend Huntington at the church building, Ida decided to visit Mattie. Had her friend returned home last night without incident? Had anyone noticed her painted face, like Blaine had hers? Her best friend didn't even know Blaine had returned. They had much to discuss.

Her route to Mattie's led past the minister's home. The good man strode along the boardwalk just outside it. She hurried to catch up to him. "I hoped I might meet you."

"Qui wouldn't come after all?" He sounded sincerely sorry.

"Trying to meet on shopping days poses problems." Ida frowned. "I have to think of something else."

"Perhaps I can help." The reverend looked down at the boardwalk before meeting Ida's eyes. "I should have offered this when we first spoke of it, but I questioned how appropriate it would be."

"You've got my interest." Ida twisted the strings on her handbag.

"I teach a class to a few young Chinese men on Thursday evenings in my home. It is safer for them than meeting in the church."

"Why safer?"

"To be seen frequenting a Christian establishment would put them in danger. The Tongs forbid conversion to Christianity."

Ida's eyes widened. She had no idea anyone could forbid knowing Jesus. "How is it all right to visit your home?"

"The Tongs recognize a church building as a symbol of Christianity. They don't know who I am or where I live."

"You want me to see if Qui will join the class?"

The minister nodded. "But, Ida, the young men attending the class will likely not welcome a white woman—they won't trust you."

"Because it's still dangerous."

Reverend Huntington nodded. "They literally risk their lives for these classes, not just from the Tongs. Plenty of citizens in our community would strongly disapprove if they knew."

Ida thought a moment. "I'll speak with Qui. What time on Thursday?"

He provided the details, and each went their own way. As Ida hurried to Mattie's, the minister's words dominated her thoughts. Encouragement swelled within. Those young men were willing to risk everything to hear about Jesus! How many more might there be if given a safe opportunity?

Mattie's mother opened the door at Ida's knock. "I thought you might come by today."

"Is Mattie home?"

"Yes. However, I'm not sure you are fit company for her."

Uh-oh. Mattie must have been caught last night. Ida sighed. How long before her aunt knew?

Mattie's mother planted her hands on her hips. "What in the world were you thinking?"

What had Mattie said? Of course, the truth always served best, but Ida loathed getting her best friend in trouble if that "truth" had come with shadows and shades.

"I guess we weren't thinking very clearly." *Or we would never have left the church basement with the paint still on.*

"That's an understatement."

"I'm sorry. I promise it won't happen again." *Because I rarely make the same mistake twice, and this one was a humdinger.*

Guilt battered Ida's conscience. She was getting too adept at half-truths for the purpose of deceit. Did the end justify the means?

Ida didn't know what else to say. "May I see Mattie?"

"Not today. I think a few days of separation are in order." Mattie's mother closed the door.

Needing time alone with her heavenly Father to seek His direction and hopefully ease her conscience, Ida headed for her favorite place on the harbor, away from the bustle of the ships and without the distractions of other people. She quieted her mind, watching waves lapping the shore, then closed her eyes and let the seashore sounds calm her further in preparation of kneeling before the Creator of the universe. No words bombarded her brain as her soul reached upward. Time ceased to exist. Sounds faded. Smells vanished. The only reality was Ida in the presence of her heavenly Father. With it came a determination to repent of deceit and walk with integrity.

A hand touched her shoulder, jolting her back to earth. She looked up, into the face of Blaine.

"Are you all right?" He helped her stand.

"Never better." Ida brushed sand from her skirt. "How did you know where to find me?"

"I didn't." Blaine shrugged. "I used to come here as a boy when I wanted a quiet place to think."

Ida tightened the loose strings on her bonnet. "I can leave."

"No, don't go." Blaine reached for her hand. "It's lunchtime. Are you hungry?"

She hadn't been until he mentioned it. "Famished."

They strolled toward the waterfront establishments and past the saloons. Ida remained quietly thoughtful as they entered a small café catering to respectable businessmen.

After sitting at a table for two and ordering, Blaine reached for her hand. "I missed you."

"You did?" Ida grinned. "When you didn't return on Friday or Saturday, I quit thinking about you."

She laughed aloud at the expression on his face and continued teasing—after all, he deserved it for leaving without a word. "For all I knew you were having a grand time with Abigail Goldberg."

"Not at all." Blaine's face remained serious, troubled. "Wait—you know about Abigail? I mean, Miss Goldberg?"

"Oh, yes. How you've spent summers in her parents' home, escorting her to parties."

At the horror in Blaine's eyes, Ida regretted her words. Had she taken the teasing too far?

Or was his consternation a result of a guilty conscience?

How well did she actually know this man?

CHAPTER 24

Ida removed her hand from Blaine's. "Perhaps this Abigail is important to you." She intertwined her fingers in her lap. If there was something going on with the young woman in San Francisco, she'd make it easy for him to confess. She'd rather know now before giving her heart entirely away.

"Miss Goldberg's father is a business associate of my father's. I attended the university with her older brother, Samuel, and have spent two summers in San Francisco as a sort of apprentice, learning from Mr. Goldberg. Abigail has no more interest in me than I do in her."

Blaine's pained look sparked compassion within Ida. She needed to remember this was the man who had twirled her on the seashore over her declaration of loving Jesus, the same man who said he'd prayed for her, who had spoken with her uncle about courtship. Had her own flirtation with deceit made her overly suspicious of others?

She grasped his hand across the table. "I believe you. I meant only to tease. Let's not speak of this anymore."

"You're right." Blaine squeezed her hand. "Let's talk about something happy and positive. Tell me about the plans you have for the children."

"Plans for the children?" What was he talking about?

"You know, the clown paint you wore last night. Didn't that have something to do with children?"

"Not at all. Some would say the opposite." She'd tell him everything. No half-truths, no hint of deceit. Ida locked her eyes on Blaine's. "I need to know you won't overreact or try to dissuade me. I want to tell you everything. I want to trust you."

"Sounds serious indeed."

A waiter arrived with their sandwiches. They bowed their heads, and Blaine thanked God for the food.

He no sooner uttered the "amen" than Ida jumped into her story. She told him about the costumes, the face paint, their changing into and out of the dresses in the church basement, about trekking down Second Street and being thrown out of Kitty Farris' Joy Emporium, about the five-steps-to-salvation pamphlets they'd placed all along the boardwalk being tossed into the street, about not finding the woman from the drugstore, and the complete failure of the mission.

As she related the events, Ida watched Blaine's face carefully. Expressions flitted across—surprise, confusion, interest—some harder to interpret than others. Fortunately, the disapproval she feared did not show.

Ida lifted her chin and straightened her shoulders. "So, as you can see, it has nothing to do with children." As a way to say, "that's it," she bit into her ham and cheese sandwich.

What should he say? Dare he discourage this scandalous scheme of hers? He should!

But he couldn't betray her trust in him with a negative response, regardless of how shocking her story. She'd begun the tale asking for his understanding. If he disappointed her now, would she ever be open with him again?

"How did you get your aunt to agree to your plan?"

"She didn't." A blush covered Ida's face—making her even more beautiful in his view. "She objected over the humiliation I'd bring to the family if I were discovered, which is why I thought of the disguise. That way I didn't exactly disobey."

"I'm not sure she'd see it that way." If he convinced Ida she ought to respect her guardians' rules, then he wouldn't be the bad guy. He could be supportive of her and at the same time share her disappointment in the inability to carry out the plan based on her aunt's objections. What had she called it? Project Save Second Street Souls.

A little manipulative, don't you think?

Where did that thought come from?

What if, instead of coming up with a way to cancel the project, he helped her? She wouldn't abandon it, regardless of his or her aunt's opinion. The issue wasn't whether or not the women on Second Street needed Jesus. The challenge was reaching them without soiling Ida's reputation.

He had an idea. "Ida, let's finish lunch, then come with me."

The brightness in her eyes, the curve of her lips, were all he needed to induce a hearty commitment to assisting in the crazy scheme.

Ida picked up her sandwich. "I can walk and eat at the same time. Where are we going?"

"To Wells Drug Store."

Using long strides to keep up with Ida's skippy gait, Blaine marveled at the purity of the young woman beside him. All it would take to win his mother over would be time spent with this amazing young woman. How could anyone with even half a heart not love her?

At the drugstore, Blaine addressed the clerk. "Miss Dempsey and I were here over a week ago on a Sunday afternoon."

"Yes, I remember." The clerk wiped the counter with a damp cloth. He nodded at Ida. "You ordered ice cream and sat over there." He pointed at the table they had occupied.

"While we were here, a woman came in requesting medication." Blaine slid a one-dollar bill across the counter toward the clerk. "I need to know her name."

The worker pocketed the money. "You'll have to give me more information. A good many women frequent our business. Can you describe her?"

Ida jumped in. "She is about my height, with sad blue eyes and light brown hair, and she wore an ostrich feather in her hat."

"Hmm. Anything else?"

Blaine shuffled his feet. "She appeared, perhaps, um. . .maybe. . .um, to be a resident of Second Street." His voice dropped to a whisper.

The clerk shook his head. "I don't know."

Blaine slid another dollar bill across the counter but kept his fingers on it. "I paid for her medication."

"It might have been either Meadow or Esther." The clerk eyed the money under Blaine's hand. "Most likely Esther."

"Thank you." Blaine left the dollar on the counter, then turned to leave. He looked back. "If she returns, tell her we are hoping to speak with her." He held up another bill between his fingers before pocketing it.

The clerk nodded then resumed swabbing the counter.

"You are brilliant," Ida gushed as they left the store. "We have a name."

"Two names, actually." Blaine took Ida's arm as they crossed the street. "Meadow and Esther."

"I want it to be Esther." Ida lifted her skirt to avoid the muddy ruts.

"Why?"

"Because it's a biblical name." Ida beamed up at him. "Like my Aunt Ruth's."

How did one look from this woman make his heart beat double time?

"Your help with this means everything to me." She rose on her tiptoes and kissed his cheek.

The softness of her lips on his face sent tremblings through him, the kind that made him want to lift her off the ground and twirl her in the middle of the street. He controlled himself this time. "It's important to me as well. Are you ready for the next step?"

"Yes! Wait. What is our next step?" Ida shielded her eyes against the sun that had suddenly poked through the fog.

"*My* next step is to ask around for Esther. Your next step is to trust me to do it."

"Ask now. Do it now." Ida grasped his hand and headed for Second Street. "Ask at the Joy Emporium. I'll wait outside."

Blaine leaned on his walking stick. "Ida, you can't be seen in that neighborhood, especially not loitering outside a brothel."

"Oh. Right."

Inappropriate thoughts of kissing her pretty pout invaded Blaine's mind. He lifted his eyes from her face to the sky.

"I've an idea." Her pout evaporated. "I'll wait for you at the waterfront—you know, where you found me earlier. It can be our special place." Ida dropped his hand and bounced lightly toward the harbor barely a couple blocks away. She waved before rounding the corner.

What could he do? He'd told her to trust him to take the next step. He hadn't thought he'd be taking that step so soon.

Well, why not? To be seen in the district during the early afternoon would be less likely to generate gossip than an evening visit. If discovered, he could claim he sought one of the sailors from the ship that just docked.

The ship! His father believed him to be overseeing the unloading of cargo from one of their ships. How long had he been gone? He pulled his pocket watch from his vest. Where had the time gone?

He strode toward the busy port, hustling past the shipping office and onto the dock. Crates crowded the pier in disorganized stacks.

His father stood in the middle of the chaos, gesturing and barking orders.

CHAPTER 25

"Forgive my delay, Father." Blaine sidestepped around a stack of crates. "I can take over now."

His father glared at him. "Yes, you will. And after you've sorted this out, I expect to see you in my office." He shoved a fistful of papers into Blaine's hand.

His mind on Ida, Blaine watched his father stride away. He signaled one of the lads who often hung around hoping to earn a bit of cash when a ship arrived. He pressed a fifty-cent piece into the boy's hand. "You'll find a young lady around the bend a bit south of here waiting on the beach—her name is Miss Dempsey. Tell her I've been delayed and will call on her after dinner."

"Yes, sir." The boy grinned and ran off.

Blaine turned his attention to the disorganized mess awaiting him. It took the rest of the afternoon to get it under control. By the time he finished, the shipping office was dark and the door locked.

He trod home, upset with himself. His father had a right to be disappointed in him. He'd failed miserably on a day that had begun with so much promise. And what could he tell Ida? He couldn't risk visiting Second Street now that evening had come.

Because of responsibilities to his father, he'd failed Ida, and because of devotion to Ida, he'd failed his father. He alone deserved blame—not them. He'd tried to please both, not considering his priorities, acting rather rashly, like a boy distracted over minutia instead of a mature college graduate in his twenties ready to join adulthood.

He hastened to the Dempseys' residence, eager to explain his afternoon. Had the lad found her and delivered the message? He'd not seen him to confirm it. How long had Ida waited for him? Was she upset?

The maid answering the door informed him Ida was not home. She offered no details.

Heart in his throat, he raced to their special place on the shoreline. Could it be possible she never received the message and continued to wait for him? As his feet pounded the boardwalks, his mind repeated over and again, "I'm sorry, Ida. Sorry. Sorry." Left foot, right foot. "Sor-ry. Sor-ry."

No one walked the shore or sat on rotted pilings. Even the seagulls had abandoned the spot. Both relief and disappointment crowded his emotions. He yearned to see her. The idea she might have waited hour after hour for him burdened his heart.

Head hanging, shoulders slumped, he slogged home.

Pratt took his hat and coat in the foyer. "Did you lose your cane, sir?"

"Left it in the office—don't worry about another one, I seem to have recovered fully." Blaine hadn't thought about his concussion all day—and he'd certainly been active enough for lingering dizziness or a headache to pester him. He'd experienced neither condition.

"I assume my parents are at dinner?"

"Yes, sir, along with guests."

Guests? His father had said nothing about visitors.

Blaine sprinted up the stairs and quickly changed into more suitable clothing for a meal with company. The idea relieved him. With others in attendance, his father wouldn't berate him for the afternoon's bungle. His mother would be in a hospitable mood as well. He washed his face, combed his hair, and downed the stairs two at a time.

"You're just in time, Blaine." His mother greeted him as he entered the dining room. "We've only now begun." She gestured for him to take a seat.

Next to Stella Sutterman.

After receiving the message from Blaine, Ida picked her way along the shoreline toward the docks. When close enough to make out his form, she watched him gesturing and directing the activity on the wharf. Before returning to work, had he inquired about the mysterious Esther?

She doubted it. As she observed him, the trace of frustration she'd experienced after receiving the message dissolved. He had a job. Responsibilities. She'd witnessed Wallace being chastised for showing up late for work—or not showing up at all. Blaine wasn't like her cousin.

Their lunch together had been spontaneous, likely taking longer than Blaine's father expected, putting Blaine in a difficult spot because of her.

She'd like to discuss everything with Mattie, but that wasn't possible at the moment.

Even understanding why Blaine had to delay their meeting, impatience hounded Ida as the afternoon waned. Project Save Second Street Souls needed to move forward. Determined to forestall more delays, she left the pier and hurried to the church. As she had done the previous day, she slipped into the basement and donned the slinky red dress, deciding against the face paint. Without Mattie to help apply the rouge and eye shadow, she'd make a mess. Wouldn't the large, feathered hat hide her face sufficiently?

Cracking the door open, Ida peered out onto the street and boardwalk then dashed out and away toward the Joy Emporium. As she neared the forbidden district, she slowed her pace and attempted to strut in the fashion she'd witnessed the night before. Once she adjusted to the embarrassment, it was kind of fun.

As she and Mattie had planned, she remained on the opposite side of the street. Awkwardness returned as she strolled alone. The project had been much easier with Mattie by her side—not that she'd give up. What did a little discomfort matter when women's souls were at stake?

A roof extended over part of the boardwalk, providing Ida with a sense of cover. She leaned against the rough outer wall of a building advertising "Live Entertainment." The early afternoon hour made it a good place to loiter, to observe the comings and goings of others. Ida waited in the shadows, fascinated by the movements of a lifestyle so different from her own.

And not so different as well. Women greeted one another, exchanged pleasantries, and smiled. Take away the provocative clothing and painted faces, and they'd blend in with the ladies' auxiliary.

Well, they'd have to walk a little differently.

And clean up their vocabulary.

She sent up prayers for each woman in her view. "Dear heavenly Father, bless that woman with the yellow parasol. Bless that one over there with the limp. Please, Father, bless the woman with the loud laugh."

The sun set lower in the sky as the dinner hour approached. She couldn't linger much longer. "Please, Father, let me find Esther."

A group of five women clustered less than a block away. One told a story, making the others chuckle. A few words floated Ida's way. Although straining to listen, she failed to understand the gist of the tale. Then the name Esther reached her.

She drew nearer to the group. Was Esther among them, or the subject of their gossip? None of the faces she could see reflected the one she sought; three of the five were turned away from her.

Being shy or hesitant would get her nowhere. She inserted herself into a small gap in the huddle. "Good evening, ladies. Excuse me—did I hear you mention Esther?"

The chatter stopped as all eyes centered on her, none of them belonging to the mystery woman from the drugstore. The woman telling the story met her gaze. "Who are you, and what do you want with Esther?"

Ida extended her hand in a gesture of social politeness. "I'm Ida. New to these parts. I believe I've met Esther previously and hoped to speak with her again."

It was mostly the truth. She'd not actually "met" Esther. She had seen her before and truly hoped to speak with her.

"Are you working around here?"

"I'm hoping to." Another deceitful answer. She knew full well what type of "work" the questioner referred to. Her answer reflected her hope she would soon be doing the Lord's work.

"You look a little young." One of the women cocked her head. "Where do you know Esther from?"

Pointed questions were harder to hedge on. Ida dipped her head and backed away from the group. "I've an appointment I must not be late for. If you see Esther, will you ask her to meet me at Wells Drug Store tomorrow?" She sauntered from the group, doing her best imitation of a sultry sashay. At the corner, she glanced back and saw the group watching her. She waved and turned down the street, away from their stares.

Now to return to the church, change her clothes, and hurry home in time for dinner.

Such a day it had been. An unexpected lunch with Blaine, acquiring his support for her mission, and before that the encounter with Reverend

Huntington and the possibility of a Bible study for Qui that even Aunt Ruth would approve.

Nor was the day over. Blaine would call that evening. Wait until she told him about her recent adventure!

CHAPTER 26

Exuberant over the potential meeting with Esther and the success of finding a Bible study opportunity for Qui, Ida entered the dining room. Her cousin slumped in his seat, apparently unhappy over something. Poor Wallace.

After the mealtime prayer, Aunt Ruth addressed Ida, her countenance reserved. "How did you spend your day?"

A trick question—or did her guilt induce unwarranted suspicion? Did they already know Mattie's mother wouldn't let her see her friend? Or about the meeting with Reverend Huntington? Anyone could have witnessed them speaking on the street. Had she been seen in her disguise coming or going from the church? How she yearned to tell everything! Fear of rebuke pushed aside her determination not to deceive.

"I had lunch with Blaine." An absolutely true statement.

"How nice!" Aunt Ruth's smile appeared genuine.

"He's to call this evening after dinner." Would that do? Guilt over her secrets attacked, preventing making eye contact with either guardian.

Wouldn't her aunt and uncle be thrilled about the potential for Qui to know Jesus? How could they disapprove with Reverend Huntington behind the plan? Perhaps she could begin there.

"Before that, after I left Mattie's house, I ran into Reverend Huntington." Ida paused. Might it be a mistake to disclose the Bible study with Qui before she spoke to the housekeeper in person? Ida glanced at the faces around the table. Wallace appeared relieved—maybe having the attention on her distracted from his woes. Uncle Harvey swirled the wine in his goblet. Only Aunt Ruth peered at her curiously. She'd continue. What was that saying, *in for a penny, in for a pound*?

"He asked me not to broadcast the information; however, I'm sure he didn't mean I couldn't tell my family. He teaches a Bible class in his home to interested Chinese and has invited Qui to join them." She looked expectantly at her aunt, anticipating surprise mixed with pleasure. She received neither. Her aunt's brow furrowed, and her lips formed a tight line.

Uncle Harvey set down his wineglass. "Do you mean to tell me the minister of our church associates with *them*?"

Uh-oh. What had she done? Reverend Huntington hadn't instructed her to keep the classes a secret, but it was implied. That her aunt and uncle would be opposed to teaching the Chinese about Jesus hadn't occurred to her. Her aunt's expression and her uncle's tone of voice indicated otherwise.

"Yes. In his own home—not in the church itself."

Her uncle's face reddened. "That's not going to continue. The church leaders won't stand for it once they know." He picked up his fork and stabbed the meat on his plate. "I wouldn't be surprised if it cost him his job. It should."

As the truth regarding her guardians' prejudice grew obvious, emotions attacked Ida, first sadness, then anger. She didn't know how to handle the flash of fervor raging through her veins. She absolutely could not sit passively in the presence of these two people. She stood, knocking over her chair. Words bombarded her mind. None made it past her trembling lips.

Tears flowed as she raced from the room through the foyer and slammed the front door behind her.

"Good evening." Blaine greeted Mr. and Mrs. Sutterman and took the chair his mother indicated next to Stella. "I apologize for my tardiness. However, in my defense, I was unaware we'd have the pleasure of company tonight." He directed the last of his comments to his mother, realizing the possibility that his father might not have known either.

He recognized the situation as open warfare. He wouldn't wait for the enemy to strike. Better to be on the offensive. As he accepted a portion of roast lamb from the servant circling the table, he continued talking. "I've plans immediately after dinner and won't be able to linger."

"Cancel your plans." His mother placed a roll on her bread plate.

"I'm so sorry, Mother, but that I cannot do." He turned to Stella, sitting beside him. "You know Ida Dempsey, of course."

Stella nodded. "Yes. She's a sweet little girl."

"Mr. Sutterman." Blaine's father commanded the conversation. "I hear you're helping Carson with his latest construction project."

"Have to do something to keep the unemployed loggers busy."

"All this unseasonable rain isn't helping things." Blaine's father helped himself to a serving of roasted carrots.

"How was the weather in San Francisco, Blaine? I heard you visited the city recently." Stella batted her eyes as she addressed him.

"Damp and foggy." In order to avoid further conversation with Stella, Blaine shoveled food into his mouth. He caught his mother's disapproving glare. She wanted him to be her charming, obedient son and entertain Miss Sutterman. He'd not play her game, not at the expense of misleading the young lady. His meal only half eaten, he scooted back his chair. With a sweeping gaze, he smiled at the Suttermans. "Perhaps you've not heard that I am courting Miss Dempsey. She is expecting me."

Mrs. Sutterman's eyes widened as her brows shot up. She glanced at Blaine's mother. "No, we had not heard."

"Not to worry—it's a recent development. I'm sure not many are aware." Blaine rose. "In fact, as I've not had opportunity to announce anything, it's possible my parents invited you here tonight so you could be one of the first to know."

He counted on Mrs. Sutterman passing along the gossip, hopefully squelching any more impromptu dinner parties with eligible young ladies.

His mother's pursed lips and flushed face warned him he had overstepped.

But she had fired the first shot.

Perhaps he should have held back the cannonball.

He'd pay for it later. Regardless, right now he'd visit Ida, and for the moment that was all he cared about.

Whistling as he strolled down the street, Blaine buttoned his overcoat. Summer in Eureka did not come with overly warm evenings, but at least it wasn't raining. He hoped Ida would welcome an after-dinner walk. Sitting in a stuffy parlor making polite small talk with her guardians did not appeal to him.

As he considered the scene he'd just left, he chuckled to himself. He'd been away from home so much of his time growing up, his parents didn't really know him. They had an idea of him, a vision of who they wanted him to be, and he didn't want to disappoint them. Even so, he refused to be a puppet. Hopefully, with no more damage than a little embarrassment on their part, he'd made that point at dinner.

As he walked toward the Dempseys' door, it flew open and out stumbled Ida, teary-eyed and red-faced, straight into his arms.

CHAPTER 27

Blinded by anger and tears, it took Ida a moment to realize whom she'd bumped into. When she recognized Blaine, she melted into him, gaining strength from his arms wrapped around her. He spoke so soft and low she couldn't make out the words but took comfort from his soothing tone. They stood as one until Ida shivered.

"Would you like to get your coat?" Blaine held her just far enough away to see her face.

"No!" Ida pulled herself back into his chest. "I need to leave."

The door opened, and Wallace handed out her coat and hat. He opened his mouth as if to say something, then snapped it closed and quietly shut the door.

"To the harbor?" Blaine helped her put on the outerwear, then intertwined her arm with his.

As they sauntered along the boardwalks, Ida's self-control returned, and her sobs subsided. What a blessing to have someone walk beside her, someone to comfort her without asking what upset her, seeming to understand that presently words were beyond her ability.

The moon shone from a rare clear sky bespeckled with sparkling diamonds. Even the wind had abated, although a chill remained in the night air. The harbor was calm, heavy with the scent of seawater and wet sand. Ida breathed in the smells of the shore and let the night sky's reflection on the water minister to her soul.

"I've behaved badly, I'm afraid." She sighed as she untangled her arm from his.

"Never. I don't believe it possible for you to do so."

"But I did. I'll have to apologize, only not yet. I want to stay here a bit longer." Ida squeezed Blaine's hand. She didn't want to ever let go.

"Do you want to talk about it?"

"I should. You have a right to know that somehow, in a flash, I've developed a temper. A horrible, terrible, disgusting, vile temper. It snuck up on me, which is no excuse, and I didn't know how to handle it."

"Your temper snuck up on you?"

"Most definitely." Did he understand? Ida searched his face for clues to his thoughts. She recognized compassion without judgment in his eyes. If he knew what she'd done, judgment might still surface.

"I've had that experience." Blaine led her along the shore, away from the wharves and lumber mills, the full moon lighting the way. "Sometimes anger will produce a nervous energy that fills me until I think I'll explode if I don't do something. When I was at the university, the punching bags in the gym helped dissolve the rage." They stopped walking. "Do you want to punch me?"

"Are you teasing?"

"Maybe a little."

"But you understand, I can tell. I've never felt that way before. Anger is scary."

They continued strolling along the shore as the moon rose higher.

Blaine put an arm around her shoulders. "Do you mean to tell me that in all your seventeen years, you've never gotten angry?"

"Not like that. I've been disappointed, frustrated, annoyed—this was different." Shame hunched Ida's shoulders and kept her face pointed to the ground. "I actually wanted to hurt someone." She glanced at Blaine, then at the water. "I've never wanted to hurt anything—let alone a person—before."

"Spiders? Do you sometimes want to hurt spiders?" A teasing tone layered Blaine's words.

"Not even spiders. I call for Wallace to take them outside."

His smile reached her heart, further dispelling the negative emotions. "I want to tell you what happened, but how was your day? I got your message—thank you for sending it—so I went to the wharf and watched you work."

"You did?"

By the way Blaine stood a little straighter and raised his eyebrows, Ida knew the idea pleased him. "Those sailors sure responded to your orders."

Did he just puff out his chest? Ida suppressed a giggle.

"Ida, I'm sorry I left you waiting. I didn't want to."

"I know. You have a job and people depending on you." She wanted to reassure him she understood he couldn't drop everything at her bidding. "I know you couldn't have had time to inquire about Esther."

"And you're all right with that?"

"Yes, partly because I understand your situation, and also because I have a lead myself." Ida paused to let the information settle. "I may be meeting Esther tomorrow at the drugstore."

"How did you manage that?" Blaine shook his head in wonder. "Did you speak with her?"

"Not directly with her." Ida recounted her afternoon experience to him, how after dressing in disguise, she'd visited Second Street and engaged in conversation with the group of women and how she thought they'd deliver her message to the mystery woman.

Did his face betray his thoughts? He hoped not. If he'd thought for a minute she'd put on that disguise again and loiter in that neighborhood, he'd have completed the errand to find Esther himself, regardless of his father's disapproval. Now here she was, pleased as punch over her success, but at what cost? Had someone seen her and reported it to her guardians, and they'd reacted strongly? Was that the reason for her emotional state when she bumped into him? It could have all been avoided. "You didn't trust me to find Esther? You risked going yourself after we talked about this?"

Joy drained from Ida's face. "It isn't a matter of trust, Blaine. You were busy, and I couldn't wait."

"Why? Why couldn't you wait?" Blaine modulated his tone. "Is that what happened to upset you? Did your guardians discover where you'd been?"

Ida stepped back. "No. I don't believe anyone saw me." She dipped her head. "I thought you'd be happy I made a connection. I thought you were with me in this." She turned away from him.

"I am on your side, but Ida, you must show some discretion." He placed his hands on her shoulders. "Please look at me."

He felt her shoulders rise with a deep sigh. She faced him, biting her lip, tears glistening.

That he had robbed her joy struck him hard. Those tears shining in her beautiful eyes were his fault. Why chastise her? For caring enough about lost souls to put love into action? She hadn't a selfish bone in her body, and he'd just squelched her spirit.

If that were possible, which, he suddenly realized, it wasn't.

Sweet, gentle Ida possessed inner strength and devotion. Whether or not he supported her, she'd not back down. Wasn't that the kind of woman he'd prayed for? So why try to restrain her?

"I'm sorry, Ida." The words sounded hollow, even to him. "It is exciting to know you might meet Esther tomorrow. Do you know what you'll say?"

Ida shook her head. "I guess I'm hoping the words will come."

"They will." Blaine tenderly took her hand. "I know they will." He turned back toward the street, bringing Ida with him. "Do you want me to accompany you to meet her?"

"No. This is something I should do myself."

He felt her pull back, dragging her feet. "It's getting late." He released her hand. "Shouldn't we get you home?"

"Do we have to?"

"No, but Ida, we can't stay out all night."

"I don't want to go home."

"Why?" Blaine could guess at her reason, but he'd rather hear it from her. There'd be nothing he could do to remedy her reluctance, yet he could listen, he could sympathize.

"I grew so angry at Aunt Ruth and Uncle Harvey that I stormed from the house. I'm sure that upset them, but in truth, I'm still mad. I don't think I can look at them." Tears glistened on her cheeks.

"What happened?"

"I told them about the Bible classes Reverend Huntington teaches in his home." Ida continued on, explaining her guardians' reaction.

Blaine listened, this time not hiding his surprise. He agreed with Ida—why disapprove of teaching the Chinese about Jesus? Her guardians' position didn't make him angry, just confused.

He'd been to Chinatown that morning. He'd seen the squalor, smelled the stench, felt the desperation. The idea had been growing within him that this could be a project worth his time and attention. He hadn't formulated a concrete plan. Maybe he'd tackle the sewage issue. Perhaps a visit to the mayor to start with.

Besides that, introducing the Chinese to Jesus would change their lives like nothing else. It could free them from the violence of the Tongs. Make their community safer. Blaine sincerely believed Jesus was the answer to everything—even the poverty and crime in Chinatown.

Ida tugged on his hand. "But even worse, Blaine, a thousand times worse, is Reverend Huntington could lose his job over this. And then what will happen to his students? He told me there were those in the community that disapproved of teaching the Chinese, but I never dreamed he meant my own aunt and uncle. I've made a terrible mistake!" Resolve accompanied the distress emanating from her eyes. "I have to go to the reverend's home and warn him. Who knows how quickly my uncle might act, and the reverend will be caught off guard. And this is all my fault!"

CHAPTER 28

"The hour is late, Ida." Blaine took her arm again as they crossed the street. "I need to get you home soon, and tomorrow morning I'll make sure the reverend is aware of potential trouble."

"I'm the one who caused it. I need to tell him." Ida's chin rose slightly.

Blaine knew the meaning of that look. "It's highly unlikely your uncle will do anything before morning. Please let me take you home. Your aunt and uncle don't know you are safe with me. They will be worried."

"I didn't think of that." Ida drew in a deep breath. "Wallace knows I'm with you, but I doubt he said anything to them."

As Blaine and Ida meandered back to her home, his thoughts continued on what steps he could take to make a difference in Chinatown. Besides the mayor, maybe a visit to the sheriff. Chinatown was a part of Eureka—smack-dab in the middle of the city. Couldn't the law do something to curb the violence? For that matter, didn't the gangs have to arrive by ship? Couldn't the shipping companies do something to keep them out?

He'd discuss his ideas with his father. The meeting that morning among the Eureka businessmen had been about doing something, and that's what he wanted.

Too soon, they arrived at Ida's front door.

She hesitated on the steps. "I have to go in, don't I?" It wasn't really a question.

"Remember your aunt and uncle love you." Blaine kissed her forehead. "However, if you like, I'll linger here in case you need me."

"Or you could come inside with me!" Ida grabbed his hand, looking at him with hopeful eyes.

Should he? Although late for a polite visit, did that matter when this woman he cared for needed him? He opened the door and gestured for Ida to enter.

She continued to grip his hand.

A light burned in the foyer, and another leaked from beneath the closed parlor door. Straightening her back and striding with determination, Ida entered the room. Blaine followed a step behind.

Her aunt stopped pacing and rushed to her. "Oh, my dear, we were so worried." She glanced at Blaine while embracing Ida. "Thank you for bringing her home to us."

"Of course." Blaine nodded. Could he leave now, or did Ida still need his moral support? He waited awkwardly near the door.

Ida pulled back from her aunt and faced him. "I'll see you tomorrow?"

"Yes." Another awkward moment passed. "I can let myself out."

His comment fell on deaf ears as Ida's aunt drew her to the settee, and both women talked at once. Could they even hear each other?

He sauntered toward his home, not eager to face what he suspected awaited him. He had no doubts his mother would have something to say about his behavior at dinner. He felt no guilt over his actions—he'd do it all again—but disappointing his mother brought him no joy.

Ida never felt more loved than at that moment in her aunt's embrace. She'd behaved immaturely, yet was met with unconditional, sincere affection. "I'm so sorry for my actions tonight."

"It's all right, dear." Aunt Ruth patted her hand. "All's forgiven. But you did worry us frightfully."

"I didn't mean to. It won't happen again." A piecrust promise? No. Ida meant every word. She also fully intended to continue seeking ways to teach Qui about Jesus. How, she didn't know. To not disappoint or worry her aunt and uncle again meant hiding her actions, a thought that tugged at her conscience. They loved her dearly and believed they were doing the right thing. How could she fault that?

But they were wrong, and she'd never convince them otherwise. Her actions regarding Qui distressed them, and, if possible, she'd protect them from knowing—but not at the expense of her mission to Qui or the Second Street Souls project.

Wouldn't they have a conniption fit over that!

"What are you smiling about, dear?" Aunt Ruth's eyebrows raised.

She was smiling? "I guess because I'm so grateful for you and Uncle Harvey. You are very good to me." She cast down her eyes. "You didn't deserve my outburst."

"Enough about that." Aunt Ruth rose. "And now that you're home, I'm free to retire for the night." She headed toward the door. "I'll see you in the morning."

Ida remained in the parlor, mulling over her day, until hunger pangs reminded her she'd not eaten her dinner. She wandered into the kitchen and nabbed an apple from the fruit bowl, her mind focused on Qui.

No doubt the cook heard them talking at dinner. Her fear of Aunt Ruth's disapproval would keep her from attending the meetings at the reverend's house—if they were even allowed to continue. Ida would have to think of something else. So might the reverend! She shuddered involuntarily, anticipating his response to her blunder.

What neutral place might she and Qui meet? Maybe the drugstore, or the café by the wharf? No, it would have to be more private, somewhere that wouldn't call attention to a Bible-toting white girl speaking with an older Chinese woman.

Tomorrow she'd ask Blaine if he had a suggestion.

Awakened by birds warbling from the maple tree near her window, Ida rose early, before the household stirred. She slipped out the door and half-ran, half-walked in the direction of Chinatown, planning to meet Qui again. She'd prefer to speak with her at home, but after last night's debacle, she couldn't risk her aunt or uncle overhearing her plans.

A short, caped figure shuffled quickly toward her along the boardwalk. The early hour lacked sufficient light to discern male or female. Ida quickened her pace. As she drew near, Qui's face grew perceptible.

"What missy doing here? Not safe." Qui scowled.

"I've an idea." Ida handed Qui a Bible she'd taken from her uncle's library. "Inside you'll find a piece of paper with a scripture verse written on it. When you can, look up the verse and read it."

"What mean 'look up verse'?"

CHAPTER 29

Ida scolded herself. She was an idiot. Well, maybe not exactly an idiot—but certainly not tactful. Why did she assume Qui could read English? And if she could, that she'd understand how the Bible was organized? Scripture, books, chapters, verses, New Testament, Old Testament, none of it would mean anything to someone raised not going to church and Sunday school.

"We'll read it together until you learn a little more." Ida smiled encouragingly. "This is a Bible. Reading it is how we know about Jesus."

"Is sacred book?"

"Yes, very much so."

Qui produced a rare quick smile as she hugged the Bible to her breast. "I have sacred book to learn about Jesus."

If Ida had any doubts about this part of her plan, the glow in Qui's eyes erased them all.

When had she clutched a Bible to her chest? Possibly never. This woman hungered to know the truth. Nothing would prevent Ida from teaching her.

As they neared her house, Ida whispered to Qui, "I'm going in the front door so no one suspects we were together."

Qui nodded in that way she had of rocking her entire upper body.

Luckily, the foyer was empty as Ida entered. Unluckily, she met her aunt on the staircase.

"You've been out already? My goodness, and before breakfast!" Aunt Ruth paused mid-step.

"The birds woke me this morning with their jubilant singing, and I couldn't go back to sleep."

"I daresay you'll need a nap this afternoon before the ladies' auxiliary meeting." Her aunt continued down the steps.

Ida plodded to her room. She'd forgotten about the auxiliary meeting held in Mrs. Zander's exquisite parlor, something she usually looked forward to. She imagined Jesus smiling at the women planning fundraisers for missionaries, their eagerness to fill those barrels, their busy hands sewing garments for the poor and needy. Mrs. Alexander always had amusing stories about her brood of children, and sweet Mrs. Bickel brought tasty treats. Sometimes the chatter turned gossipy. Showing up ensured she'd not be fodder for the rumor mill. Not attending left that door wide open.

Would her relationship with Blaine be the topic of choice if she didn't attend?

Could she fit everything into the day? She planned to visit Mattie, if her mother would allow it. Her best friend still didn't know Blaine had returned, and she wanted to tell her about the potential meeting with Esther—who might appear at the drugstore anytime.

Ida expected to be at the drugstore most of the day. If Esther didn't come by three o'clock, she'd forgo the auxiliary meeting, even though Aunt Ruth would be disappointed at her absence.

First, she had to find Reverend Huntington to confess her blunder and warn him about Uncle Harvey's reaction. If her uncle disturbed a meeting at the pastor's home, his Chinese students might never risk it again, and it would be her fault.

Ida dropped to her knees, hastening a prayer prompted by guilt and fear. When she arose, beams of sunshine flowed through her window. Heaven-sent to chase away her negative thoughts? The day would work itself out. It always did.

Eager to get the hardest part over—namely, warning Reverend Huntington—Ida downed the eggs and toast placed before her, drank a glass of milk, nodded to her aunt, and bounced away from the breakfast table before Uncle Harvey finished his first cup of coffee. Typically, neither she nor her aunt engaged in conversation during this first meal—Uncle Harvey didn't like what he termed "mindless chatter" to begin his day. Engrossed with the morning paper, his head hidden behind the pages, he seemed to notice neither Ida's presence nor her departure.

On the way to the reverend's house, Ida changed her mind. She'd go to Mattie's first. Maybe her best friend would accompany her. She could use the support.

Mattie opened the door at Ida's knock. "You can't come in."

"Can you come out?"

"No." Mattie shook her head. "You got me in a lot of trouble. I tried to explain it was just face paint. It wasn't as if I'd paraded down Second Street or anything." Mattie rolled her eyes.

Ida understood the veiled message. Mattie hadn't told her mother the whole truth. Good to know. Better would be to know exactly what she'd said. That information couldn't be given at the moment though, not knowing who was listening inside. "Will she let us be friends again ever?"

"Mattie, shut that door!"

"Yes, Mother." Then her friend whispered, "Tomorrow at church," before disappearing behind the closed door.

Ida slogged away from the house, disappointment coating her like a foggy mist.

A long-haired, matted, gold-colored dog zigzagged along the rutted dirt street, nose to the ground, tail wagging. He bounced up to Ida, drool dripping from his jowls. "Go away." Ida brushed him aside.

The dog sprinted in a circle around her, his ears flopping like a lady's handkerchief on a clothesline. "I said go!" The animal sat in front of her, blocking her way. He looked up and barked. Hoping he'd move, Ida grabbed a stick from the side of the road and tossed it. It flew up, but not far. The dog chased after, catching it in the air before it hit the ground.

Ida continued toward the reverend's house. She didn't count on the mutt bringing back the stick or almost tripping her as he dropped it at her feet. "You just want to play, don't you, Goldy?" She picked up the stick again, and this time tossed it farther down the street. The dog chased it at full speed. When he tried to stop, his paws tangled with each other and he rolled head over heels past the stick. Unfazed, he bounced back, grabbed it, and loped to Ida.

The sight of his ungainly gait and flopping ears along with the stick clenched in his drooling mouth dispelled Ida's disheartened mood. As sometimes happened, once she began laughing, she couldn't stop. All the way down the street toward her destination, she tossed the stick and the golden dog retrieved it, with Ida giggling robustly.

Her next toss veered left, flew farther than she meant, ricocheted off a picket fence, and smacked Reverend Huntington on his buttocks.

She should stop laughing. There was nothing funny about assaulting an unsuspecting person from behind, but the yelp he emitted and the look on his face as he turned, combined with Goldy scrambling to stop, overrunning the stick, and again losing control of his legs and rolling over, tickled Ida all over again.

Tears rolled down her cheeks as she covered her mouth, trying to hold back her giggles.

At the minister's stern countenance, Ida sobered. "I'm very sorry. Are you all right?"

"Startled is all. It isn't every day I'm attacked walking on my own street."

"I'm not very good at throwing."

"Were you aiming for my head?"

The dog dropped the stick at the reverend's feet and sat.

"Does your friend here have a name?" Reverend Huntington picked up the stick as strings of drool slathered from the dog's panting mouth.

"Oh, he doesn't belong to me. I call him Goldy. I think God sent him to cheer me."

"You needed cheering?"

Ida nodded. "Actually, twice today."

Reverend Huntington raised his eyebrows. "And it isn't even noon yet."

"And I believe a third time is imminent." Ida swallowed hard, then confessed her error about the reverend's classes. She described her uncle's reaction and his threat about the minister's job. All sense of lightheartedness disappeared like ice dropped in boiling water. "I'm afraid I've caused a lot of trouble. I'm so sorry."

"I don't imagine Qui will be attending the class after all." The minister tossed the dog's stick.

"I didn't get a chance to invite her. I'm sure she heard my uncle's loudly expressed opinion. She won't risk his wrath." Ida sighed. "Will you have to cancel the classes?"

"Dear Ida, this is not the first time I've faced resistance to something I am doing or want to do. I can handle it."

"You mean you won't cancel the classes?"

"Absolutely not. However, that doesn't solve the problem for Qui."

Ida sighed. "I gave her a Bible this morning, and you should have seen the look on her face. You'd have thought I'd given her a million dollars. But I made a mistake. She can't read English."

Reverend Huntington tossed the stick again for the panting dog. "How about if we give her one she *can* read?"

"You have a Chinese Bible?" Ida wrapped her arms around the minister and squeezed. "Oh, thank you, thank you, thank you!"

"All right. That's enough." He cleared his throat and backed away. "Wait right here, and I'll get it now."

Ida tossed the stick as she lingered on the boardwalk, thinking what a morning it had been, up and down like a teeter-totter. Would the rest of the day be as unpredictable?

CHAPTER 30

When Blaine arrived home, neither parent awaited him in the parlor or the drawing room. He had hoped to get the uncomfortable conversation over with. Instead, he spent the evening hours praying in his room and reflecting on Ida.

His life certainly wouldn't be dull or boring with her in it. What could he do to convince his parents she was the right one for him? Definitely a God-size issue. He'd fallen asleep praying for a solution.

He awoke after dawn with a looming sense of dread. Not even his morning devotions dispelled it. Maybe he'd take a cue from Ida and stroll along the shore. It brought her peace; might it do so for him? He raided the icebox for leftover ham and cheese, stuffed them between two halves of thick sliced bread, and headed out the door before anyone in the household stirred.

Dew sparkled on every blade of grass and flower petal. The eastern sky showed hues of pink as the sun rose above the horizon. One could never determine for certain what the weather might be. A rainy morning often gave way to a sunny afternoon and vice versa. He sauntered along the uneven boardwalk, not meeting a soul. Even the docks lacked their usual hectic activity. The outgoing tide left a wide shoreline along which small crabs scuttled.

Blaine perched on a beached log and watched the rhythm of the water, noting it slowly receding. Rocks, once submerged, showed barnacle-covered tops, and thirty minutes later their rounded, pocked middles. He stilled his mind and let his Creator speak to him through the world He'd created. Finally, the peace he sought filled his soul.

Shouts from the wharf alerted him that the morning had grown old. He hurried to the office of Prescott and Son, expecting to find his father scowling at his late arrival. But neither his father nor any employees were inside. He sat at his desk and scrutinized the latest bill of lading.

He'd gotten halfway through when footsteps sounded on the hardwood floor and both his parents entered his small cubicle. To say it was unusual for his mother to accompany his father to the office was an understatement. What could it mean?

Blaine rose. "Good morning, Mother, Father."

"We missed you at breakfast." His mother sat on a wooden chair against the wall.

"I woke early and thought I'd stroll down by the water. Time got away from me." Blaine returned to his seat behind his cluttered desk. "I looked for you when I arrived home yesterday, as I knew you might want to speak with me about dinner." Better to broach the subject himself, bring it out in the open, and get it over with.

"You are aware, then, of the embarrassment you caused us." No compassion or hint of understanding showed in his mother's eyes.

"I'm aware you'd prefer I choose Miss Sutterman or Miss Goldberg over Ida." Blaine believed a direct approach saved everyone time and energy. "I hope you'll reconsider and give Miss Dempsey a chance."

His father stepped forward. "We hope you'll reconsider and give Miss Sutterman the same chance."

"I can't do that." Blaine rose from his chair. "Surely you understand that the choice of a wife must be mine." He turned to his mother. "You expressed to me your displeasure of Miss Dempsey based on her suspicious parentage, yet you said nothing about failings in her character." He faced his father. "You do business with her uncle and mix in the same social circles. As you requested, I have sought a companion among gentlemen's daughters. I am not going to abandon Miss Dempsey."

"I'm very sorry to hear that." His mother pursed her lips and nodded at his father.

He strode closer to Blaine's desk. "I'll give you the week to reconsider. If you remain stubborn and oppose your mother's wishes, then I'll be forced to reconsider you as a partner in Prescott and Son."

The words smote straight into Blaine's heart. All his life he'd been preparing to join his father in the shipping business. He'd never considered other options, had never wanted to. "You can't mean that, Father.

How does my choice of a wife affect my ability to contribute to our business?"

His mother responded. "It speaks directly to your loyalty to your family."

"Mother, you don't even know Miss Dempsey. If you'd give her a chance, you'd love her as I do."

Love her? Did he already? Because of his certainty God had chosen her for him, he was *willing* to fall in love. Could he claim that so soon? His heart responded with a resounding yes.

"You don't know her either, yet you're ready to declare love?" His mother shook her head, lips taut. "She's bewitched you, and the sooner you recognize this folly, the better for all concerned."

"It seems to me, Mother, with all due respect, that the only people concerned are myself and Miss Dempsey. And to set the record straight, she has not pursued me. I have sought her." Did he dare reveal his prayer for a wife and God's answer? Would it have any effect on their judgment? Likely they'd disregard it as nonsense.

His mother rose. "We've said all we need to say. You understand our position. The choice is yours."

"You have a week." His father followed his mother out of the office.

Did his father truly share his mother's viewpoint, or did he follow her lead to keep peace between them? If he could speak to his father alone, might he be persuaded otherwise? Together, over time, with respect of course, they could alter her opinion. Mr. Dempsey made it clear the courtship would be long. Time was his friend.

Meanwhile, he'd make himself invaluable to the company. He'd be on the dock for every arriving and departing ship. He'd streamline the process of loading and unloading. He knew enough from his summers with Mr. Goldberg that their accounts receivables could be more efficient, resulting in faster payments. He would double-check every bill for accuracy and make recommendations to cut costs. Blaine carefully walked through the building, looking for ways to improve the setup of rooms and offices.

He'd fight for the dream of partnering with his father.

Clutching the Chinese Bible in her hands, Ida headed for the church, debating whether she should forgo wearing the red dress. In the end, she decided to risk it one more time. If—when—Esther showed, she wanted no barriers. She wanted the poor woman to feel they were on equal ground, that she was not some do-gooder above her in social standing.

Inside the basement, she deposited the Bible beside the manger, retrieved the dress from behind the nativity scene, slipped into it, and donned the oversize hat.

The roads were busier than before, perhaps because of the time of day. As other pedestrians passed Ida on the boardwalk, she kept her eyes down, avoiding all contact. She did the same with the buggies she met. As she entered the drugstore, she released a huge sigh of relief. She couldn't be sure she wasn't recognized, but no one stopped her, and she'd heard no exclamations of surprise.

At the counter, Ida ordered a pot of tea and two cups, then positioned herself at a table near the window where she could also keep an eye on the door. A slow hour passed. Then another. It neared noon. She dared not pour a third cup of tea because a trip to the necessary room might cause her to miss Esther.

At every tinkle of the bell attached to the doorframe, Ida's heart skipped. Would the clerk notice her loitering and request she move? A steady stream of customers kept him occupied, and he appeared not to notice. As time slogged by, she closed her eyes to pray. "Please, Father, let her show up."

When she opened her eyes, she spied Esther paused in the doorway, staring at her. She wore everyday clothes and looked as respectable as any woman in the ladies' auxiliary. Ida rose and hurried to her. "Please, will you come sit with me?"

Esther followed her to the table and perched on the edge of the chair. Ida poured tea, realized it was cold, and apologized. "I'll get more."

"Don't bother. I'm not staying."

"But you came." Ida reached to touch her hand. Esther pulled it back.

"I came to tell you to leave me alone."

"I don't mean you any harm; in fact, I'm eager to be your friend." Ida tried to meet the woman's eyes, but her gaze flitted from window to tabletop to floor—everywhere but at Ida.

"I've all the friends I need. I do not want to see you ever again. Do not come to my place of business. Do not ask for me by name. Stay out of my life." Esther walked away then looked over her shoulder.

"And never wear that dress again."

As Ida hastened along the streets, Esther's last comment rang repeatedly in her mind. Why did the woman care what dress she wore? What did it matter to her? The demands to leave her alone made sense—sort of. The comment about the dress did not.

The woman had intrigued her before, and now, rather than be discouraged, the disastrous encounter convinced Ida she shared some sort of connection with Esther. A ridiculous idea, of course, but it couldn't be shaken.

Project Save Second Street Souls had suffered a setback, definitely not a death punch.

Not by a long shot.

CHAPTER 31

As Ida slipped into the church basement and dressed again in her own clothes, Esther's words repeated themselves in her mind. She'd asked—no, the tone of her voice *demanded*—that Ida leave her alone. That she stay out of her life. The mystery surrounding her increased. Why such intensity behind her words? Wouldn't a more normal reaction be to find out what Ida wanted before rejecting what she had to offer?

And when it came down to it, how was the way Ida dressed any of her business? Why even care?

Normally, she'd discuss such a puzzle with Aunt Ruth or Mattie, but she couldn't speak with either. To tell Blaine carried risk—he might listen objectively, or be upset she wore the dress again.

What about Reverend Huntington? Could she confide in him? She'd have to explain her actions, and that would be embarrassing—and possibly freeing at the same time. Her conscience nagged her over deceiving Aunt Ruth. Confessing to the minister might ease the guilt. Given the opportunity, she'd do it all again even though she disliked walking the fine line between flagrant disobedience and subtle deceits. Neither suited her. The minister might have insights into the strange encounter and what she should do next.

First, she wanted to give Qui the Chinese Bible and report her reaction back to him. She stuffed her dress behind the manger, pulled the Bible from its hiding place, and hurried out the door. Later she'd retrieve both dresses and discard them away from the church—what would a missionary think if they showed up in a barrel! Giggling over the imagined reaction, she hurried home.

Wallace and Qui were discussing something in the kitchen when Ida arrived. They stopped talking as soon as she entered. "Am I interrupting something?" She snagged a cookie from a cooling rack.

"No. Mister Wallace just leaving."

Her cousin stomped out the kitchen door, scowling.

Ida watched him leave. "What's the matter with him?"

Qui picked up a knife to chop an onion. "He's a man. That's enough."

"I'm not supposed to be alone in the kitchen with you, so please don't go anywhere. I'll be right back."

"Where I go anyway?" Qui hacked at the onion as if it had committed a hideous offense.

Ida found Aunt Ruth in the foyer putting on her coat, gloves in hand.

"Oh my, you can't go to the meeting like that." Her aunt raised her eyebrows. "Goodness, look at your hair. Well, hurry up. I'll wait."

"Yes, Aunt, I'll hurry. First, will you come to the kitchen with me?"

"Why?"

"You don't want me to be alone with Qui, and I have something to give her." Ida darted toward the kitchen.

"Ida, what are you up to now?" Aunt Ruth's skirts rustled as she hurried after her.

"Will you put down the knife for a minute, Qui? I have something for you." Ida produced the book hidden in her skirts. "This is from Reverend Huntington. He wants you to have it."

Qui's forehead wrinkled. She cocked her head to one side. "I already have sacred book. Remember you give me this morning."

Ida glanced at her aunt, whose brows furrowed. "Yes, Qui, but this one is written in Chinese."

The cook's eyes widened. "A sacred book in Chinese?" She wiped her hands on her apron and took the Bible from Ida. "I read about Jesus in Chinese?"

"Uh-huh." Ida drew in a deep breath. "And if Aunt Ruth agrees, the three of us can discuss what you read while you make dinner or lunch or whenever my aunt thinks suitable."

"Very kind. Thank you." Qui bowed and bowed again, the book clutched to her chest in the same manner as she had the English Bible she'd received earlier.

Ida turned to her aunt. "I know we have to go. I'll just be a minute." Before her aunt could comment, Ida dashed up to her room. She washed her face, pinned her hair back in place, and skipped down the stairs.

Aunt Ruth waited near the front door. As they strode side by side on the boardwalk, she linked her arm with Ida's. "You, my dear girl, are a wonder. I never know what you'll think of next."

"You mean like teaching Qui about Jesus?"

"That's exactly what I mean."

Ida glanced sideways at her aunt. "I know you don't approve of mingling with the Chinese in general, except Qui is our cook. I love her, don't you?" Ida didn't give her aunt time to respond. "And if she wants to know Jesus, can't we teach her?" Again, she continued talking. She didn't want to hear excuses, denying the potential for a study. "Qui isn't just anybody. She's practically a member of our family. And if we teach her, she can teach others, and they'll teach others, and one day all of Chinatown could know Jesus, and the Tongs wouldn't have control anymore, because Jesus is the answer for everything."

"Yes, dear. But you see, the Chinese have their own religion." Aunt Ruth patted Ida's arm. "I appreciate you telling me your plan and not hiding it. It shows what a good heart you have—naive, but lovely."

As Ida began to defend herself as passionate, not naive, her aunt stopped her.

"Just to make sure you understand, Ida, we will not be teaching Qui about Jesus. We care for her, but she is not one of us. Period. She has her own religion, her own way of thinking about things. It isn't possible for her to understand. You'd succeed only in confusing her. You will forget this crazy idea."

"Aunt Ruth?"

"Yes, dear one?"

"Don't some of the missionary barrels go to China?"

Blaine dove into the disorganized receivable accounts, sorting them by date, then alphabetically, the oldest first with delinquent invoices set aside for immediate attention. He kept an eye out for his father's return, hoping to speak with him without his mother present. He suspected her influence prompted his father's threat to reconsider his place in the family business. If they could talk man-to-man, he hoped to defuse the situation.

Shortly after noon, his mother stormed into Blaine's office, red-faced and spewing venom with such velocity, he couldn't understand a word. It had to be a serious matter indeed. Had something happened to his father?

"Mother, please calm down." Alarmed over her state of mind, he rushed from behind his desk and directed her to sit, then knelt in front of her and took her hand. "Take your time and tell me what is wrong."

"I warned you, but would you listen? Now the worst has happened and you, Blaine, are to blame." She dabbed her eyes on a lace handkerchief. "In less than a day, rumors about you and Ida have spread like wildfire—I feared Stella Sutterman would gossip to everyone in town—and just as I predicted"—his mother closed her eyes and shuddered—"she's soiled our good name forever."

"Stella soiled our good name?"

"Don't be daft, Blaine. Ida Dempsey did. The little hussy."

Ire pushed Blaine to his feet. "I'll not listen to you speak of Ida with such language. She is the purest, most virtuous young woman I've ever met."

"Is that so? Then explain why several trustworthy people witnessed her dressed as a—as a *prostitute* parading around town in the middle of the day. Virtuous, my foot. Do you have any idea what people are saying? Any idea of the irreparable damage done by your ridiculous speech last night and then this? The Suttermans are having a field day!"

"If our good name can be so easily damaged by the act of one young lady, then it didn't have much foundation to begin with." Blaine wished he could deny Ida's actions. The story was likely true, or at least portions of it. He seriously doubted she "paraded around town." She had likely visited Second Street in disguise.

Part of him surged with pride. Arguably, her zeal lacked wisdom. While he preferred she'd use more discretion, he admired her spunk and determination. Life for him would be easier, more peaceful, if he didn't have to defend her to his family and their friends. But he hadn't prayed for a peaceful life; he'd prayed for a purpose-filled one.

Blaine helped his mother to her feet. "I do regret that Miss Dempsey's actions have upset you. It may help to know I am aware of her disguise and the reason behind it. You see, she is concerned about the women in that part of town. She's named her mission Project Save Second Street Souls. She hopes to gain their acceptance by appearing as one of them in order to teach at least one of them about Jesus."

"That's the most ridiculous thing I've ever heard. You're too smart to believe such a falsehood." She wagged a finger in Blaine's face. "I told you about her parentage. The apple doesn't fall far from the tree."

As she strutted from the room, the realization dawned on Blaine that for him to attempt to sway either parent in favor of Ida was a losing proposition. First of all, because Ida would never fit into his mother's world of proper decorum, and second, because he didn't *want* her to change enough for that to happen.

He had to decide whether or not it was God's plan to expose Ida to the constant criticism and disapproval that joining his family would bring.

He loved her too much for that.

CHAPTER 32

After praying in the office and not receiving a definitive answer, Blaine left, ready to act as his conscience dictated. He didn't need a week to decide between Ida and his mother, for that's what the issue boiled down to.

He'd choose loving Ida every time. Which meant he had to let her go. Teachings in Corinthians that he'd known from childhood repeated in his mind. *Love is patient, love is kind. . . . It is not self-seekin. . . . It always protects. . . .*

To continue their relationship would be selfish of him. He loved her enough to protect her from a future of never measuring up, from the cruel words and harsh looks sure to come from his mother. He wouldn't subject her to that.

But he hated that his mother would think she'd won.

As he hoped, Mr. Dempsey was in his office and willing to see him. He greeted him with a warm handshake and smile. "How are you, Son? To what do I owe this visit?"

"May I sit, sir?" Blaine removed his hat.

"Of course. Hmmm. You look very serious indeed."

"I'm here on a difficult matter." The words stuck in Blaine's throat. He couldn't meet Mr. Dempsey's eyes. "First, I want to say I am more in love with Ida now than when I first spoke to you of courtship."

Mr. Dempsey cleared his throat. "Now see here, young man. I made it very clear when I gave my permission that neither I nor Ida's aunt are eager for her to wed so young. I am standing by that. No profession of love will alter my mind."

"Of course not, sir. I'm not asking you to. This shames and burdens me deeply—I am asking to cancel our courtship arrangement. I cannot continue a relationship with your niece."

Dempsey's face reddened. He bristled. "And why not?"

"I'd rather not say."

"I see. And have you spoken to her about this?"

"No." Blaine twisted the brim of his hat, unable to raise his eyes from the floor.

"I will not pass along a message for you, if that's what you're thinking." Dempsey pursed his lips. "I thought better of you. Perhaps it's all for the best. Obviously, you're not worthy of her."

"You are right. I am not. She would undoubtedly make me the happiest man in the world; unfortunately, I cannot guarantee her joy as my wife."

"And why is that?" Dempsey's tone softened.

Blaine risked a glance up. For reasons he didn't understand, he desired this man's good opinion. "May I speak freely?"

At Dempsey's nod, Blaine continued. "My parents, specifically my mother, are intent on choosing a wife for me, and they have someone else in mind. My father has threatened my position in our company if I continue a relationship with Ida."

"I understand. A young man must protect his livelihood."

"No, sir, that's not it at all. I've dreamed all my life of joining my father's business. Even so, I'd give it up in an instant for Ida." Blaine fixed his gaze on Dempsey. "What I will not do is ask Ida to wed into a family that does not cherish her as I do. My mother has many good traits, and I do not mean to disparage her, but she is set against Ida and will not relent. What kind of a man would I be to bring such a person as your niece into my family, knowing the depth of my mother's feelings against the match?"

"Am I to understand that you wish to nullify the courtship arrangement because you wish to protect Ida from your mother's ill temper?"

"That's part of it."

"Pshaw. Once she gets to know Ida, she'll love her as we all do. It's just a matter of time." Dempsey picked up a pen as if to end the conversation and return to work.

Blaine stood in preparation of leaving. "I wish that were true. My father has given me a week to break off the relationship on pain of not allowing me a place in our shipping business. He means to manipulate me into accepting my mother's terms. They may get what they want regarding Ida, but I will seek employment elsewhere anyway." He didn't add that he'd never agree to marry any young lady they put before him. If he couldn't have Ida, he'd remain single.

Dempsey put down his pen. "Do you mean to say you'll not continue with Prescott and Son Shipping?"

"I will not." He shook his head. "Truly sir, I *cannot*."

"Have you any money set aside?"

It seemed an odd question. Blaine hesitated before answering. "Yes. My grandparents set up a fund for me, which I had access to when I turned twenty-one. I've had no need to spend it. Why do you ask?"

"I'm looking for a partner. If you're willing to invest in my sawmill, I can put you to work here as a junior partner. I've been saving the position for Wallace; however, he seems uninterested."

Silently, Blaine let the words sink in. A partner in a sawmill?

Dempsey continued. "Consider not only whose family Ida might join, but the other side of the coin. You would be a most welcome member of our family."

The plan to finalize the filling of the missionary barrels necessitated a change of venue from Mrs. Zander's parlor to an upstairs classroom in the church. The ladies' auxiliary meeting droned on forever with discussions regarding fundraisers and worthy causes and setting up committees and who should be responsible for what. Ida never enjoyed this part of the meetings; she endured them to please her aunt. Shouldn't they quit talking and move to the basement, where the precious barrels awaited?

It wasn't that their projects were without merit, but Ida yearned for a more intimate, personal touch to add meaning to the charity. As the interminable meeting continued, she fidgeted and her mind wandered.

Her aunt's refusal to allow her to teach Qui about Jesus dominated her thoughts. How could these women be satisfied with sending their cast-off items to places such as China and not care about the same people in their community? The hypocrisy of it battled within her, creating judgmental feelings. She couldn't remain still another minute.

"Excuse me," she whispered to her aunt. "I need to use the privy." After visiting the outhouse, she went around to the basement door and retrieved her and Mattie's dresses, hats, and face paint. As she stuffed them into a bag she'd brought along for that purpose, her aunt's voice—the high-pitched voice she used when angry—sounded from the stairs along with clomping feet.

Another voice, louder and more intense, indicated an argument. Over what, Ida could not comprehend. The staircase door burst open. Mrs. Prescott stormed through, appeared startled to see her, then pointed. "You want proof. Well, here it is." She marched to Ida, ripped the dresses from her hands, and flung them in Aunt Ruth's face. A dozen women crowded on the narrow stairs, craning their necks and hushing one another.

"Now, what do you have to say?" Mrs. Prescott folded her arms across her chest and lifted her chin as if in triumph.

"I'm sure Ida can explain." Aunt Ruth picked up the red dress and folded it as if it were a costly garment. Glaring all the while at the intruder, Mrs. Zander did the same with the green one.

Before Ida could find the words to respond, Mrs. Prescott turned on her. She pointed a finger in Ida's face, almost touching her nose. "You won't charm your way out of this one, dearie. More than one trustworthy person witnessed your antics, saw you enter and leave this basement. Saw you wearing that scandalous red dress, parading in broad daylight like a brazen hussy."

Mrs. Alexander inserted herself between Ida and Mrs. Prescott. "You will speak civilly, or leave."

"Oh, I'm leaving, all right." She turned to Ida's aunt. "My son recants his proposal for courtship. We will not have our good name and reputation trod through the mud by an illegit—"

"That's enough!" Elderly Mrs. Bickel tapped her cane almost on the toes of Mrs. Prescott, then hobbled to join Mrs. Zander and Mrs. Alexander as a wall protecting Ida.

Ida's heart wilted as the impact of Mrs. Prescott's words hit home. Blaine wanted to end their courtship? He sent his mother to deliver the message, not even willing to explain it himself? Her missions so far had been miserable failures, and now this.

And then these women—the same ones she thought insufferable with their endless planning and discussing charity events—came to her defense like mama grizzly bears protecting their cub. While it didn't come close to soothing her heartbreak over Blaine's message, their compassion kept her from completely losing control.

"What's going on here?" Reverend Huntington pushed his way

through the group of bystanders. "Mrs. Prescott, I had no idea you were interested in joining our women in their charity efforts."

"Humph."

Mrs. Lee stepped forward. "She's not here for charity. She barged in and disrupted our meeting, accusing sweet Ida of improprieties."

"For which I have proof!" Mrs. Prescott's lips curled as she reached for the red dress.

Ida's aunt blocked her way.

"Reverend, I've made a terrible mess of things." Tears slipped down Ida's cheeks.

The minister gestured for her to come to him. He placed an arm around her shoulders. "I suppose our little secret is out." He looked at the astonished women around him. "You see, Miss Dempsey talked with me about her Project Save Second Street Souls, and I encouraged her to proceed."

He directed his gaze at Ida. "How did it go today? Did you make any headway?"

Mrs. Prescott's mouth dropped open. She inched back toward the door. The women blocked her escape.

CHAPTER 33

"Am I to understand, Mrs. Prescott, that you are accusing Miss Dempsey of impious behavior?" Reverend Huntington raised his eyebrows.

The room immediately hushed, with the only sound the occasional creak of floorboards overhead. Ida fought the urge to hide behind the nativity manger. Cringing inside, she held her breath, head down, waiting for more of Mrs. Prescott's venom.

The woman responded meekly—as meekly as possible for a woman such as Mrs. Prescott. "I was informed of certain shocking actions. Perhaps they were in error."

Reverend Huntington nodded. "I know we can count on you to correct the error, not to let malicious rumors escalate out of control." He headed for the stairs, then turned. "Miss Dempsey, I'd like to speak with you before you leave, please." He directed his gaze pointedly at Mrs. Prescott. "I'll be meeting with Reverend Rich later today. You attend his church, I believe."

Mrs. Prescott nodded.

"Hmmm." The reverend ascended the stairs.

The women's auxiliary members surrounded Ida, offering words of comfort for her and expressing outrage over Mrs. Prescott's charges. A barrage of questions flew at her from all corners.

As the humbled woman backed out of the room, Ida felt sorry for her. She wanted to ask if they could walk together and maybe arrive at a better understanding, but her intuition hinted now was not the time.

What would Mrs. Prescott report back to her son? He loved and respected his mother, as a son should. How would he react to her humiliation suffered at the hands of Reverend Huntington?

That blessed man!

What would have happened if he'd not interrupted when he did?

Ida envisioned frail Mrs. Bickel whacking Mrs. Prescott with her cane. She smothered a smile and responded to the questions born of curiosity without a hint of accusation.

Yes, she had worn a disguise on Second Street.

Yes, she had spoken with some of the women.

Yes, she went in broad daylight because her timidity disallowed going at night.

No, she didn't see any men.

Over thirty minutes passed before the women tired of bombarding Ida with questions and headed to their homes, forgetting all about the half-filled barrels.

Alone with Aunt Ruth, Ida shoved the dresses into the bag. "Will you go with me to speak with the reverend?"

"If you wish."

"I do." Ida's deceit had gnawed continually at her conscience. She'd noticed her aunt remaining in the background, listening to her respond to the women's questions, noticed the sad look in her eyes, the slump of her shoulders, the slight trembling of her hands. She'd hurt this dear woman who loved her as a mother. Whatever Reverend Huntington had to say, she wanted Aunt Ruth to hear.

What would he say? She deserved a dose of "I told you so."

Aunt Ruth knocked on the office door. At the response "it's open," she nudged Ida to enter first.

Reverend Huntington stood, gesturing them to sit. Aunt Ruth did, as Ida remained standing. "Thank you, Reverend, for defending me. You warned me about potential trouble, and I didn't heed it."

"Are you speaking of trouble in the basement, or on Second Street?"

"Second Street." Ida stared at the floor.

"Did they gobble you up and spit you out?"

"Yes. One in particular." Ida rubbed her forehead. "And, really, I couldn't figure out why. You know the lady I told you about, the one Blaine helped in the drugstore?"

"Yes." The reverend returned to his seat.

"I discovered her name, and yesterday I approached her, um, colleagues and asked them to deliver a message to her to meet me at the drugstore today, and she did! I'd almost given up, but she came. Then she told me to leave her alone. She said she never wanted to see me again. And then the strangest thing, she told me not to wear that red dress again."

Ida sighed. "Are you going to say, 'I told you so?'"

"No. I've an important question for you." Reverend Huntington steepled his fingers. "Mrs. Prescott backed down when confronted by your friends. But you must understand, it's not the last you'll hear of this, not only from her. Others in the community who don't know you like the auxiliary women do will run with this scandal. You will face additional scorn, heavy with judgment. And your mission so far has not produced the results you want. My question is, how do you feel about all this?"

Ida glanced at her aunt, who sat silently, hands folded in her lap, eyes downcast. She'd never witnessed her so quiet. She'd prefer a reprimand!

How could she express her jumbled emotions? "I'm heartbroken that Blaine no longer wants to court me. I'm remorseful that I've hurt my dear aunt. I'm perplexed as to how to proceed next, but I'm not ready to quit." She met Reverend Huntington's eyes. "I'm not giving up."

Blaine left the Dempsey sawmill, needing time to think. He'd like to consult Pratt, but he wished to avoid encountering one of his parents at home. Nor did he desire to go to the harbor, where his father's ships docked. A ride in the redwoods might provide clarity. He circled behind his home to the stable and saddled Prince. He rode to the picnic site and revisited the spot where he'd first seen Ida, where he had his first inclination God had chosen her for him. He dismounted and strolled around the meadow, remembering their conversation. Passionate feelings stirred within him.

If he turned away from Ida, he'd regret losing her the rest of his life. If he continued courting her, she might regret it the rest of hers.

He could not easily discard his long-held dream of partnership with Prescott and Son. "I want both," he cried aloud to God. "I want a life with the woman You've chosen for me and a relationship with my father." He waited in silence on his knees, head and hands lifted toward heaven.

He remained in the solitude of the giant trees until the sun set, still undetermined as to what to do. He mounted Prince and rode him back to town, resolved to visit Ida and talk things over with her. She might have a perspective different from his.

He knocked at the Dempseys' door and was shown into the drawing room, where Ida sat, tearful, with her aunt, drinking tea.

What had he interrupted? "Should I come back later?"

"No." Mrs. Dempsey rose and gestured for him to take a seat. "I've been anticipating your visit. May I pour you a cup of tea?"

"No, thank you." Blaine attempted to put the pieces together. Had Mr. Dempsey related their afternoon conversation? Blaine sat next to Ida on the settee and reached for her hand.

She squeezed his, keeping her eyes downcast. How much had Mr. Dempsey revealed? Why such sorrow? "Have you spoken with your uncle?"

Ida shook her head.

"Should we have?" Mrs. Dempsey sat opposite him and Ida.

"I don't know." Blaine took both of Ida's hands in his. "Will you tell me why you're upset?" He wished Mrs. Dempsey would leave the room so he could converse with Ida privately.

"It has been an eventful day," Ida's aunt answered. "Overwhelmingly so."

"For me as well."

"So we've heard."

Ida kept her head bowed. He felt her hands tremble. "Will you go for a walk with me?"

"I don't think that is wise." Mrs. Dempsey stood. "I recommend you say what you must and be on your way."

"Might I speak with Ida alone, please?"

"Do you wish me to leave, dear one?"

Ida shook her head.

What had he done to make her not want to be alone with him?

She released her hand from his and stood beside her aunt. For the first time, she met his gaze. Sorrow seeped from her eyes, trickling down her cheeks. "Please, may we get this over with?"

"I'm at a disadvantage. Obviously, something has happened to cause you to doubt me, but I don't know what."

Mrs. Dempsey put her arm around Ida. "To begin with, you could have had a private conversation with Ida regarding your change of mind instead of sending your mother to deliver the message and that in front of a roomful of people."

"Exactly what message are you referring to?"

"Did you ask her to deliver more than one?" Mrs. Dempsey's eyes narrowed.

"I didn't ask her to deliver *any*."

Ida lifted her eyes at his response.

Mrs. Dempsey's tone remained accusatory. "Did your mother inform you of Ida's actions this afternoon regarding her Project Save Second Street Souls?"

"Yes, she did." Blaine directed his answer to Ida. Her gaze remained glued to his face.

Ida's aunt continued. "And did you react to the information by sending your mother to announce the annulment of the courtship agreement?"

"I most definitely did not. I would never do that. Ida, you've got to believe me." What had his mother done? She'd gone too far this time.

"But you did discuss the option," Ida spoke softly.

How could he respond? It was not a simple yes or no answer.

CHAPTER 34

Blaine's emotions drove him to his feet. "All afternoon I've been praying for the Lord's direction."

Mrs. Dempsey interrupted him. "So you've considered disavowing the courtship agreement." She stiffened.

"Yes! No! Well, not like that." Blaine's pulse rose. A growing fury threatened to overwhelm his self-control. "I love Ida!" He spoke louder than he intended. "I only considered breaking our agreement to protect her from my mother's vitriol." He paced about the room. "So, yes, I prayed about how best to show my love." He stopped in front of Ida. "Not to reject you."

"You love me?" Her voice trembled. "Like forever love me?"

He reached for her hand, and she let him entwine his fingers with hers. "I'm never happier than when I'm with you." He drew Ida into his arms and pressed her head against his chest. Her heartbeat merged with his. "My dearest angel, I want to spend the rest of my life making you happy."

"You can't." She pushed back and lifted her face to peer into his. "My heavenly Father is responsible for my joy—and for yours. You cannot protect me from this world's trials. You don't need to, because I have His defense and refuge." Her eyes glistened as she whispered, "But I'm glad you want to try. I love you too."

He stopped her speech with a kiss, gentle at first, then growing with passion. Who was this little woman to speak such wisdom and stir his heart like no other ever had or could?

When Ida pulled from the embrace, flushed and breathless, Blaine realized he'd forgotten the presence of her aunt.

She stood with her back to them, rearranging flowers on a side table.

So that was kissing. No wonder people did it. Ida leaned in for another. But Blaine whispered, "I think that's enough for now."

"Why?" Didn't he like it? She sighed.

"Your aunt may not approve."

Ida giggled and whispered, "She's not looking."

"Right now, we need to talk." Blaine pulled her to the settee. She considered tugging back. Talking didn't interest her. She wanted to explore this kissing thing.

Aunt Ruth turned around. "Yes, Ida, we must have a conversation." She took the chair nearest them. "You may have questions, Blaine; however, I reserve the privilege of going first." She directed her attention toward Ida. "Reverend Huntington came to your rescue today. Still, I wonder how much he actually knows about your project."

"Truthfully, not much." Ida met her aunt's gaze. "But I want to tell you." She squeezed Blaine's hand. "And you too." She looked at the flowered carpet before continuing. She'd known this day would come, only she'd hoped to report better results than she'd garnered so far. Neither project—teaching Qui nor Project Saving Second Street Souls—had gone as she'd hoped. Maybe if she explained her belief that God had placed these people on her heart, Blaine and Aunt Ruth would understand she couldn't quit. Her past deceit tore at her conscience—but how much more guilt would she feel if she refused her heavenly Father's bidding?

Passion for her projects surged through her. She rose and paced a moment, seeking the right words.

"We're waiting." Aunt Ruth raised her eyebrows.

Please, heavenly Father, help me know what to say. "It's no secret that I believe the world will be a better place when people everywhere understand the love Jesus has for them. I don't have access to Africa or Asia, but I do to the hurting people in our community."

"Yes, Ida. We've had this discussion before." Her aunt's hands fidgeted—a sure sign impatience grew within.

Ida rushed her next words. "I made over your old red dress to look like fashions common on Second Street, and I made contact with a woman Blaine and I encountered in the drugstore that Sunday we went for ice cream."

"That's what you told Reverend Huntington." Aunt Ruth leaned forward in her chair.

Ida put her hand on Blaine's arm. "Blaine helped me discover her name. Then with the help of others in that neighborhood—"

"By that neighborhood, you mean Second Street?" Aunt Ruth's lips drew a thin, tight line. "You went there attired in the red dress? How many times?"

"Not lots, Aunt Ruth, and except for today, I've been very careful. I remembered what you said about shaming our family. I thought if I went in disguise no one would recognize me, and the thing you feared wouldn't happen."

"That didn't exactly work out, did it?"

"Not at all like I planned. And I'm truly sorry." Ida paused. Should she continue, or wait for the lecture brewing in her aunt's mind?

"All right, what else?" Aunt Ruth's eyes remained cold, not a look leveled at Ida often—or actually ever.

"I met with the woman today in the drugstore." Ida squeezed Blaine's arm and switched her attention from her aunt to him. "You don't know about this part. Anyway, without asking why I wanted to meet with her or drinking the tea I offered, she told me never to seek her again, to stay out of her life forever."

"Well, there you have it." Aunt Ruth shrugged. "You've heard the saying 'You can lead a horse to water, but you can't make it drink.' You've done your best." She sipped her tea.

"That's not how I feel." Ida rose from the settee and knelt beside her aunt. "The woman isn't a horse, and she doesn't *know* she's thirsty. I can change my tactics, figure out some other way to connect. I can't give up."

At the sound of the dinner bell, Aunt Ruth left the room.

"I should go." Blaine rose.

Ida extended her hand toward him. "Won't you stay for dinner?"

"I'd like to. However, there's a matter I want to discuss with my mother."

"It won't be pleasant, will it?" Ida imagined what that conversation would entail. It couldn't be one he looked forward to. "Everything worked out. Can you let time smooth over the prickles?"

"I can't let her speak to you the way she did. Nor can she continue to interfere with my private life."

"I think that's what parents do—because they love us so much, you know. They want the best for us." Ida sensed Blaine's ready protest. "Of course, we have our own lives to live. I think it may be difficult for mothers especially to let go."

"I can't believe you are saying this. You're asking me to ignore how she treated you?"

Ida nodded. "No real harm was done." She didn't add that, since it ended with her first kiss, maybe it was worth it.

"You're amazing. Yes, I'll stay for dinner." Blaine escorted her to the dining room.

After Uncle Harvey asked the mealtime blessing, Ida looked around the table at the people gathered, her heart swelling with affection for each of them. Wallace appeared more chipper than usual, her aunt less animated. She couldn't read Blaine.

Her uncle opened the conversation, directing his words toward Blaine. "I don't suppose you've had time to decide on my offer."

"No, sir, the afternoon's been busier than expected."

Ida swallowed a bite of roasted chicken. "What kind of offer?" Blaine hadn't mentioned a meeting with her uncle, probably because there'd been no time.

Blaine coughed into his napkin. "I find myself in need of employment, and your uncle has generously offered me a position in his company."

Ida's eyes widened. Wow! Big news indeed. "I thought you were set to join your father's shipping business." She sobered. "What happened?"

Blaine grimaced. "The topic does not make for pleasant dinner conversation. It's something we can discuss later." He forked green beans into his mouth.

"Nonsense." Uncle Harvey spooned boiled potatoes onto his plate. "There's nothing unpleasant about offering an astute, ambitious young man a partnership. I thought Wallace might occupy the position; however, he's shown neither interest nor, I daresay, aptitude."

Was that the reason for Wallace's cheerful disposition? He'd been freed to pursue another course? A glance in his direction proved otherwise. Rejection appeared frozen on his face.

"I've an appointment elsewhere." Wallace tossed his napkin onto his plate, scooted back his chair, and exited the room.

Compassion for him filled Ida's heart. He must not have known about his father's decision. She feared he'd act rashly over being excluded, as if Blaine had usurped his position as the only son. She'd find him later, get him to confide in her, assure him that no one could take his place as his father's son.

"How was your day, Ida?" Uncle Harvey slathered butter on a warm yeast roll.

"Somewhat eventful, actually." What if she told him she'd been kissed for the first time? The thought made her giggle inside. Neither could she talk about Mrs. Prescott's accusation in front of the ladies' circle, or Esther's reaction at the drugstore.

She could share part of that. "I've been seeking a way to establish a relationship with women who work on Second Street to teach them about Jesus. So far, none of my efforts have succeeded."

Aunt Ruth cleared her throat loudly. She glared at Ida through wide, anxious eyes.

Her uncle cut into his chicken. "In my opinion, that's an exercise in futility—a waste of your time, but I know you, Ida, you'll have to learn that on your own. It's a tricky business. You can't very well show up in that part of town on your own. If I were you, I'd volunteer to help Dr. Marsh."

"How would that help?"

"The women are checked every two weeks for health concerns. You might assist Doc during his rounds. It would give you access without raising eyebrows."

Ida jumped up from her seat, rounded the table, and hugged her uncle's neck. "Thank you! That's perfect!"

Aunt Ruth's fork dropped to the floor.

CHAPTER 35

After dinner, Mrs. Dempsey invited Blaine to join them in the parlor.

"Thank you, but I must decline. I've business to attend to at home." Blaine couldn't procrastinate confronting his parents any longer. He didn't know yet whether he'd accept Mr. Dempsey's offer. He did know he'd not continue with Prescott and Son under the present circumstances. Although Ida made a good point about no harm being done, he couldn't ignore his mother's actions. Unless he made a stand, the harassment would continue.

Ida walked with him to the door. "I wish you could stay."

"Believe me, I'd rather visit with your family in the parlor than face what I'm compelled to do at home." Blaine took her hands in his. "I'll see you tomorrow." As he bent to kiss her forehead, she lifted her face, and he got the tip of her nose instead.

"Can we do that other kiss again? The one where we close our eyes?" Her face raised to his, eyes already closed.

Blaine willingly complied.

As he strolled home alone, he reflected on the day—one he'd not soon forget—and found himself detouring along the wharf. Moonlight reflected on the dark water as gentle, rolling waves lapped against the shoreline one after another in a constant rhythm. Lifting his face to heaven, he breathed in the salt air. He stood in the presence of his Father as his spirit filled with a sense of peace and power. Assurance bathed him in the knowledge that God would go before him. He uttered no words, asked for nothing, letting contentment clothe him as he simply paused with a thankful heart. Barking seals interrupted his private communion, reminding him a conversation lay ahead at home. He was ready to face whatever awaited him.

In the foyer, Pratt took his hat and coat.

"Are my parents in the parlor?"

"No, sir. They chose the drawing room tonight."

"Are they alone?"

"Yes, sir."

The ticking of the ornate mantel clock greeted him as he entered the elaborately decorated room. Both parents sat before a small, glowing coal fire, his father puffing on his pipe and perusing a newspaper as his mother read a book. Neither looked up as he approached.

Blaine cleared his throat. "I've just come from the Dempseys'."

His father peered at him over the top of the newspaper. "I didn't expect so quick a response from you, Son. Shows how much you're maturing."

Content to let his father's false assumption remain for the moment, Blaine perched on the empty chair next to his mother and reached for her hand. "Is there something you'd like to tell me, Mother?"

"Why? What did they say?"

He felt her hand tremble.

"Both Ida and her aunt were under the impression that I'd sent you to deliver a message."

"I never said you sent me."

"Did you speak on my behalf without consulting me?" That he maintained control of his emotions, Blaine recognized as God's help.

His mother extracted her hand from his and rose from her chair. She stood near the fire as if warming herself. "As you are aware, I've been informed of scandalous behavior regarding Miss Dempsey. She has somehow duped Reverend Huntington, who came to her defense in front of all those women. Together they made me out quite the villain." She dabbed her eyes with her lace handkerchief. "You've no idea of the pain I've endured because of your rash actions. I don't know what can be done now. If you call off the courtship, half the town will believe I forced you to. And if you don't, mark my words, our family will continue to suffer shame at her hands."

"Mother, isn't it possible you've misjudged the girl?"

His mother left the fire and strode to a heavily draped window, her back to him. "I am never wrong in my judgment of character. She's not the right one for you, but all I can do is hope and pray you'll come to your senses soon enough."

He joined her at the window. Remembering Ida's words about the love parents have for their children, he put an arm around her shoulders. "Mother, I know you want the best for me." He planted a kiss on her forehead. "All I ask is you acknowledge my right to choose my companions and not try to manipulate my choices. May I trust you'll not pretend to speak for me again?"

In response, she laid her head on his shoulder and sobbed into her handkerchief. He wrapped an arm around her, frustrated with her histrionics, but wise enough to know he'd get no further attempting to change her mind.

He looked at his father. "I believe Mother is no longer insisting I break off my relationship with Ida. Do you also have a different opinion, Father?"

"Humph."

Not much of a reply, as noncommittal as his mother's. When he'd entered the room, he fully intended to sever ties with Prescott and Son. Now that the moment had arrived, he hesitated. Maybe he wouldn't have to after all.

It was no small thing to give up on a lifelong dream.

After Blaine departed for his home, Aunt Ruth gestured for Ida to sit beside her in the drawing room. "I chose to ignore your display of affection with Blaine before dinner." She took Ida's hand. "You are too young for such things. Mr. Prescott should have known better. Promise me it will not happen again."

Heat flushed Ida's face. "Yes, Aunt. I'm sorry." Should she confess the second kiss? Embarrassment held back the words.

After Aunt Ruth left the room, Ida sought Wallace. She found him in his room, drinking from a flask, which she chose to ignore. "You seemed upset at dinner. Do you want to talk about it?"

"No."

She plopped down on the floor beside him and leaned against the wall. "You know you can trust me."

Wallace narrowed his eyes at her and offered the flask.

"No, thank you."

"I want to be alone."

"Wallace, don't be like that. Talk to me."

He mocked her. "Ida, don't be like that. Drink with me."

She took the flask from him and set it aside. "Are you upset about Blaine possibly coming to work at the sawmill?"

"What do I care about any sawmill? If he wants it, he can have it." Wallace reached around her for the flask. When Ida kept it out of his reach, he didn't fight for it.

She waited for the right words to come as she sent a silent prayer heavenward. She ached for her cousin, whom she considered a brother. If she didn't know what bothered him, how could she help? He used to talk to her. How could she get him to again?

After a few minutes of silence, he slumped against her. His breathing indicated he'd dozed off.

After gently lowering his head to the floor, she retrieved a pillow and blanket from the bed and maneuvered him to a more comfortable position. Taking the flask with her, she tiptoed away. Alone in her room, she fell asleep praying for her cousin and for Blaine, her aunt and uncle, Qui, and the women on Second Street.

Ida slept late and awoke with Wallace occupying her mind. Then she wondered how Blaine's discussion with his parents had gone. Had he decided between his dream of partnering with his father or abandoning that to join her uncle at the sawmill?

Her next thoughts centered on his kisses. At first, she wanted to dress hurriedly and find Mattie; such major events in her life demanded sharing. But how could she do that? Mattie had been attracted to Blaine as well, and discussing a first kiss with her would be unkind, to say the least. Besides, Mattie might consider it as scandalous as Aunt Ruth did.

She finished her toilet and joined her family downstairs as they prepared to leave for church services.

As Ida strolled alongside her aunt in the summer sunshine, she wondered if Blaine would meet her at the church again. Then her thoughts wandered to seeing Mattie and all she had to tell her.

Neither showed up. Ida continued to look for them even as the congregation rose to join the choir in the first hymn. Aunt Ruth frowned at her in a silent warning to stop scanning the sanctuary and face forward.

Humiliated at having to be corrected, Ida succeeded in putting all distractions from her mind and just worship—mostly.

On the walk home, Aunt Ruth spoke Ida's thoughts. "I thought we might see Blaine again today at church."

Ida sighed. "I did too."

Aunt Ruth continued, "I'm sure we'll see him later today."

"Maybe not," Wallace spoke from behind. "A ship docked early this morning. He's probably at work."

How did Wallace know about the ship? Ida chose not to ask.

After lunch, she joined her aunt and uncle in an outing through the redwoods, ending at one of her favorite beaches, where the endless motion of crashing waves polished millions of agates on a steep shore.

Immersed in the Creator's handiwork of forest and sea, Ida's disappointment in seeing neither Mattie nor Blaine vanished. Her worship in the church building had been lacking. This venture into nature inspired awe and wonder, resulting in praise and gratitude for the graciousness of her heavenly Father.

On the return trip, Uncle Harvey detailed to Aunt Ruth his meeting that morning with other church leaders about the outrageous behavior of their pastor and the steps they intended to take to halt his unacceptable association with the Chinese.

Ida held her tongue and listened.

Something had to be done.

CHAPTER 36

Blaine planned to accompany Ida to church and join her family on their pew—partly to enjoy worshipping the Lord together and partly to firmly establish his devotion to her in front of the ladies' auxiliary—and any female who hadn't received the message. As he headed out the door, though, his mother suffered another fainting spell. While his father sought the doctor, he stayed by her side, applying cool cloths and holding her hand.

As he sat quietly, his mind debated the dilemma he faced regarding Ida and his position at Prescott and Son. Nothing had been accomplished by the discussion with his parents the previous evening.

The sting of his mother's humiliation would wear off in a day or two. Something new in the community would draw the busybodies and gossips in another direction, and his mother would likely renew her campaign to rid Ida from their lives. He dreaded her next attack.

That his earlier plan to speak alone with his father would prove fruitless, he had no doubt. Although no one could accuse his father of being henpecked, in this matter his mother's wishes ruled. There had to be a way to change her opinion.

As she reclined on the parlor settee, he observed her face. Wrinkles around her eyes and lips reminded him she had aged. Did the fainting bout signal a serious decline in her health? He squeezed her hand and prayed.

She stirred, opened her eyes, then shut them again.

His mind wandered to his option to invest in the sawmill. He'd do it. Tomorrow he'd visit the bank and check on available funds from the trust his grandparents set up for him. He'd not thought much about the money in the past. He'd had no need to. Now the time had come to consider his assets and how they might be put to use.

If he continued to work with Prescott and Son, the funds could purchase a house for him and Ida. Maybe a cottage with a view of the ocean. That would please her. He pictured coming home to her waiting for him at the door. Red flowers bloomed in yellow window boxes. A white picket fence surrounded a yard with a giant maple tree offering shade in the summer. Sumptuous dinner smells wafted in the air as he approached. And Ida on the stoop, smiling, reaching her arms toward him, standing on tiptoe to greet him with a kiss, maybe a puppy bouncing around their feet.

"Ahem!" His father and Dr. Marsh stood before him.

Blaine rose and stepped aside for Doc.

"She's in good hands now." His father gestured for Blaine to follow him. "A ship has docked."

Blaine needed no further invitation. He accompanied his father toward the pier.

"What were you thinking about back there?"

"Ida. A home with her."

"I thought you ended that."

"Then you haven't been listening." Blaine shook his head. "I don't need any more time to consider your threat."

"Not a threat, Son. Consider it motivation for you to do the responsible thing."

"Father, it has always been my greatest desire to join you in business. I've never considered any other option."

"Good. Just what I wanted to hear." His father increased his pace.

"Let me finish, please." Blaine hesitated, searching for a way to keep peace with this man he'd looked up to all his life and still follow the path God set before him.

"I'm waiting."

"If you force me to choose between a partnership with you or a relationship with Ida, I choose her. Actually, Father, the decision is yours. You can accept I've chosen Ida and allow me to prove my worth to the company, or you can turn away and force me to use my skills elsewhere. Either way, Ida is part of my future." Blaine softened his voice. "I believe you know what I'd prefer."

"You're giving me an ultimatum?"

"Not at all, sir. Just explaining the facts."

The ship had come into view with its lowered gangplank and sailors already beginning to unload cargo. Blaine began directing the activity as his father skirted around the crowded dock, making his way to the gangplank.

Like most cargo ships, this vessel was outfitted to handle a few passengers. Although summer weather enticed more travelers to visit than during other months, not many chose a freighter for their voyage. His father paused at the end of the gangplank, then took baggage from the hand of a young woman and escorted her along the dock.

As they drew nearer, Blaine recognized Abigail Goldberg.

What? Had the entire morning been a ploy to keep him home and available when Miss Goldberg arrived?

That would explain his father's nonchalant attitude toward his wife's health.

At first, Blaine couldn't believe his eyes. Then, as Abigail and his father neared, irritation flamed into anger. Did his father truly believe he could be dissuaded from Ida by flaunting other young ladies before him?

Enough was enough. But no good would be served by causing a scene on the docks. Blaine strode past the two without so much as a nod. Abigail smiled and reached out her hand as he passed. She must have felt his censure as he continued on. He didn't care.

Even though being rude solved nothing, the anger bubbling inside prevented him from acknowledging her. Ignoring his father's repeated call, he sought the ship's master to receive the bill of lading. He devoted his energy to the ship's cargo, not even noticing when his father and Abigail left the wharf or where they went. The task kept him busy the rest of the day, into the evening, with enough mental exercise to put his troubles out of his mind.

When his work concluded, the anger crawled back. Although hungry and tired after a day in the sun and wind, on his feet without a break, he determined not to return home. All day he'd held the thought of seeing Ida in his mind. He couldn't show up sweaty and dirty—and he couldn't go home, not in his present state of mind.

He retrieved his bicycle from behind the office and pedaled toward the sawmill. Why, he didn't know. He needed a destination, and the mill came to mind. It being a Sunday, the mill was shut down.

Could he adapt to this type of work? Of course he could. Did he want to? Every part of his being said yes, but he couldn't give an answer he'd have to live with born of anger.

Nor could he stay away from home forever. At some point, he needed to return, take a bath, get his belongings.

Get his belongings?

And take them where?

As he pedaled, he chided himself. What was he, a moody teenager running from his problems? He expected more from himself. He'd be cordial to Abigail. Introduce her to Stella Sutterman and other young ladies in town. He could maintain his independence without churlish behavior—with the help of God.

His route home from the sawmill took him through a neighborhood he rarely visited. Two-story, neatly kept homes lined the street, although none appeared as opulent as his residence. One had a sign in its window: Room for Rent.

A solution sent from God, or a mere coincidence he chose this path home? Blaine didn't believe in coincidences. He leaned his bicycle against the picket fence, strode through the gate, and knocked at the door. The elderly lady answering the knock introduced herself as Mrs. Bickel.

"Please forgive my untidy appearance. I've just gotten off work and saw your sign in the window."

"You work on Sundays?" Mrs. Bickel frowned.

"Not usually. When a ship comes in, I have no choice."

"Hmm." She looked him up and down as if trying to decide to let him enter.

"I can come back tomorrow if you prefer."

"You're here now. Come on in." She showed him to a spacious upstairs room boasting a writing desk situated under a large window, a substantial armoire, two upholstered armchairs facing a stone fireplace, and an ample bed—more than adequate for his needs.

Before agreeing to lease to him, she drilled him on his habits—she'd tolerate no drinking, late nights, or female guests upstairs. And she'd need a reference from his pastor.

"What did you say your name is again?"

"Blaine Prescott, ma'am."

"Any relation to Mrs. Florence Prescott?"

"She's my mother."

"Oh." His inquisitor frowned.

Ironic that a mention of his family might work *against* him. "You know my mother?"

"Not really." Mrs. Bickel pursed her lips. "Met her a few times. Most recently when she barged into our ladies' auxiliary."

It didn't take finely honed observation powers to note this potential landlady did not fancy his mother. Perhaps he could redirect her attention. "You are acquainted then with Miss Ida Dempsey?"

For the first time since he'd entered the dwelling, the diminutive matron smiled. "Most definitely. A dear girl."

"I heartily agree. She and I are courting."

Mrs. Bickel's eyes widened, and then an understanding, compassionate look took over. "My dear boy, the room is yours. I'm happy to be a part of your escape."

Before Blaine mounted his bicycle to return home, he lifted his eyes heavenward, his heart full of gratitude. The route he'd taken was definitely not a coincidence.

Excited to share with Ida what he'd done, he bicycled to her home and knocked on the door. Mr. Dempsey answered—and raised his eyebrows.

"Please forgive my appearance. I know I'm a mess. Two ships came in, and I've been working all day. I hoped to speak with Ida a moment. I've something important to tell her."

"Go home and take a bath." The door closed.

CHAPTER 37

The knock at the door brought Ida to the top of the stairs. She heard Blaine's request to see her, his explanation for his appearance, and Uncle Harvey's reply. Not pleased with her uncle, she retired to her room.

Something hit her window. A tree branch? No. Wrong sound.

Another hit.

She doused her light, opened the window, and peered into the darkness.

"Down here."

Both hands held high, Blaine waved then blew her a kiss. "I'll see you tomorrow. I promise!"

Ida blew a kiss back and watched him disappear into the night. Every negative thought evaporated like fog under attack from the sun. She fell asleep, a smile in her heart.

Morning found her well rested and eager to begin the day. Immediately after breakfast, she followed her uncle's suggestion and visited Dr. Marsh, arriving at his office before his first appointment of the day.

"I'm sorry to intrude. I wondered if I might have a moment of your time." Ida fidgeted, suddenly nervous to approach the doctor with her proposal. He'd taken care of her all her life, but she didn't feel close to him. Doses of terrible-tasting concoctions usually accompanied his appearance. As unfair as it seemed, she associated his presence with discomfort.

"I have a few minutes. How can I help you?" His smile encouraged her.

Ida explained her mission and her uncle's suggestion that accompanying the doctor on his rounds might open the door to reach Second Street women.

Dr. Marsh listened intently as she rambled, finally interrupting her. "If you are offering to assist me in my care for the women on Second Street, I am willing to accept. I insist on having another female present with me at such times. Currently, Nurse Scott fills that role. It is an assignment she's not fond of. She will be happy to be replaced. I tend to the women on the second and fourth Tuesdays of every month, in the early afternoon." He paused, slowly shaking his head. "I don't expect you'll get the results you're hoping for. It is likely you'll be disappointed."

His acceptance of her offer overshadowed his expression of doubts. "Thank you!" Ida bounced from his office, excited for this new opportunity and wondering how she could bear waiting almost two weeks until the doctor's next rounds. On the one hand, it gave her time to figure out how to approach the women she'd meet, but on the other hand, it felt ages and eons away. Talking with Mattie would help—dare she try?

She crossed the street and headed south toward Mattie's neighborhood. As she neared Chinatown, she paused. The street was mostly vacant, as were the boardwalks on both sides. Previously, Ida hadn't been overly curious about the area. However, as she scanned the quarter, it occurred to her that to effectively relate to Qui, she should know more about her environment, culture, and traditions. Aunt Ruth's opposition had been based on distinct differences between themselves and the Chinese. Exactly what were those differences?

Ida had never been specifically forbidden from Chinatown, so in venturing there, she'd not be disobeying any rules. She'd heard tales of violence, rumors of opium dens and illicit gambling parlors—certainly not places for moral young ladies to visit, but what could it possibly hurt to wander around outside in the middle of the day?

A stench emanating from under the boardwalk assaulted Ida's senses, causing her eyes to water. Not even placing a handkerchief over her nose helped. As she swatted at the myriad flies buzzing around and strolled along the row of unpainted wooden buildings in varying degrees of dilapidation, she grew aware of eyes behind cracked and darkened windows following her progress. None of the signs above the doors were in English. She had no idea what or who lurked behind them.

Another strong smell wafted onto the street from a pair of opened windows. This odor hinted of fish and spices she could not identify, perhaps in preparation of lunch. At the creaking of the uneven boardwalk behind her, she glanced over her shoulder. Several men dressed in dingy white dungarees, their hair caught up in single braids dangling down their backs, stopped in their tracks. They spoke to one another in what sounded like gibberish to Ida's ears. A few women peering from doorways she'd just passed ducked back inside.

Ida increased her pace to match her pounding heart, amazed at the otherworldly aura of this neighborhood. No more than one block long, it felt as foreign as if she had traveled the distance to China itself. She reminded herself that she walked a street in Eureka, her hometown, with naught to fear. Still, a sense of danger dogged her steps.

Movement across the rutted dirt road caught her attention. Another group of four or five men, dressed similarly to those behind her, carried a red flag with a golden dragon in its center. Did it have a special meaning?

Resisting the urge to glance behind her again, Ida forced herself to slow her breathing. She clasped her hands together to still their trembling and lifted her chin in an attempt to show a confidence she didn't feel. How could one block be so long?

"Ida!"

Was that Wallace? What was he doing here?

From a narrow side door, he leaped to her and took her arm, pulling her along. "Hurry up." She nearly ran to keep up with his stride. And then they were at the corner, across the street, and the sense of danger vaporized.

Outside the fruit stand, Wallace stopped and swiveled Ida to face him. "What in the world are you doing?"

"I could ask you the same." Ida pulled her arm away.

"It's none of your business." Wallace grabbed her arm again, his grip tight.

The look on his face, coupled with the pressure on her arm, shocked Ida. What was her cousin up to? Then, in a blink, critical judgment fled and her heart softened. "Wallace, we're friends, remember?"

"Did you follow me here?"

"No. I hadn't a clue you were anywhere around."

"Then what were you doing?" He released her arm.

"Nothing! I was on my way to see Mattie, and on a whim, I thought I'd see Chinatown. I want to teach Qui about Jesus and thought if I understood her culture a bit better, I'd be more effective."

"That's it?" Wallace nudged her to continue walking. He smoothed back his hair. "All sorts of things go on there. Weird things. Mysterious things."

"Things you find intriguing?" Ida met Wallace's gaze. "Aren't you supposed to be at the sawmill?"

Wallace planted a smile on his face. "Oh, little Ida, don't you worry about me. I'm always where I'm supposed to be."

"Do you resent Blaine?" Ida determined not to let her cousin weasel out of a discussion she knew he didn't want to have.

"He's fine."

"Wallace, please. Tell me what's wrong."

"Nothing."

"You've forgotten who you're talking to. It's me, Ida. Remember I'm your friend, on your side. And I know you. So out with it."

Wallace drew in a deep breath and exhaled. "Maybe later. I can't right now. There's nothing for you to worry about." He turned on his heel and darted away. Before he rounded the corner toward Chinatown, he looked back and waved, calling out, "Nothing to worry about."

After Wallace disappeared, Ida abandoned her plan to seek Mattie. Experiencing Chinatown had awakened something inside her, a feeling of fervent compassion coupled with an acute sense of impotence. Reverend Huntington had warned her she was no match for the women on Second Street, but no one had counseled her about the inhabitants of Chinatown. And Qui lived in that dangerous squalor! Aunt Ruth had tried to tell her.

What was it like for the cook to come and go every day, a foot in two worlds so completely opposite one another? How many others experienced the same situation? Every household Ida knew employed Chinese men and women as housekeepers and cooks. Maybe not every household—Mattie's family didn't—but certainly all of Eureka's upper class did. Did they know the living conditions of these people? The stench and condition of the buildings distressed Ida. Worse, the entire block reeked of hopelessness. A result of the absence of God?

That couldn't be. The Creator existed everywhere. He loved the world. That included the residents of Second Street as well as Chinatown.

Ida hurried home, sat at her desk in front of her bedroom window with its view of the harbor, and opened her Bible. An urgency pushed her to note scripture after scripture she should share with Qui. They'd read some of them together as soon as she finished the list. She'd chop onions or peel hard-boiled eggs or do whatever busied Qui in the kitchen to make the time.

That Aunt Ruth would disapprove bothered Ida, yet she had to risk it. Some things were too important to set aside.

Lunch came and went, and still, Ida pored over the scriptures. As she read each one, her conviction increased. This God she worshipped deserved nothing less than her whole heart. How could she not share His love with those unfortunate souls who didn't know Him?

Armed with more than fifty passages, she skipped down the stairs and into the kitchen. Qui kneaded bread dough for the next day's meal. "Missy hungry?"

For the first time, Ida understood Jesus' words "man shall not live by bread alone, but by every word that proceedeth out of the mouth of God." Having Qui read the scripture meant more than food.

"Let me knead the dough, and you read this—do you have your Bible here?"

"No. You not knead right." Qui returned to the lump of dough. "Bible hidden."

"Then I'll read to you." Ida opened immediately to John 3:16.

For the next thirty minutes, Ida read and Qui listened as she prepared food. For Ida, the passing time felt like seconds. She could have continued indefinitely, but Wallace interrupted the session. He and Qui exchanged a look that puzzled Ida.

She glanced from one to the other. "What's going on?"

"I could ask you the same thing." Wallace grabbed a cinnamon jumble from the cookie jar.

"Qui is learning about Jesus." Ida poured a glass of milk and handed it to him.

Wallace downed the milk and took another jumble. "Qui and I need privacy."

"Why?"

"If I explained that to you, we wouldn't need the privacy."

CHAPTER 38

Staying out late the previous night allowed Blaine to escape dealing with his parents until morning. He arrived at breakfast prepared for a confrontation.

He was not disappointed.

His mother waited until he sat. "What do you have to say for yourself?"

His father set aside the morning newspaper.

Although several sarcastic retorts ran through his mind, he chose to reply with respect. "I apologize for not better communicating my plans. It seems to be a trait in our family."

As he forked a bite of ham into his mouth, he noted Abigail's absence. Would this be a good time to announce his change of residence?

"Let me be perfectly clear." His mother glared at him. "Last night will not be repeated. We require your presence at dinner and after for the foreseeable future. That should be simple enough to remember."

"I'm sorry to disappoint, Mother. I have plans and will not be able to accommodate your request."

His father scowled. "It wasn't a request."

His mother continued as if Blaine had said nothing. "You might want to write this down. This week, dinner, as I said. On Saturday, I've planned a picnic. Miss Goldberg hasn't seen our lovely redwoods. On Sunday next, we'll host a welcoming party for her on the lawn. I'll let you know the schedule for the following week as soon as I've finalized the plans."

Blaine ate his eggs without responding to his mother. She'd interpret his silence as acquiescence, but he'd recently learned that arguing with her was futile.

Abigail joined the meal, bright and cheerful, all smiles and pleasantries that he knew to be false. He detested the charade. Downing his coffee, he rose from the table. "I'll see you at the office, Father." He nodded to Abigail and his mother, then made his escape.

In all those months—years actually—dreaming of the day he'd graduate from the university, make a permanent home in Eureka working for his father, he never once imagined the reality he now faced.

Unnerved by Wallace and Qui's secret, Ida headed to the docks. Unnoticed by Blaine, she watched him direct sailors loading a ship. Seeing him in this element increased her admiration of him. He exuded confidence without lording it over the laborers, and he wasn't above getting his hands dirty as he helped them.

She found it impossible to observe him without remembering that first kiss—the kiss Aunt Ruth disapproved of, the kiss that couldn't be repeated.

Turning from the docks, she headed to one of her favorite residential districts, which just so happened to include the street on which the Prescotts lived. Taking her time to enjoy the fragrant flower gardens surrounding the mansions, her thoughts wandered back to her visit with Dr. Marsh. Everything about that plan felt right. Uncle Harvey had suggested it, so Aunt Ruth couldn't possibly disapprove. She'd be serving the women with humility and compassion. She envisioned the process, smiling to herself. How could she wait two weeks to begin?

As she continued down the street, a young lady she didn't recognize strolled her way, carrying a lacy umbrella and dressed in finery not often seen in Eureka, even among the upper class.

Ida smiled as she neared. "Please don't think me rude, but that is such a lovely dress. I daresay it's not from the West Coast."

The young woman smiled back. "No. I insist my seamstress provide the latest French fashions."

"Here in Eureka?"

"Oh, goodness, no. I reside in San Francisco. I'm here at the invitation of the Prescotts. Do you know them?"

"Yes, we are acquainted."

"I'm so glad. Then you'll be at the welcoming party they are hosting for me. We will be great friends, I predict. I don't know anyone here except dear Blaine."

Dear Blaine?

What welcoming party?

As Blaine concluded his tasks for the day, his father met him at the office door. "A young lady is here to see you."

Ida? No, his father wouldn't look so chipper.

Abigail sashayed to him, linking her arm with his. "Can we talk a minute?" She pulled him back outdoors.

"I'm on my way to see Miss Dempsey."

"A delightful young lady. I had the pleasure of meeting her this afternoon."

She had Blaine's attention. "How did that happen?"

"Not important. Can we talk?"

"Do I have a choice?"

"Don't be difficult. Besides, you owe me."

"How do you figure that?"

"You didn't keep your promise in San Francisco."

"I made you no promises, Miss Goldberg." Blaine remembered Sam's warning about his sister, that she would be angry at his departure and seek revenge. Was that what this was about? "Walk with me."

"Where?" Abigail raised her eyebrows. "To Miss Dempsey's?"

"Why not?" Blaine didn't know what Abigail had up her sleeve, but wouldn't it foil his mother's scheme if Ida and Abigail became friends? "You can get better acquainted with my future fiancée."

"I don't intend to be in Eureka long enough to make friends." Abigail kept up with Blaine's long strides.

Although he knew the answer to the question, Blaine asked anyway. "Why are you here?"

"I followed you, of course."

Not the response he expected. "My father didn't send for you? Your parents didn't force you?"

"As if they could." Abigail stopped under a leafy maple tree. "No, this time the joke's on them. They believe you broke my heart when you left—my mother still believes you wrote that sickeningly sweet note to me. You'd laugh at how easily I convinced them to allow me to come to Eureka."

Blaine shaded his eyes against the setting sun. "Why leave Chester?"

"I didn't. He'll be here soon. I'm staying only until he arrives."

Blaine struggled to hide his shock at Abigail's implication. "Are you sure this is the route you want to take?"

"No, it's not my first choice at all. My mother and father have made it my only option."

He refrained from voicing his disagreement with her scheme. Who was he to advise anyone on how to deal with overbearing parents?

Certain that he'd come after dinner, Ida waited for Blaine on the front porch swing. She wanted to speak with him alone; if he came inside Aunt Ruth would insist he join them in the parlor and privacy wouldn't be possible. So much had happened! She couldn't wait to tell him the results of her visit with Doc, her experience in Chinatown, her success reading scripture with Qui. She wanted his perspective regarding Wallace. Did he have any idea what her cousin might be doing in Chinatown? How was it connected to the secret he shared with Qui?

The appearance of Miss Goldberg and the upcoming party took priority in her mind. When did Blaine discover she was coming? Why hadn't he mentioned the party? Ida trusted Blaine, but Mr. Prescott's words on the dock the morning Blaine sailed away niggled like a pesky insect. She'd mentally swat the conversation away only to have it return—not like a big buzzing bumblebee—more like a persistent, annoying mosquito. Could there be any chance at all that Blaine was false to her?

Honeysuckle bushes released their sweet fragrance into the cooling air as she paced to and fro from them to the stone shell-shaped birdbath.

A couple strolled nearer—wait, not a couple! Blaine with that Miss Goldberg clinging to his arm.

So much for time alone.

Blaine separated from Abigail and greeted Ida with a peck on her cheek. "You've been waiting for me?"

"I've had quite a day and have so much to talk about." Ida drew in a breath and glanced at his companion. "It's nice to see you again, Miss Goldberg."

"Don't say what you don't mean." Abigail lifted her chin as if daring Ida to contradict her. "You are hoping to have time alone with your dear

Blaine and weren't expecting me at all." Her eyebrows arched.

Rarely was Ida caught speechless. This was one of those times.

Blaine broke the awkwardness. "Openness and honesty in all its glory." He chuckled.

"I'll not spoil your evening." Abigail turned to leave. "I'm perfectly capable of taking care of myself, especially in this backwoods excuse for a town."

What was the ancient saying? Keep your friends close and your enemies closer? Miss Goldberg might not be an enemy, but she definitely wasn't a friend. "Please come inside and meet my aunt and uncle."

Abigail stopped, looked Ida's house up and down, and frowned. "No thank you, I'd rather not."

Did she mean to offend with her superior tone? Usually, Ida easily ignored uppity attitudes, but this woman got under her skin. Because of her familiarity with Blaine? Was she jealous? Ida shook off the idea.

"Perfectly capable of taking care of yourself?" Ida linked her arm with Abigail's. "Eureka isn't the size of San Francisco, but what we lack in population, we make up for in disreputable districts."

"Really? In this backwoods town?"

Ida bristled again at Abigail's haughty air. In every way, this newcomer presented herself as superior. It shouldn't bother her. But it did.

"Let's walk, shall we?" She glanced back at Blaine. "Will you escort us around town?"

Not waiting for an answer from him, Ida led Abigail away from the residential district. Blaine followed as they strolled to the edge of Chinatown. Maybe if it hadn't been evening, not much would have been going on, but the summer night brought out rival Tongs. One didn't have to speak Chinese to understand the hostility in the voices shouting back and forth, to feel the tension, to smell gunpowder mixed with the sewage.

Ida sensed Abigail's anxiety, felt it herself. She led her reluctant companion away from Fourth Street, hurrying down H to Second. Red lights glowed from upper-story windows, and scantily dressed women wearing red lipstick and painted eyes leaned against doorways from which loud music and raucous laughter poured.

"I've seen enough." Abigail refused to budge farther down the block.

"We still have to visit the saloons along the waterfront where the sailors congregate," Ida teased.

Blaine stepped between the two, grasping an arm of each. "It's my turn."

Ida couldn't imagine where he would take them. She'd shown Abigail the worst parts of Eureka to prove her "take care of myself" attitude wrong. What had gotten into her? If she'd been trying to compete with Abigail's superiority, she should have led her past the theater and finer restaurants.

Perhaps that's what Blaine had in mind. No. He took them away from downtown, closer to the residential neighborhoods. He escorted them down a slate walkway leading to a modest two-story home, removed keys from his pocket, and opened the door.

In the narrow entryway, he called out, "Mrs. Bickel?"

Ida tugged on his arm. "Why are we bothering her at this hour?"

"I want to show you my new residence."

Abigail grinned and patted his back. "*Dear* Blaine. I didn't think you had it in you."

CHAPTER 39

Mrs. Bickel's cane tapped on the hardwood floor as she hobbled into the entryway, a frown creasing her forehead until she spied Ida. Then a smile lit up her face.

"I know you forbade late nights and females upstairs. I hope you'll allow me to share this change with Miss Dempsey." Blaine grinned. "If we are disturbing your rest, we can return earlier tomorrow."

Abigail cleared her throat.

"I've forgotten my manners." Blaine introduced his landlady to Abigail. "Miss Goldberg is visiting from San Francisco, and Ida and I thought to show her around town."

From the corner of his eye, Blaine watched Ida, trying to decipher her reaction to his big news. Her smile appeared sincere.

Did she have any other kind? Her lack of duplicity endeared her to him. She wouldn't play games like his mother. Or Abigail.

Unless that was what prompted the tour of Eureka. Some sort of competition between her and Abigail?

"I said, what do you think, Blaine?" Abigail nudged him.

All three women focused on him expectantly.

He had no idea what they were talking about. He should admit his mind had wandered. Instead, he blurted, "I agree with Ida."

Giggles resounded, first from Mrs. Bickel then from the other two.

"What's so funny?" Blaine looked from one laughing female to another. Heat crawled from his neck to his face.

No one answered. As the laughter subsided, Mrs. Bickel dabbed her eyes with a handkerchief. She allowed the three to trek up the stairs to inspect Blaine's new quarters, while she remained on the ground floor to "save" her legs.

Blaine opened the door to the room with a flourish, hoping the light mood continued, hoping for Ida's approval.

"This is perfect." Abigail looked especially impressed.

Why did she say that? It wasn't grand at all. Clean, but definitely not opulent.

Blaine grasped Ida's hand. "What do you think?"

"It's lovely."

He met her gaze. Her eyes indicated she held something back. Of course she did. He'd not said anything about seeking lodging. She likely had questions she'd not ask in front of a stranger. He'd pictured this moment differently. It should have been him and Ida alone.

Abigail ran her hand along the back of the upholstered chairs, peered out the window, and opened the armoire. "I daresay there's more space here than one person needs."

What was she getting at?

Ida released Blaine's hand. "We should leave. It's late, and my aunt doesn't know where I am."

Back downstairs, Blaine apologized to Mrs. Bickel for the interruption to her evening and escorted Ida and Abigail toward the Dempseys'.

"When are you moving in?" Abigail linked arms with him. The narrow walkway necessitated Ida follow behind them—or step into the street.

He didn't need the forlorn look on Ida's face to prompt him into action. He disengaged from Abigail and placed an arm around Ida. He felt her stiffen, realized his error, and linked arms with her.

"I asked when you are moving in." Abigail followed barely a step behind.

"I hope Saturday. However, I've not had an opportunity to tell my parents." Blaine kept his eyes forward to better detect any reaction from Ida. She'd grown uncharacteristically quiet.

"Did you forget about the picnic?" Abigail stepped on the back of his heel.

Ida glanced up at him, her eyes lacking their usual sparkle. He didn't know why this beauty beside him was hurting. He could think of only one thing to do.

Get rid of Abigail.

Hadn't the woman boasted she could take care of herself?

Blaine stopped at the corner. "Miss Goldberg, I believe you'll be able to find your way home from here." He pointed up the lighted street. Yes, he was being rude, but since he had to choose between being impolite and hurting Ida's feelings, he'd pick being impolite.

Abigail's narrowed eyes displayed her displeasure. "Of course. Or I can wait here. I'm sure you won't be long."

"Suit yourself."

Ida shook her head. "No, Blaine. I'm nearly home, and you can't leave Miss Goldberg standing on a corner." Before he could stop her, she dashed across the street.

As he started to follow, Abigail grabbed his arm, pulling him back. "She's right, you know."

He shrugged away from her. "If you don't want to stand on the corner, then don't."

He dashed off, almost colliding with a horse-drawn buggy at the intersection, losing precious minutes in his chase after Ida. He reached the Dempseys' home just as she stumbled inside. "Wait!" he shouted.

She glanced back. And slammed the door.

"What is all that commotion?" Uncle Harvey scowled at the foot of the staircase.

"I'm sorry. It's nothing." No longer able to hold back her tears, Ida dashed past him up the stairs and into her room.

Confused and frustrated, she plopped on her bed and wept into her pillow. How she longed to vent to Mattie. Too many feelings! How to sort them out?

She shouldn't have slammed the door. That was a mistake. Immature, to say the least. That Goldberg woman brought out a beast within her. How? Why?

The evening had not gone as planned. How could such a promising day end so poorly? There'd been so much on her mind to share with Blaine. Apparently, he had news as well.

He hadn't mentioned a desire to move away from his parents. It could be a good thing. She didn't know. He hadn't told her about leaving for San Francisco, or about Uncle Harvey's employment offer. He'd said nothing about his family expecting a visitor—who did Abigail Goldberg think she was anyway—or about a picnic, or any type of welcoming party.

As if she'd attend!

The knock on her door didn't surprise her—Uncle Harvey likely said something to her aunt about her slamming doors and bolting upstairs. Aunt Ruth entered, attired in her dressing gown, her hair already undone and hanging loose. She sat on the bed. "You worried us, dear one, leaving as you did without explanation and remaining gone so long." The rebuke held no harshness of tone.

"I'm sorry." Tears coated Ida's cheeks, dripping off her chin. "I wanted to speak with Blaine, but then he showed up with that Miss Goldberg." Sobs stifled her words.

Aunt Ruth put an arm around her, drawing her closer. Ida leaned her head against the comforting shoulder.

"Who is Miss Goldberg?"

Ida took the handkerchief her aunt handed her and blew her nose. "A friend of the Prescotts from San Francisco. I don't like her one bit. She's all uppity and snooty, and someone should teach her manners."

"Oh my. I've never heard you speak so harshly of anyone."

"I could say more."

"Well, it's my experience that after a tough night, things often seem better in the morning." Aunt Ruth rose from the bed.

Ida didn't want her to leave yet. "I was rude to Blaine. None of it was his fault. I treated him poorly. And I didn't get to tell him about my visit with Dr. Marsh."

"You've already seen the doctor?" Aunt Ruth drew in a sharp breath. "I meant to talk to you about that."

"It's all right. I don't begin until the twelfth. Doc said I'd be doing his nurse a favor by attending the women with him. He insists on another female present, and the nurse doesn't relish the assignment."

"Of course not. You'll find it distasteful as well. In fact, after discussing the matter with your uncle, he agrees with me that it isn't a suitable activity for you."

"I don't mind the unpleasant aspects, because it opens the door for me to teach about the love of Jesus without shaming our family in any way."

"Dear one, it's my and your uncle's job to protect you from such influences as you'll find in that neighborhood. You'll have to give your regrets to Dr. Marsh. We cannot allow you to accompany him. Would you like me to speak to him for you?"

It was too much. After the successes of the day, then the disappointment of the evening with Miss Goldberg, to also have her aunt shatter her plans for Project Save Second Street Souls pushed Ida past the point of tears.

So things would be better in the morning?

For whom?

CHAPTER 40

Ida awoke with swollen eyes and a drippy nose. She'd fallen asleep full of anger and resentment, but her aunt's words proved true. The bleakness of the night mellowed with the morning sun.

As she prepared for the day, it occurred to her that she hid as much—maybe more—from Blaine as he did from her, although she didn't mean to *hide* anything. Possibly he didn't either. She hadn't had an opportunity to share yesterday's events with him. Was it the same with him? Until they had a chance to talk, she'd give him the benefit of the doubt.

Nevertheless, she owed him an apology. Did he owe her one? Maybe.

After breakfast, she read scripture with Qui in the kitchen despite her aunt's request to leave the cook alone. Until God revealed another time and place, she had to take the risk. This morning, the Bible study served two purposes: First and foremost, it quenched Qui's thirst to know Jesus. Second, it served as a distraction from Blaine and Miss Goldberg.

Midmorning, Wallace again interrupted their session and again required privacy with the cook. Ida suspected he was up to no good. What could she do? Would discussing the situation with Blaine offer insights or at least a different perspective?

Blaine.

If she showed up around noon, might he eat lunch with her again, giving them time alone to talk?

After notifying her aunt of her intentions, she left the house and strode to the docks. No ships remained in the harbor. Dare she bother Blaine in his office? An aversion to speaking with the elder Mr. Prescott gave her pause. She hesitated outside the building and decided against entering it.

A restlessness provoked by unresolved business—namely clearing her conscience regarding how she had behaved toward Blaine—prevented her from returning home.

Would it be a mistake to visit Mrs. Bickel? Ida meandered into the tidy neighborhood. The elderly woman wouldn't be expecting her to call. How would Blaine view it? She could claim that a desire to thank Mrs. Bickel for defending her at the last ladies' auxiliary meeting prompted the visit. But that would be deceit. Drawing her to Mrs. Bickel was Blaine's upstairs room.

A horse-drawn wagon with a few crates and barrels stood outside. Blaine's belongings? Possibly.

She drew near and rubbed the horse's nose. A man in denim overalls exited the house and hefted one of the crates from the bed of the wagon. "Hello there." Ida smiled. "Beautiful day, isn't it?"

The man nodded. "Good day, Miss." He continued toward the house with his load.

"Are these Mr. Blaine's possessions?"

"I suppose. Either that or he's a thief." The man chuckled as if he'd made a grand joke.

"Is he here?"

"No. Don't know where he is. I'm just following instructions to deliver the load to this address."

Ida followed the laborer inside. Mrs. Bickel remained out of sight, perhaps in the parlor. Ida continued up the stairs behind the hired worker. He set the crate down in the middle of the room and left, Ida supposed, to bring in another one.

She tapped on the lid of one of the boxes. Inside were Blaine's personal effects. Curiosity nipped. Unfortunately—or perhaps fortunately—opening the container required a crowbar. Ida didn't have one.

After the worker brought in another load, Ida followed him down the stairs. She cleared her throat loudly in the narrow entryway. "Hello? Mrs. Bickel?"

"Who is it?" a voice answered from the front room.

"It's me, Ida Dempsey." She entered the room, smiling. "I saw the wagon outside and thought perhaps Mr. Prescott was here."

"Do have a seat, dear Ida." Mrs. Bickel rose from her chair on unsteady legs. "He'll be back in a moment."

"Don't get up. I'll not bother you."

"Nonsense. You can join me for lunch." She sat and rang a bell from the side table.

A bent over, wrinkled woman resembling Qui—except much older—shuffled in. She stared at Ida and frowned.

Mrs. Bickel spoke loudly, almost a shout. "Yoke, bring us lunch, please."

The woman made no reply. She turned and left the room.

"Yoke's hard of hearing," Mrs. Bickel explained.

Ida sat near her. "How are you today?"

"Fine as frog's hair." The elderly woman settled back in her chair. "I believe I made a good decision renting the room to your Mr. Prescott. I like company and don't have the pleasure very often. You're the second young lady to call today, and it's barely past noon."

The second visitor? Her mind jumped immediately to Miss Goldberg. Had she come? That was ridiculous. She'd have no reason. "I'm glad to know you enjoy company."

Blaine's voice sounded from outside.

Along with a female voice Ida immediately recognized. Jealousy flashed through her. She pushed it back. That Miss Goldberg! Really! "It sounds as if you're about to get a third visitor."

Mrs. Bickel frowned and shook her head. "Not her again."

Laughing as she entered, Miss Goldberg called out to Mrs. Bickel. "I've returned with Mr. Prescott. Don't mind us though. I'm helping him get settled."

The elderly lady pursed her lips then whispered, "You better go with them, Ida. I don't trust her."

Ida caught Mrs. Bickel's gaze. "Neither do I." She rose and strode to the entryway. "Is the workman finished unloading the wagon?"

Blaine spun around to face her. "You're here!" He pushed past Miss Goldberg and took Ida's hand. "I stopped by your house. No one answered."

"I went to the wharf, thinking you might be at work. I need to tell you how sorry I am for the way I acted last night. I should never have run away and closed the door in your face." Ida didn't care who overheard her apology. If she held it in, she'd burst.

"No, I'm the one who needs to apologize." Blaine squeezed her hand. "Yesterday was terrible. I'm so sorry." He led her out the door as the horse and wagon drove around a corner. "Do you have time to talk?"

Ida nodded.

"Let's go to our spot near the harbor." Blaine wanted nothing more than to be with her. He'd been tormented last night and all morning over the way they'd parted. When he'd not found her at home, he feared she was avoiding him. He hooked his arm with hers, bringing her close to his side.

"What about Miss Goldberg?"

"Haven't you heard? She can take care of herself."

Blaine sought privacy. He needed to talk with Ida to inform her of the recent events and to erase any doubts spurred by the intrusion of Abigail. He wanted no interruptions.

They found their spot and settled in the sunshine. He had so much to say, as apparently so did she. The words gushed from her—good news about a doctor and Qui, bad news about her aunt's demands, upsetting news about her experience in Chinatown, and worry over Wallace. He wrapped his arms around her and listened. His turn would come. For now, he rejoiced that they were together and that she trusted him with her feelings and thoughts and ideas.

She leaned into him, quiet and calm. "Your turn."

Where to start? With Abigail's appearance? With the picnics and parties his mother had planned? With his frustration over his father's demands? With the decision to rent the room and how he knew God led him to it?

Yes, that's where he'd begin.

He feared discussing Abigail—that he wouldn't have the right words to explain so Ida could understand. As he talked, she snuggled against his side, her head on his shoulder. When he broached the subject of Abigail, he expected her to pull away or question his motives. Instead, she intertwined her fingers with his and made no critical comments.

When he finished, she pulled back and met his gaze with tear-filled eyes that overwhelmed him with deep affection. Her lids closed as she lifted her lips to meet his.

CHAPTER 41

Wednesday during his lunch break, Blaine deposited half of his trust fund into the care of Mr. Dempsey. "I want to invest in the sawmill, but I'm not ready to commit to employment. May I have more time to consider?"

"You have other options?" Mr. Dempsey produced a contract for Blaine to sign, making their partnership legal.

"Not really. I'd like to work things out with my father even though I know I indicated otherwise."

"Take the time you need." Mr. Dempsey shook Blaine's hand. "Family matters can be complicated."

The next few days Blaine devoted himself to Prescott and Son, determined to be an invaluable asset to the company, to prove his worth to his father.

When he spoke with his parents about the room he had taken, they simply wished him well. He ate dinner the rest of the week with the Dempseys, growing fonder of Ida as well as her family, especially Wallace. He saw him as a frustrated young man, seeking his way to manhood. He hoped to help.

To appease his mother, he attended the picnic on Saturday and the lawn party on Sunday, both times accompanied by Ida. His mother addressed them politely; his father ignored him—or was just too occupied talking business with other guests. Although Ida appeared cheerful, she clung to his arm the entire time. He didn't remain long at either gathering. Living away from home spared him his mother's criticism. He had no idea what she'd find fault with; no doubt there would be something.

Monday morning, Blaine dressed for work with trepidation. He'd been given a week to decide between Ida and his father's business, and that deadline passed on Saturday. He'd already told his father that, if forced to choose, he'd take Ida. After that conversation, he worked every day in the office or on the docks. Discussions between them had been minimal and restricted to business matters. Had he done enough to nullify his father's ultimatum?

As he headed toward the company office, praying as he pedaled, Blaine braced himself for what he might find. Would the doors be locked? Would his desk be cleared out? He knew the shipping schedule with nothing due in port until tomorrow, so he'd not be needed on the wharf until then. If he was still employed.

His father met him at the door. "Another meeting has been set regarding the Chinese affair."

Was this an invitation to attend? Blaine fell into step with him. Their conversation along the way focused on the meeting, who would be there, and the most recent issues. "Remember, you're new. I expect you to listen and learn."

"Of course, Father. Thank you for including me."

The rhetoric against the Chinese had been volatile at the previous meeting; this time the hostilities intensified to a new high. A white woman from an elite neighborhood had been found unconscious outside an opium den, bruised, with torn clothing. Reportedly she knew neither what happened nor how she got there—an abominable crime!

More of the same suggestions—evict them all, burn down the block, take them deep into the forest and leave them without provisions—stampeded the room. Blaine remained silent while protests filled his mind. The way he saw it, the problems discussed were symptoms of underlying issues. Tackle those, and the contemptible manifestations would take care of themselves.

Back in the office, Blaine waited for his father to say something, either about the quality of his performance or to dismiss him from the premises. They worked the rest of the day with only walls separating them—without conversation. Covering up difficulties as if they didn't exist ate at Blaine. Several times he rose from his chair, determined to broach the conversation with his father. Each time, he sat back down.

He hoped Mr. Dempsey meant what he said about taking the time he needed.

Ida finally met with Mattie and told her all the details of what had happened since they'd been together—except about the kissing.

Being the best friend she was, Mattie declared she loathed, detested, and abhorred Abigail Goldberg. When could she meet her?

Ida had grown increasingly nervous about reading the Bible in the kitchen with Qui, basically right under her aunt's nose. Did Mattie have a suggestion?

"Can't you go to her house after dinner?"

"She lives in Chinatown and tells me it's dangerous if I get too near."

"Are you afraid?" A light shone in Mattie's eyes. "We could go in disguise."

"You are much more adventurous than I."

"Until I get caught." Mattie's eyebrows puckered together as she thought. "You said Blaine rented a room. What about there?"

"Of course! Maybe sweet Mrs. Bickel will let us use her parlor."

"Good." Mattie chewed her bottom lip. "One problem solved. Now, how are we going to join the doctor on his rounds, since your aunt has forbidden it?"

"We?"

"Why do you get to have all the fun?" Mattie pouted. "Will you ask him if I may come?"

Ida woke early the second Tuesday in August. Eagerness to finally get back to Second Street fought with unease over disobeying her aunt and uncertainty over what her tasks for the doctor would entail. She wished she understood her aunt's perspective. No shame or humiliation would occur over helping the doctor. Nurse Scott suffered no disrespect because of it.

Life grew increasingly complicated. Once upon a time, she obeyed her guardians without question, without a hint of doubt they were always right. Lately, the ideals that mattered most to her were the very ones they disapproved of.

Not everything. They liked Blaine—a lot. But teaching Qui about Jesus? Reaching out to the women on Second Street? They didn't understand she could more easily cut off her right arm than stop either mission. Well, maybe not literally, but while disobeying her aunt grieved her conscience, going against what she believed Jesus called her to would grieve her soul.

Mrs. Bickel eagerly agreed to let Ida use her parlor to teach Qui. Ida said nothing about keeping it a secret from her aunt, so the permission came with risk her aunt might find out. They'd met only once so far, on Sunday afternoon, Qui's day off work. The elderly woman's live-in servant, Yoke, joined them. Ida doubted how much Yoke understood, as she sat quietly during the entire session. Qui's questions demonstrated a desire to find truth. They also indicated she'd been reading the Chinese Bible on her own.

Guilt attacked when Aunt Ruth praised Ida for visiting Mrs. Bickel later that evening. Blaine told her not to worry about it—the good she did deserved commendation. Although his words contained an element of truth, Ida's conscience rebuked her deception.

Today she'd add more duplicity to her crimes because nothing would stop her from assisting the doctor.

After lunch, Ida easily escaped the house without being questioned. Aunt Ruth had shopping to do, and Uncle Harvey remained at work, Wallace presumably with him.

She walked with the doctor to the lobby of Kitty Farris' Joy Emporium sans Mattie. The doctor had declined her friend's offer without giving a reason. After being ushered into the small, windowless room in which the exams were conducted, Ida realized there wasn't space for anyone besides the "client," herself, and the doctor.

Gas lights on all four walls brightened the closet-like, whitewashed room. Across from the door stood a low, polished table with a wooden chair next to it. A narrow, high desk squeezed next to the door, reminding Ida of a miniature pulpit. It held a quill and inkwell.

The doctor handed her a sheaf of papers and nodded toward the desk. "They are in alphabetical order by name—only first names are recorded." He chuckled. "Many don't use their real names, but I don't care."

Standing behind the desk, Ida looked at the top paper.

Doc pointed to it. "As you can see, here is the name. Then the dates and results of prior examinations. I want you to add today's date on this line. Depending on my diagnosis, you'll enter codes from this list."

She recognized the word "lice." But what in the world was syphilis? Gonorrhea? How did one even pronounce them? Ida didn't ask. She needed this job to connect her to Esther and the others. She couldn't risk Doc thinking her unqualified.

He continued instructing her. "Then on the next space you'll record any treatment given."

He rubbed his graying goatee.

Something bothered him. She smiled. "Thank you for allowing me this opportunity."

He shook his head. "When you came to my office, I might have been overly influenced by your enthusiasm for—what did you call it—Project Save Second Street Souls?" He grimaced. "You're very young—too young to witness what happens in here."

"Please, give me a chance." She picked up the quill as if ready to begin. "Anyway, I'm here and Nurse Scott isn't, so should we begin?"

Dr. Marsh opened the door and ushered in the first patient. "Good afternoon, Miss Delight."

The middle-aged woman looked like anyone Ida might see in church or attending an auxiliary meeting. She glanced at Ida and sat on the low table.

Embarrassed that she'd been caught staring, Ida shuffled through the papers, finally finding Delight's name. The papers might be in alphabetical order, but the patients arrived without regard for that. Ida entered the date in her neatest penmanship: Tuesday, August 12.

Doc began by examining the woman's mouth. Finished with that, the woman lay down on the table and hiked up her dress.

Maybe she was too young for this.

CHAPTER 42

Twelve women.

That was how many Doc examined in the tiny room, and how many charts Ida recorded for him. With each opening of the door, her heart rate increased. Would Esther be next? She wasn't. In fact, she didn't show at all. Two weeks ago, she had. Her chart indicated no problems. Not like some of the others.

After a diagnosis of syphilis, two women received mercurous chloride, a compound resembling white salt. One complained about missing her monthly and received a pill to set herself right—whatever that meant. Another received written permission to return to work.

After the appearance of the first patient, Ida refrained from staring. Doc opened the door, greeting each woman with respect. A few of them asked about his wife and family as if they were close friends. Some noticed Ida standing behind the desk and inquired about Nurse Scott.

Not once was there an opportunity to mention Jesus.

As they sat together in the garden swing after dinner, Blaine comforted her. "You can't expect miracles the first day."

"When can I expect them?" Ida removed her shoes and rubbed her stockinged feet.

Blaine put an arm around her shoulder, and she leaned into him. He kissed the top of her head. "What is it they say? 'All in good time.'"

"I didn't have a good time at all." Ida shivered. "I never heard of two of the illnesses he checked for. Doc suggested I might be too young to be there."

"You don't have to continue."

Ida lifted her head to look into his eyes. "Absolutely, positively, I'll continue. Do you think just because something is hard, I'll quit?"

"Not at all." Blaine patted her shoulder. "But I wouldn't think less of you if you chose another way to continue Project Save Second Street Souls."

"Do you have another way in mind?"

"No."

The next day, her talk with Mattie went much differently. They met in Ida's bedroom after lunch and sat cross-legged on the floor, neither caring about their unladylike posture. At first, her friend expressed disappointment that she hadn't been allowed to help, and then she plied Ida with questions.

"How many women did he see? "Did Esther come?" "Were they nice to you?" "Did anyone recognize you from before?" "Nurse Scott gets paid for the work; will you?"

Ida had her own questions. "One of the women needed a pill to 'set herself right.' Do you have any idea what that means?"

Mattie shrugged. "You could ask your aunt."

"Two of the women were given a medicine that looked like salt. They can't, um, work until Doc gives them the go-ahead." Ida's brow wrinkled. "They were not happy about that at all. Doc warned them severely. He said he'd be reporting their condition to the madam. One of them had sores in her mouth." Ida paused. "Some of them had fake names."

"How do you know they were fake?" Mattie stood and sauntered to the window.

"For one, Doc said so. And besides, nobody names their babies Delight or Midnight Joy."

Mattie laughed. "What do you think our names would be?"

"Mattie! What a thing to say." Ida giggled. "Oh, I know. I'd have a Bible name."

"You mean like Jezebel?"

Ida threw a pillow at her. "Let's go outside."

The young ladies meandered from the house toward the waterfront, Ida's favorite destination even before Blaine arrived.

Abigail, along with Mrs. Prescott, met them as they passed the Congregationalist Church on G Street. Surprising Ida, they not only nodded politely but stopped to talk.

"How are you today?" Ida's pulse quickened every time Blaine's mother came near.

"I'm well enough." Mrs. Prescott's permanent frown indicated otherwise. "And how is your aunt?"

"Very well, thank you." Would that be enough? An exchange of meaningless pleasantries, then she and Mattie could continue on their way.

Abigail's fake smile made Ida want to make a silly face, maybe stick out her tongue and cross her eyes. She resisted the urge.

Mattie cleared her throat. "I don't believe I've met your house guest, Mrs. Prescott."

"No, you haven't. Come along, Abigail. I'm eager to return home."

Abigail turned to her hostess. "You know, I've meant to visit Miss Dempsey, but dear Blaine is always around. Would you mind if I join these ladies on their walk?"

Mrs. Prescott hesitated before replying. "Suit yourself." She strutted away.

"Ida and I are on an errand. You'll probably not want to join us." Mattie's smile appeared every bit as fake as Abigail's.

Abigail sighed. "Another afternoon with Mrs. Prescott, and I'll drown myself in the sea."

Mattie's eyes widened.

"Not literally, of course." Abigail touched Ida's arm. "You'll have pity on me, won't you?"

What could she say? Spending one afternoon alone with Mrs. Prescott might be enough for Ida to want to jump into the sea.

"If you're so miserable, why don't you go home?"

Leave it to Mattie to be rudely direct.

"I will as soon as Chester arrives."

Mattie and Ida exchanged glances.

"Who's Chester?" Mattie raised her eyebrows.

As the trio strolled along together—not toward the harbor as Ida initially intended, but along the boardwalk lined with shops—Abigail explained. Chester was to have met her within a couple days of her arrival. Weeks had passed, and she'd heard nothing. Something or someone must have delayed him. The worry kept her awake at night.

Against her will, the story softened Ida's heart. She knew how it felt to be separated from someone she cared about and wouldn't wish it even on an enemy.

Mattie, on the other hand, rolled her eyes. "It's been weeks, and you've heard nothing? He isn't coming, sweetheart. You might as well go home."

Blaine relaxed in his position at Prescott and Son Shipping. As the days melted into weeks and nothing was said about his continued courtship with Ida, he accepted that his father had changed his mind and his position at the company held strong. Mr. Dempsey showed no disappointment in the development. With a friendly handshake he told Blaine the position was still his if he ever wanted it and, regardless, he remained a partner in the sawmill.

A month passed, and he received no paycheck from his father. An oversight? Not desperate for funds, since he had the inheritance from his grandparents, Blaine debated whether or not to bring it up. He would. Didn't scripture say the workman was worth his wages or something like that? Nor did he wish to fritter away his remaining trust fund. They guaranteed a future with Ida.

As he and his father walked back to the office after another volatile meeting with Eureka's businessmen, his father appeared in a mild mood. The lumber industry had slumped, and not nearly as many logs or milled boards were exported on his ships; nevertheless, the vessels continued transporting other goods up and down the coast. He should bring up the subject of his pay.

"Father, I believe there's been an oversight. I've not received any compensation for my work at our company."

"Nor will you until you return home and give up your courtship of Miss Dempsey."

His father's words smote deep. "Haven't I proved my value to the company, to you?"

"It isn't your value to the company that's in question. It's your loyalty to your family, as your mother clearly expressed."

"I am committed to Ida. Why won't you accept that? She is a God-fearing, chaste young woman from a reputable family. Even if that were not true, what type of man would I be if I let others dictate to me whom I can and can't associate with? Surely, Father, you see that this choice must be mine."

"What I see is you have not acquiesced to my stipulations."

"For weeks you've accepted my work. Where is the integrity in that?"

His father stopped walking. "You are questioning my character? This conversation is over."

His father strode away, leaving Blaine on the boardwalk. To be rejected by this man cut him to the marrow, actually robbed him of breath until outrage pushed aside the shock.

A scripture flooded his mind. *A man's heart deviseth his way: but the Lord directeth his steps.*

A cry from his heart flew toward heaven. "Please, Lord God, lead me in your way."

With the prayer came an answer.

Blaine knew his next step.

CHAPTER 43

"Mr. Dempsey, if the offer still holds, I'm ready to commit to working at the sawmill."

Blaine's future father-in-law smiled broadly. "Glad to hear it! Sorry you were unable to work things out with your father. His loss is my gain." He patted Blaine on the back. "The rainy season came early this year, which affects the loggers and, of course, our production. This will give you time to learn about the industry without pressure. When do you want to begin?"

"Immediately. Even today." A new task would take his mind off the crushing conversation with his father. He needed to look forward to a new future, not behind at what he'd lost.

"Today is not convenient. How about Monday of next week?" Mr. Dempsey rubbed his jaw. "Plan to come in the afternoon."

"You won't need me for full days?"

"Not right away." Mr. Dempsey walked him toward the door. "In a week or so, I'll be forced to lay off about half my employees. They'll not take kindly to being let go as it is. I can't appear to be hiring someone from the outside at the same time."

Blaine left the sawmill, mulling over the conversation. Half days. It didn't take much wisdom to understand business was slow. The lumber industry had always been seasonal, similar to fishing, but layoffs this early were not typical.

Unemployed workers—the basis of the complaint against the Chinese. White men without jobs at the expense of cheaper labor. But few, if any, Chinese worked at the mill. Perhaps the discord centered around the Chinese occupying jobs the out-of-work mill workers would seek.

An idea leaped into Blaine's thoughts. Spending the afternoon at the sawmill would allow him to continue working at Prescott and Son in the morning. In that capacity, he could hire unemployed mill workers to help with loading and unloading the ships. That would be good for the community.

He wouldn't be paid for it.

He doubted he'd be paid by Dempsey either. Had he invested in a failing venture?

Maybe.

But he trusted God to direct his steps. Back to Prescott and Son?

Or was that an idea born of his inability to let go of his dream to work with his father?

Only God really knew.

Blaine smiled to himself. He'd be an asset to both companies. Who knew what might come of it?

Ida waited impatiently for two weeks to pass before she could again accompany Dr. Marsh. She wondered how Esther had avoided the examination, as they were a requirement for such employment in Eureka.

At the next session, she asked Doc about women not showing up for the examinations.

"Some work both here and in Arcata. Maybe a few of them avoid the appointments; however, most come willingly. They recognize the examinations protect their health as well as their"—the doctor cleared his throat—"um, clients."

Although Esther appeared at the third session, she didn't look Ida's way. Frustration built. The women she saw regularly responded now to her smile and at least nodded when she wished them a good day. So far she'd found no way to bring Jesus into nonexistent conversations. At the fourth session, she approached the doctor with a new idea. "Young girls growing up don't dream of this profession, right?"

"No, Ida. Most come into it out of desperation. A few think they'll meet a rich man who will fall in love with them and offer marriage. Honestly, that is a pipe dream. Not many opportunities are available to poor, uneducated young girls. I don't condone their choice, but neither do I condemn them."

His words encouraged her to continue with her thoughts. "Do you think lack of education is behind it all?"

"Not all of it, but a good portion. There are those who made bad choices in their youth and are stuck. They need to eat and have a roof over their heads. Once they start down this road, it's almost impossible to get off."

"Especially if they can't read and write?" Ida chewed her bottom lip, her gaze locked on the doctor.

"Yes, my dear girl. Now where is all this questioning headed?"

"What if I offered free lessons? Would they come?"

"You mean teach them to read?"

"Exactly."

"I thought you wanted to teach them about Jesus."

"I do. I'll use the Bible for the lessons." Ida held her breath, waiting for Doc's next comment.

He shook his head. "You are something, Ida Dempsey. I believe it's a great idea. Whether or not they'll come, I can't say."

When she told Mattie, her friend grew excited. "Let's make posters. We can put them up all around town. Where will you teach them? Will it be one-on-one, or in a group? Will you give each one her own Bible? Where will you get them? Do you even know how to teach someone to read? Can I help? Should we wear our costumes, so they'll trust us?" Mattie waggled her eyebrows.

Blaine listened intently to Ida's new plan. This amazing woman. Certainly not a quitter. He understood persistence and tenacity. Respected it.

As he suspected, neither his father nor Mr. Dempsey offered a paycheck for his services. He showed up every morning at Prescott and Son and every afternoon at the sawmill. Mr. Dempsey assured him that his investment would pay off come spring. Whether or not it would, Blaine didn't know. He kept his expenses to a minimum, spending carefully to stretch his funds as long as possible.

Even so, he had an idea how he could help Ida. It came with a cost but answered one of her questions. He took her hand. "Come with me."

Although umbrellas protected their heads from the November downpour, by the time Ida followed Blaine into Wells Drug Store, the hem of her skirt was muddied and dripping.

"What are we doing here?"

"You'll see."

The clerk that had helped them discover Esther's name greeted them. "I don't suppose you are after ice cream this morning."

Blaine answered, "No. We'd like to discuss a business arrangement."

"I'm listening."

"Miss Dempsey needs a place to conduct a class where women on Second Street will be comfortable. If you allow us to hold the classes here at your tables, we'll be purchasing sodas for each attendee."

"How often?"

He looked to Ida for the answer.

"Three days a week."

The clerk rubbed his jaw. "How many women?"

"Not sure." Blaine kept his voice confident. "Having people in your store will bring in others, if for no other reason than curiosity. More visitors means more business."

"What time of day?" The clerk gestured at the empty space before them. "I could use more business in the morning."

"No, early afternoons work best," Ida responded quickly. "My students aren't early risers."

The clerk laughed. "No, I guess they aren't."

"Do we have a deal?" Blaine extended his hand.

"On a trial basis." The clerk shook Blaine's hand. "Let's see how it goes till the first of the year."

As they left the store, Ida nearly danced beside him, squeezing his arm in her excitement.

Just the reaction he had hoped for.

"Thank you! I never considered the drugstore!" Her tone sobered. "How am I going to pay for the sodas? I don't think my aunt will give me the money."

"I'll pay for them." How long he could continue the extra expense, he didn't know. But the first of the year was not far off. He could manage, at least until then.

As they hurried back to Ida's home, windblown rain pelted them. The umbrellas whooshed inside out. By the time they arrived, both were soaked through, although, judging from the look on Ida's face, nothing dampened her spirit.

Blaine kissed her forehead in the foyer. "I have to change my clothes and go to work."

Ida's smile lit her entire face—and his heart.

That God would answer his prayer for a faithful wife with such a woman astounded him. He didn't deserve her.

Broken umbrella in hand, he dashed through the storm back to Mrs. Bickel's. He removed his shoes, hat, and coat in the entryway but still dripped rainwater all the way upstairs.

Barely inside his room, he began unbuttoning his shirt. Female sobs stopped him short.

"Abigail! What are you doing here?"

CHAPTER 44

"I don't know where else to go." Abigail wiped tears from her eyes.

"Why do you need somewhere to go?" Tears or not, Blaine didn't trust her.

"Your mother is suspicious. You've got to help me, Blaine. I don't know who else to ask." More tears flowed.

His heart began to soften. Crying women had that effect on him, even those he didn't trust. "What do you need?"

"Chester hasn't come. I know he would if he could."

"I don't know how to find him."

Abigail sniffed and dabbed her eyes with a man's handkerchief embroidered with BP. His initials. He didn't remember giving it to her. "Shouldn't you return to your family in San Francisco?"

"I can't go home, I can't. I'll just die." More sobs erupted.

Her histrionics nibbled away at his compassion. "I can book passage for your return trip. Aside from that, I don't know how to assist you."

"Didn't you hear me? I can't go home."

Blaine's patience wore thin. He wanted to remove his wet clothing and warm himself by the fire with a cup of hot coffee, then get to work. "Of course you can." He opened the door. "Please step outside while I change clothing."

Instead of leaving, Abigail turned her back to him and headed to the window. "I have to find Chester."

"Isn't he in San Francisco?" Keeping his eyes on the intruder, Blaine quickly removed his shirt and donned a dry one. What could he do about his soaked britches? He couldn't take them off with her in the room, back turned or not.

"Sam says he isn't. I believe he went north to Seattle."

"So you want me to book passage for you to Seattle? We don't have passenger ships sailing that way this time of year."

"I need you to escort me on one of your freighters."

Her words dumbfounded him. He stared at her back, speechless. After a few moments, he recovered. "Abigail, if Chester made his way to Seattle, he certainly can make his way to Eureka. Why chase after him? You've got to accept the fact that he is not the man you believe he is."

"He would be. If he knew."

"Knew what?" Exasperation blanketed Blaine's words.

"About the baby." Sobbing, Abigail sank to the floor.

Ida wasted no time creating invitations. Mattie eagerly helped. She had ideas for decorating posters and plastering them all over Second Street.

Ida disagreed. "I want this to be personal. An invitation from me to Delight. From me to Joy."

"I get it." Mattie rolled her eyes. "From you to Esther. And if we put notices up everywhere, your aunt might see one."

"I'm going to tell her what I'm doing."

"Really?" Mattie shook her head. "Why? She'll disapprove."

"It's not on Second Street, and it includes the Bible. I think she'll support the idea."

Mattie met Ida's eyes. "Have you told her about your studies with Qui?"

"No."

After dinner, Blaine asked Ida to sit on the porch with him. "I have to tell you something—privately."

Ida retrieved her wool coat and scarf. "You'll have to sit really, really close."

"That's what porch swings are for." He winked at her.

As they sat together, Blaine appeared nervous.

"What's wrong?" Ida wanted to show him the invitations she'd made, but whatever was on his mind seemed more important. "Did something happen with your father again?"

"No. It's Abigail."

"Oh." Ida had mixed feelings about the young lady. She felt sorry for her over all the time she had to spend with Mrs. Prescott, but mostly the woman annoyed her. Fortunately, she had little trouble avoiding her most of the time. "I can't believe she's still here."

"That's what I want to talk about. She wants me to escort her to Seattle. She thinks she'll find Chester there."

"Are you going to?"

"No." He paused. "I do think I should escort her back to San Francisco, though."

Ida studied his face. What else bothered him? She couldn't trust her feelings regarding Abigail. Anything related to her rubbed her wrong. She didn't want him to go—she didn't trust the little snob.

She'd have to repent for her bad attitude. Why was it easier to feel compassion for Qui and women like Esther than for Abigail?

Blaine touched her hand. "What are you thinking?"

"Abigail annoys me." She could say that much. He already knew it anyway.

"She needs a friend right now."

Ida straightened her back and removed her hand from his. "You want to be her friend and accompany her home, all the way to San Francisco? Your mother will be pleased." As soon as she said the last words, she regretted them. It was the type of catty thing Abigail would say. "I'm sorry. I shouldn't have said that."

"I won't go if it distresses you."

This man supported her ideas, cheered her on, and worked to help her succeed even when he didn't fully understand. Couldn't she do that for him? "If Miss Goldberg needs an escort home, I can think of no one better than you to do so."

"Do you mean it?" Blaine cupped her cheeks in his hands, lifting her face to meet his gaze. His eyes bored into hers, probing into her heart as if trying to see beyond her words.

Goodness, she wanted to kiss him.

But not only was this not the right time, she'd promised Aunt Ruth no more kissing, a promise she'd already broken once. If she couldn't obey her aunt regarding working with Dr. Marsh and teaching Qui, she could at least try harder to follow the no kissing rule.

She kept her gaze locked on Blaine's. "I mean it. I believe it must be important, or you wouldn't go." She couldn't trust Abigail; she did Blaine.

With a strong wind blowing in from the north, the ship made port in San Francisco in a day and a half. Blaine had wired Mr. Goldberg of their travel plans, hoping the man would meet them at the wharf. But not even Samuel greeted them.

Abigail had taken a lot of persuading to board the ship. That his mother might be suspicious of Abigail's condition did much to convince her. She had no resources of her own to find a way to Seattle, let alone secure food and lodging. She had begged with many tears, but Blaine refused to give her the money—not because she couldn't pay it back, but because he saw her plan as folly. Alone in a city without family or friends could force her to take desperate measures. Wasn't that how some women ended up on Second Street?

His conscience forbade him from being a part of a scheme with such risk. He didn't believe for one minute that Chester would let her find him.

Abigail's steps grew slower and slower as they strolled up the hill toward her home. "I'm afraid." She clung to Blaine's arm. When the house came into view, she stopped. "Will you marry me, Blaine? Just to give the baby a name? Just to save my reputation? It wouldn't have to be for long. We could get married now. You wouldn't have to stay here. I could claim I hate Eureka—the truth—and you have to go back for your work. Then you could return to Ida. Please, Blaine."

Blaine disengaged his arm from hers. "Miss Goldberg, the answer is no."

"Don't look at me like that." Her narrow eyes bespoke anger boiling inside. "You owe me, *Mr. Prescott.*"

"I have always treated you with respect. Your suggestion offends me to my core." In the back of his mind, an alarm sounded, warning him to keep control. Words from the book of Proverbs whispered to him. *A soft answer turneth away wrath.*

He didn't listen. "You came to Eureka, insinuating yourself uninvited into my life. You've been rude to the woman I love. You've lied to your parents and plan even more deceits. No more, Miss Goldberg. No more."

Blaine stomped away, breathing hard, feeling the heat from his neck to his face. More angry words pummeled his thoughts. Down the hill he trod, kicking at rocks and mumbling. Not until he reached the docks did he notice his whereabouts. The port, so much larger than the small harbor in Eureka, boasted more ships than his town saw in a week. Foreign tongues added to the hectic activity and sense of chaos.

He'd been mugged and left unconscious not far from where he stood.

Where would he stay the night? Fog rolled in as daylight waned.

He had no idea which direction to go.

CHAPTER 45

As Blaine wandered the streets, his anger gave way to self-reproach. He should not have lost his temper. He should not have spoken as he had to Abigail. He sent a prayer of repentance heavenward. Should he return to apologize? No. That would give her false hope. He'd send a note.

Soon after, he found himself in front of a building with the words YOUNG MEN'S CHRISTIAN ASSOCIATION engraved above the door. They had no rooms for rent but sent him in the right direction to find suitable lodging. As he sat in a wooden chair gazing out the narrow window in his second-story room, the exertion of the past two days caught up with him and hunger gnawed.

His thoughts turned to Ida. If he hadn't left on this fool's errand, he'd be with her now, eating a fine meal in a warm house. He missed her. Missed the sparkle in her eyes when she looked at him. Missed her quick smile and the lilt of her voice. Missed her energy and passion for her projects. Once he returned, he'd never leave her again. Tomorrow he'd find the first ship headed north and be on it.

At breakfast, Aunt Ruth discussed plans for Thanksgiving.

"I hope Blaine will be home in time." Ida emitted a deep sigh.

Aunt Ruth set down her fork. "I'm sure he will. He won't want to delay a return trip."

"He said he'd be back by the twenty-fifth. I know the tides and wind can add days to any voyage." Again, Ida sighed.

"Or speed the journey along." Aunt Ruth flashed a smile. "What do you have planned for after church today?"

"I'll visit Mrs. Bickel."

When Ida arrived at her elderly friend's home around two o'clock, Qui met her at the door. "I read my Bible. I read like you say. I finish list you give me."

Ida's dampened mood lifted when she saw the light in Qui's eyes. They'd been reading scripture together every week for months. Qui had many questions that showed her genuine interest. "I will give you others."

"That good, but I have question." Qui opened her Bible. "It tell story here of Philip. He teach Ethiopian."

"Yes." Ida opened her Bible to the book of Acts. She began to explain the special festival in Jerusalem.

Qui interrupted her. "Ethiopian ask why he not be baptized."

"Qui, are you interested in baptism?" Ida's heart leaped to her throat. Could it be? Was this Chinese woman ready to defy the Tongs ruling her neighborhood and acknowledge Jesus as her Lord?

"We have plenty water."

Ida glanced at Yoke. How had Qui's enthusiasm affected her?

The older Chinese woman appeared to be sleeping.

"Qui, do you believe that Jesus is the Son of God?"

As Qui emphatically bowed her assent, tears filled Ida's eyes. Such an answer to her morning and evening prayers! But why was she surprised? Didn't her heavenly Father promise to honor her requests?

What should she do? She'd not anticipated this development so soon. "Wait right here." She stopped at the door. "Don't go anywhere. I'll be right back."

Not caring that proper ladies did not hike up their skirts and run, Ida dashed through the neighborhood, all the way to Reverend Huntington's parsonage and up the ramp leading to his front door. Out of breath, she pounded her fist against it.

He opened the door, worry etched on his face. "Are you all right? Has something happened?"

"Qui wants to be baptized."

A broad smile broke out. "Well done, Ida. Well done."

"Can you come?" Her breath still came in gasps.

"Right now?"

Ida nodded.

"Just a moment." He returned with his coat on and hat in hand.

As they walked along—Ida could not induce the minister to run—she asked him what trouble Qui might face over her decision.

"She's not the only convert. I believe she knows one young man—Wei Lum—who has also professed his belief in Jesus as his Savior. So far, no one has threatened him."

After a good night's sleep and a full stomach, Blaine saw things in a better light. He better understood Abigail's desperation. Depending on how her family reacted, it could spell her ruin. Before boarding a northbound ship, he sent a note apologizing for his lack of compassion and expressing his good wishes for her future. In no way did he consider her untoward request. Apologizing for his angry words was the best he could offer.

The wind continued blasting from the north, hindering the vessel's progress. Two and a half days passed before he saw Eureka again.

He didn't expect to see Ida waiting for him on the dock, but there she stood, the wind whipping her wool coat around her. "How did you know I'd arrive today?"

"I didn't. I've come every day." She gripped his arm, leaning into him. "I've got news I could share only with Mattie."

"Something happened on Second Street?"

"Not yet. You'll never guess. Qui believes in Jesus."

Blaine stopped in the middle of the wharf, forcing seamen to go around him. "That is amazing news."

"We'll keep studying, of course. She's so eager to learn. I believe it's contagious. I find myself more interested in reading God's word as well. This morning my prayers lasted through breakfast."

"You are quite a woman, Miss Dempsey." Blaine resumed walking along the pier, his dour mood erased. "I have so much to be thankful for."

"I know! Isn't God amazing? I can't wait until tomorrow when I hand out the notices for the reading classes."

Blaine walked Ida home, enjoying her presence beside him. Even her pout when he couldn't stay delighted him. His absence had been unplanned, and he needed to check in at Prescott and Son and the sawmill as well. "I'll be back for dinner."

As he headed toward the shipping offices, he changed his mind. He'd call on his mother first. He'd not spoken with her for weeks, not nearly as often as he saw his father. He wondered if she was lonely in Abigail's absence. On a whim, he plucked the few remaining blooms from the garden before entering.

Pratt met him at the door and greeted him warmly. "Good to see you, sir."

"Thank you. Is Mother in the parlor?"

"Yes, sir."

Blaine entered the room to find his mother alone, weeping into her handkerchief. She would not want to be seen in such a state. He silently backed out of the room, then cleared his throat loudly before taking his time to reenter. "Hello, Mother." Her forced smile wouldn't have fooled him even if he hadn't seen her tears a moment ago. "How are you?"

"I'm fine. Why wouldn't I be?"

He offered her the meager bouquet. "The last of the flowers from the garden."

Her hand trembled as she accepted them. "I'll get a vase."

"Could you wait just a moment? I'd like to sit and talk. It's been too long since we've enjoyed a chat together." He took the chair next to the one she'd vacated.

Looking at her, he wondered for the first time what her life was like. What choices had been forced upon her? Had it been her idea or his father's that he attend boarding schools? Did she wish for more children? Had she been once as cheerful and giving as Ida? What had happened to squeeze her heart so tightly? Which of her dreams died?

He wanted to take her hand and ask. He wouldn't—couldn't. Instead, he prayed silently he'd learn to view people with the same compassion Ida showed.

Every life has a story. Not all of them with happy endings. Or beginnings. Or middles. He didn't know his mother's story at all.

He stayed with her, engaging in small talk until the dinner bell rang.

"Will you stay for dinner?"

"Of course. I'd love to." The Dempseys would be expecting him, but he couldn't leave her. He'd go there after the meal.

He escorted her into the dining room, to a table set for one. "Isn't Father coming?"

A servant brought in another place setting.

"He has a meeting of some sort. I forget which one."

"Do you eat alone often?"

No answer. She took her seat, chin raised. "Blaine, will you say grace?"

He knew she meant for him to offer the prayer, but the word *grace* struck him. If a man didn't treat his own mother with grace, what kind of man was he?

CHAPTER 46

At Ida's request, Doc allowed her to open the door for the patients. She greeted the women with a smile, called them by name, and ushered them into the room after handing each the announcement of the classes, scheduled to begin Wednesday of next week.

When Esther entered, she acted as though she'd never seen or spoken to Ida. She accepted the invitation without looking at it.

Even though she had no reason to expect anything, Ida wished for more. Her inspiration for the project centered around this woman. Did it have to be so hard?

A week later, on Wednesday afternoon, Ida brought a bundle of Bibles she'd gotten from Reverend Huntington to Wells Drug Store. Mattie showed up with a slate and chalk.

"Good idea," Ida admitted. "Don't know why I didn't think of that."

Of the dozen invitations Ida handed out, three women accepted. Because the Gospel of John was her favorite, she began the lessons there. Mattie took over teaching the actual reading and proved to have a natural talent. Using the slate and chalk, she emphasized the sounds of the letters in such a way the women caught on quickly.

Within two weeks' time, the class had grown to four. The attendees worked hard for the hour each day, with Mattie directing the reading and Ida answering questions from the text.

"What does it mean 'in the beginning was the Word'? The beginning of what?"

"How could the Word become flesh? What does that mean?"

After covering the first chapter of John, they skipped to the fourth chapter for the story of the Samaritan woman.

The next week, Esther and another woman came. The group insisted on reading the same passage of scripture again and peppered her with questions—which allowed her to emphasize the love Jesus had for those outside the religious community.

Esther remained silent throughout the session, refusing to cooperate even when Mattie asked her to read from the slate.

But she returned. Every day, three days a week. She never took a turn reading, never brought up questions, never made comments of any kind.

As Christmas neared, Ida switched to the book of Luke to read about Jesus' birth. She and Mattie worked together with a natural rhythm. And the women learned.

For the last class before Christmas, Ida had wrapped each Bible in tissue paper tied with colorful ribbons and handed them out as gifts. None of the six women receiving one responded as rapturously as Qui had; still their gratitude showed in their smiles and glistening eyes.

When Ida gave Esther hers, she paused. "I wish you a very happy Christmas, Miss Esther."

"Thank you." No smile accompanied the words.

"Are you aware that Esther is a biblical name? She became a queen and saved her Jewish people."

No response.

Ida wondered why the woman even came—and how to break through the barrier.

Mattie's conversations with Ida focused less on finding a rich husband and more about wondering how she might begin her own school for illiterate adults.

After the new year, Blaine discontinued working at Prescott and Son. Maybe his value to the company would be recognized more by his absence. If his father did the work, might he miss Blaine's contributions and mend their rift?

He devoted more time to the sawmill. As he had for his father, he improved the accounting practices. He learned how to do each man's job in the mill. The experience helped him understand the workings of the business. Because of his knowledge of shipping, he negotiated better prices for getting the lumber to market.

With more time at his disposal, he met with his mother weekly, just to chat. Rarely did their conversations contain any substance. He wished to dig deeper into her life, more than her committee meetings and social activities, to understand her. He trusted that could come with time.

To honor both parents, he spent Sundays with them, attending church and dining afterward as well. Conversation with his father carried more substance only when discussing the Chinese problem. Blaine didn't hold back his doubts and questions. At his father's invitation, he continued to attend the irregularly scheduled meetings of the businessmen. In doing so, he grew immune to the hostile rhetoric. It was all talk, no action—nothing would come from it. He'd like to see measures taken—such as fix the sewage issue and improve the tenement buildings. To his disappointment, no one agreed with his proposal that bettering the living conditions would ameliorate the issues.

Ida remained the highlight of every day. Whether on the front porch swing, or in Mrs. Bickel's parlor, or walking along the harbor shore, she chattered effusively about the progress with her Second Street project, giving him part credit for the success—after all, if he hadn't thought to speak to the clerk at Wells Drug Store, she wouldn't have a place to meet. And if he didn't fund the refreshments during the classes, would the clerk allow them to continue? He especially appreciated that she asked his opinion on how to answer Qui's questions.

Esther's appearances confounded him. "Do you think she attends for some other reason than the reading lessons?"

Ida shrugged. "She sits stiffly, hands folded in her lap, never making eye contact with me or Mattie. I don't direct questions to her anymore. I've seen her laughing and talking with the other women before class. I can't say for sure—it seems she's only cold and hard around me."

"Curious indeed." Blaine couldn't imagine Ida offending or intimidating anyone. He puzzled over how to help, perceiving Ida's challenges as his. His need to protect her urged him to action.

To do what?

When February descended with its customary wind and rain, Blaine's frustrations mimicked the weather. What exactly was he doing to make a difference in the community? He'd prayed for a partner devoted to the Lord, and God had provided Ida, but how did he live out *his* devotion?

He could help the Chinese. No bigger need existed in the community. Qui might have ideas where he could start.

"I made a New Year's resolution, and here it is the beginning of February, and I've not fulfilled it." Ida chewed her lip.

"How can I help?" Blaine smiled inside. What was she up to now?

"At dinner tonight, I'm going to confess to Aunt Ruth and Uncle Harvey what I've been doing at Wells Drug Store."

"I thought you changed your mind, since you didn't bring up telling them again." Blaine raised his eyebrows. "What about the Bible studies with Qui and Yoke?"

Ida shook her head. "I can't. That's Qui's story to tell, and she's afraid she'll lose her position here, afraid the wrong people will find out in her neighborhood, and of the persecution that could result. I'm not sure she's right, but I can't go against her decision." Ida paused. "The classes are different. I'm the only one afraid. No, that's too strong a word. I'm not *afraid*, just aware that Aunt Ruth especially will not understand, and I truly dislike disappointing her."

"I'll be right beside you." Blaine squeezed her hand.

His support meant she could do this. What would life be like without him? She intended never to find out.

The pleasant aroma of pork roast wafted from the kitchen clear to the front porch. Even though she was determined to reveal her actions, Ida's nerves caused her to stumble on the steps leading to the door. She dropped her coat on the floor instead of on one of the hooks on the hall tree. When Blaine pulled out her chair at the table, she missed the seat. Without his quick reflexes, she'd have ended up on the floor.

After her uncle said grace, Blaine grasped her hand under the table.

It was time. She could do this. "I've something I'd like to discuss with you, Aunt Ruth, Uncle Harvey."

"Of course, dear one." Aunt Ruth smiled encouragingly. "Are you considering joining Mattie in teaching illiterate adults to read?"

"No, this is something I've been doing now for about six months."

"Oh." Her aunt's smile vanished. "Go on."

Ida directed her attention toward her uncle. "I'm sure you remember suggesting I help Dr. Marsh with his rounds in order to avoid Second Street and still connect with the women there."

Uncle Harvey nodded. "I also remember that on reviewing that suggestion, we decided it an inappropriate occupation for a young lady."

"Yes, you did advise against it. And you were right about the reason. However, I've been assisting Doc twice a month since late summer."

A frown puckered her aunt's eyebrows together. Her lips drew taut.

Blaine squeezed her hand three times—a signal they'd worked out to use when in the presence of his mother. Three squeezes meant "I love you."

Although difficult to do, Ida continued. "There's more. A little while before Thanksgiving, Mattie and I invited the women I've met to classes. Many cannot find other employment without an education. We thought teaching them to read could be a first step in improving their lives, in getting them off the street."

Aunt Ruth's features softened slightly. Uncle Harvey appeared sincerely interested without judgment.

"We meet three times a week at Wells Drug Store. Mattie teaches the six women who attend how to read, and I answer their questions—oh, I forgot to say we use the Bible for the lessons."

Uncle Harvey nodded approval. "That is amazing, Ida. Well done, my child."

"It is ingenious." Aunt Ruth's frown had disappeared. "Are the lessons going well?"

Tears of relief flowed as Ida rose from her chair, raced to her aunt, and threw her arms around her neck. "Thank you for understanding! Oh, thank you."

She started for her uncle, but he shook his head. "That's quite enough, my dear."

Encouraged by their response, Ida relaxed, and her tongue loosened. "So we have six women attending. They are as interested in the Bible stories as they are learning to read. I love answering their questions. Some have interesting names such as Delight and Midnight Joy and Misty Sun. One's name is Esther—"

Aunt Ruth choked on her water. She rose quickly, dropping her napkin to the floor, and rushed from the room.

Uncle Harvey followed.

CHAPTER 47

Ida's gaze met Blaine's. "What do you think that was about?"

"I can't say. Should we follow?" Blaine scooted back from the table.

"I think not. Whatever upset her, she'll want privacy. She's probably in the parlor—I didn't hear her on the stairs. Let's wait in the library."

Quietly, they opened the library door then halted. Her aunt paced the room, illuminated only by glowing embers of coal in the fireplace.

"Harvey, do you hear me? Ida met Esther. I knew we shouldn't have fabricated that story. I argued against it from the beginning."

"Yes, dear, but remember, it was the only way your sister would agree to the adoption. We had no choice."

"Oh, Harvey, I don't know what to do."

"You are overreacting. Your sister did not reveal her identity. Ida is still protected from the truth."

Aunt Ruth's sister—*her mother*—was alive? She'd been lied to all this time? Ida burst into the room. "My mother is Esther?" Before her aunt responded, Ida knew the answer. It all made sense now. The connection she'd felt, the standoffishness of the woman. She wanted to run back to Second Street and find her. If she had to bang on every door in the neighborhood, she'd do it.

Blaine grasped her arm as she turned. He whispered in her ear, "This is a shock. Don't do anything rash."

How did he know she considered rash actions?

Her need to flee propelled her out the library door. Aunt Ruth called after her. "Wait, Ida, please wait."

Ida sped through the foyer, Blaine trailing a step behind.

"I never wanted to lie." Aunt Ruth followed, shouting. "It wasn't my idea."

Once out of the house, Ida increased her speed. Blaine kept pace. She wanted to run and run and run—away from everything. Blinded by tears and confusion, she darted into the street. Blaine pulled her back from an oncoming horse and buggy.

"Let me go!"

"I can't."

Ida collapsed into Blaine's arms, sobbing. "I've been lied to all my life by the people I've trusted most."

Blaine steered her toward the shore.

Ida allowed him to direct her, but no amount of gazing at waves could help.

Nothing could.

Blaine chose a place as far from the active docks as possible and sat on the coarse sand, bringing Ida down and close beside him. Although her eyes stared unblinking at the moonlit waves, he doubted she saw them. Did she hear the squawking seagulls or feel the breeze teasing her hair? Was she oblivious to the sea smells?

Physically she leaned against him, but she seemed far away. How could he reach her? He imagined the turmoil boiling inside, and it angered him. This beautiful, sweet, innocent young woman had been struck with a devastating blow. Yet against whom could he levy his wrath? Her aunt and uncle, whose love had provided an environment for her to become the amazing woman she was? Her mother, who, by staying absent from her life, allowed her to blossom with purity and confidence? What about the father? Did he live and work in Eureka, his secret safely hidden? Did he even know?

He wished she'd speak so he'd understand what to say, how to comfort her. Everything within him wanted to fix the situation, to remedy her pain.

What had she proclaimed early in their relationship? That God was her refuge? That her peace and joy came from Him? Then that's where he'd go. He snuggled her closer to his side and prayed silently for the God of all comfort to make His presence felt within her. It was not just the only thing he could do; it was the best thing he could do.

As Blaine pressed her closer to him, Ida sensed his concern but had no resources to reassure him of anything. A part of her wished he'd leave. If he spoke, if he offered platitudes, she'd jump up and flee.

She'd been lied to all her life! She reeled with doubts of her true identity. Everything in her world felt topsy-turvy, upside down, out of kilter, as if her feet had been knocked out from under her, and she was falling, falling, falling, without any idea of where to land.

Her mother, Esther, lived and worked as a prostitute on Second Street. The occupation didn't unsettle her; the truth of her mother's existence did. It changed how she viewed herself. She'd been Ida Dempsey, blessed orphan, fortunate beyond measure to be loved so dearly by her aunt and uncle. But that was not who she was at all. Who, then? Ida with no last name, abandoned by her mother, lied to by those she had never doubted. Conceived in sin. Illegitimate.

What lies had she been told about her father? Had she seen him daily in one of Eureka's businesses, not knowing his identity? Maybe he labored as a sailor, a lumberjack, a miner? Did he even know of her existence?

Leaning against Blaine, she closed her eyes, exhausted by turmoil. Visions of Esther circled through her mind. Esther, the first time at Wells Drug Store. Esther, demanding Ida stay out of her life. Esther in the exam room, ignoring her presence. Esther during the lessons. The visions pierced like a knife through Ida's heart. Another round of sobs threatened her ability to breathe. Convulsions wracked her body.

Blaine hugged her more tightly against himself, his strong arms offering a support she neither wanted nor had the ability to refuse. She slumped against the one person who hadn't lied to her—or had he? Whom could she wholly trust?

Reverend Huntington.

She couldn't talk to him! How did one broach such a subject with someone of the opposite gender, especially a holy man?

With the changing tide, an onshore breeze brought with it a chill. It came as a comfort, something to neutralize her heart's agony, something to distract her thoughts from Esther, Esther, Esther. Lies, lies, lies.

Blaine rubbed her shoulder. He whispered, "You're cold."

Was she?

He rose from the sand and lifted her in his arms as one might cradle a child. She laid her head against his chest, wrapped her arms around his neck, and closed her eyes. Where would he take her? Did it matter?

The sound of his footsteps clomping on the boardwalk alerted her they'd left the shore. Anxious thoughts fought with lethargy. What if he took her back home? She could not face her aunt or uncle.

When Blaine's breathing grew labored, Ida whispered in his ear, "I can walk now." As he set her on her feet, she looked around, confused by the surroundings.

Blaine grasped her hand. He led her to the minister's door and knocked. When no one responded, he rapped again, harder.

"This is Thursday night. If he's teaching his class, he can't answer." Considering the jumble in her mind, how did she remember that detail? "We should leave."

"I don't know where else to go." Blaine knocked again, long and loud.

Finally, the door cracked open, and a female voice spoke. "Please come back tomorrow. We have retired for the night."

"It's all right, Blaine." Ida stumbled into the street. The stray dog she'd met before ran toward her. What had she told the minister about him? She'd thought God sent Goldy to cheer her—as if a mangy mutt could heal a broken heart. Balderdash.

The dog bounced around her with a stick in his mouth, begging to play.

How could this dog, or anything in the world, continue as if nothing had happened?

CHAPTER 48

Goldy dropped the stick at Ida's feet, annoying her. Weren't dogs supposed to be sensitive to their owner's moods?

So what—she didn't own him. "Go away, you stupid mutt."

"This isn't the dog's fault, Ida." Blaine picked up the stick and tossed it.

"Oh, really? And whose fault is it?" Ida jerked her arm from Blaine's support and stomped away. How dare he defend that dog!

"Will you let me take you home?"

Ida increased her pace. "No!" she shouted. "I don't want you to take me anywhere. Go away!"

He grasped her arm, and she faced him, pummeling his chest with her fists. He absorbed the brunt of her anger until her arms wearied. When Blaine once again lifted her in his arms, exhaustion left her limp. Quietly, he entered Mrs. Bickel's parlor and set her on the sofa. She leaned against him, her head on his chest, tears still flowing. Lulled by his hand gently stroking her hair, Ida stopped fighting sleep.

When she awoke, Blaine still sat beside her, his legs stretched out and head tilted back. Slight snores puffed from his open mouth. What would Mrs. Bickel say when she discovered Ida had been there so long? Then remembrances of the day pushed aside other thoughts.

Ida slipped out from under Blaine's arm and tiptoed to the window. Dawn lit the sky with pinkish hues. As noiselessly as possible, she covered Blaine with a granny square afghan and stole out the door. Shivering against the chill of the early-winter morning, she hurried home.

Once inside, she determined that if she encountered anyone, she'd flee again, but at the moment she sought the comfort of her room. In the foyer, she removed her shoes and crept up the stairs, avoiding the squeaky third step. No sounds greeted her as she made her way into her room. Collapsing onto her bed, she pulled the coverlet around her and muffled her cries in the pillow. She willed herself to sleep, hoping to escape the pain engulfing her heart.

≈

With an aching back and stiff neck, Blaine awoke. Where was Ida? He rose from the sofa and stretched.

"Good morning, Blaine." Mrs. Bickel sipped hot liquid from a blue-flowered teacup. "Interesting choice for a bed."

"I passed an interesting night." Blaine ran his tongue over fuzzy teeth. His mouth felt as if something had crawled inside and died. "If you'll excuse me, I'll go upstairs."

"Of course."

Taking the stairs two at a time, Blaine hurried to his room. He had to find Ida. Had she gone to Second Street after all? As soon as he finished changing clothes and had taken care of his basic grooming, he returned down the stairs. Mrs. Bickel would have to wait for an explanation—finding Ida came first. He dashed out the door, mounted his bicycle, and pedaled down the street.

The morning sun had already evaporated the night's coating of dew. Horse-drawn buggies populated the rutted lanes. Out-of-work loggers, mill workers, and miners cluttered the boardwalks outside the shops and restaurants. Blaine sped past them all. Once in the red-light district, he found himself at a loss. The late-morning hour found the boardwalk as empty as the dirt road. Ida might possibly be inside somewhere. Should he knock on doors? Call out her name?

On second thought, if this was where she wanted to be, she'd resist him dragging her away. And if she'd not come here, he'd anger the neighborhood unnecessarily.

He'd try Mattie's.

Or maybe she met with Reverend Huntington.

Possibly—very likely—he should wait until she wanted to be found. In the company of either her best friend or the minister, she was safe and didn't need his interference.

But what if she wasn't?

How could he know? When had she left? How long had she been gone?

He pedaled toward the Dempsey house. They'd be worried about her, and even though he couldn't tell them her whereabouts presently, he could assure them she'd been with him through the night.

No, he couldn't!

From his position, he saw the tall mast of a ship in the harbor, possibly one of his father's. Who was overseeing the unloading? Maybe he'd ride there.

Bad idea. If he showed up every time a ship docked, how would his father ever miss his contributions?

One thing remained for him to do.

Saddle Prince and head for the redwoods.

The majesty of the forest spoke to his soul. He never rode through the towering trees without sensing the Creator's presence. At the picnic site, he dismounted and let Prince graze as he knelt before his God. Words failed him—but the Spirit spoke for him, and he rose, strengthened and encouraged.

The sun set before he headed back toward town. He felt no regret at his lengthy absence. It had been time well spent, and surely his heavenly Father had taken care of Ida in his place. A sense of peace filled him.

He arrived to a city in chaos. He stabled Prince and found the usually stoic Pratt in a state of nerves. "What happened?"

"Mr. Kendall has been shot and killed by a stray bullet from Chinatown."

"The councilman?"

"Yes, sir. A meeting has been called at Centennial Hall." Pratt rubbed his forehead. "They're shouting to burn Chinatown—and worse."

Blaine raced to the hall, arriving in time to witness the crowd shouting down Mayor Walsh.

Reverend Huntington gained the stage and tried to reason with the mob. He denounced the death of David Kendall as a tragic accident, then said, "The people of Chinatown are as innocent of his death as I am. They pay their rent, they mind their own business, and you have no more right to drive them from their homes than you have to drive me from my home." He paused. "If Chinamen have no character, white men ought to have some."

Blaine applauded the speech.

The crowd remained unconvinced. They appointed a Committee of Fifteen to go to Chinatown and order all Chinese out of Eureka.

Blaine's protests went unheeded. How could decent folks agree to such a plan? He joined the mob headed for Chinatown, seeking any opportunity to stop the injustice.

He watched helplessly as teams of men rode out to nearby farms, logging camps, and mines with the object of forcefully bringing in Chinamen they found.

What about Qui?

She might still be at the Dempseys'. He had to warn them! He sped to Ida's house and burst through the door, shouting, "Qui? Qui, are you here?"

He found her cowering in the kitchen, Ida alongside her.

"What can we do?" Ida trembled.

"I don't know. No one is listening to reason." Blaine clenched and unclenched his fists. "They've built a gallows with a sign threatening that any Chinese seen on the street after three o'clock tomorrow will be hung."

"No, no, no," Qui wailed.

Fury gripped Ida. "They won't get you. I won't let them." How could this happen in her little town? "We'll fight them all. In the name of justice, we'll fight."

"No. I go."

"Then I'm coming too."

Ida would not let this dear woman be expelled from Eureka. She'd stand up for her. Plead her case. Urge the Christian community to stand against this wickedness.

Qui gathered her coat and basket. "I go now. Not want to hang." She shivered. "I go get my things."

Ida wrapped her arm around Qui, trying to be a buffer between her and the crazed town. Blaine led the way until they reached Chinatown. He didn't know the way to Qui's apartment, so he followed them, a rear guard for their safety.

A tangible fear choked the district. Even as the residents attempted to gather their meager belongings, looters broke into the shops and businesses, breaking down doors and shattering windows, stealing anything and everything of value.

As Ida and Qui arrived at her building, Ida turned to speak with Blaine. He wasn't there. She rose on her toes to see farther into the crowds. How had he vanished so quickly? Maybe he sought help. Would Reverend Huntington protect Qui and the others, whom he'd taught?

In her tiny upstairs apartment, Qui gathered her belongings into baskets as the mob raged outside. All through the night, Ida huddled with her, terrified of the shouted threats and sounds of breaking glass and splintering wood.

What would the morning bring?

CHAPTER 49

Ida refused to leave Qui's side. Around noon on Saturday, she peeked through the curtain of the upper-story window. Broken furniture, smashed pottery, and tattered fabric cluttered the street. The mob had dissipated.

"Come on, Qui. I believe it's safe." Ida grasped two baskets. "Let's go to the church. We might find help there."

She opened the door to find Wallace standing guard. "I'll keep your home safe, Qui, but you have to leave." He shrugged as Ida looked quizzically at him. "You're not the only one trying to make a positive difference in the world."

Qui bowed repeatedly in her way of showing obedience and respect. "Wallace protect from Tongs. He protect now."

Wallace, protector of the vulnerable? She'd never have guessed his secrets with Qui had to do with chivalry.

Burdened with the baskets, they left Chinatown. Qui scurried bent over, a shawl covering her head. Ida strode boldly. Just let someone try to stop her!

They did. Effectively.

Armed men blocked every side street except for the route leading to the pier, where two ships docked. No one touched Ida, but anytime she attempted to direct Qui off route toward the church, a rough hooligan would grab Qui and force her back.

Finally, they entered one of the warehouses where at least a hundred Chinese waited. Surrounded by their belongings, Ida prayed and trusted. Surely God would intervene. When she saw Reverend Huntington pray with Wei Lum, her faith surged. Even when the good man walked away, Ida still expected a miracle. The Red Sea didn't part until the Israelites stood at the shore, the Egyptians in pursuit. God would come through.

No one questioned her as she boarded the vessel with Qui. She supposed in their hurry to rid the community of Chinese, no one noticed, or cared, who else might be carried away.

Qui attempted to stop her. "No, missy. You not go."

"I'm coming with you. That's all there is to it. And when we get to San Francisco, we'll get on a northbound ship and sail right back."

They waited all Saturday night on board the ship in a windowless compartment with neither food nor water provided. Without the sun and moon to help understand the passage of time, Ida lost track of what day they finally arrived in San Francisco.

When the gangplank lowered, the passengers dashed off. In the melee, Ida lost Qui. She followed the masses to San Francisco's Chinatown—a much larger community than Eureka's. Tired, hungry, lost, and alone, Ida's courage flagged. Up until they disembarked, she'd held on to hope that God would answer her prayers.

She leaned against an unpainted wall under a sign written in Chinese letters, two of Qui's baskets in her hands. What now?

No one knew her whereabouts—not even herself. She'd followed the crowd, all the while seeking Qui. She had no idea even how to return to the wharf.

She had no money and no friends in this city.

Blaine paced the docks. Indian Island emerged, barely visible through the dense fog that dulled the sounds of workers preparing ships to sail with the tide. His thoughts matched the dreariness of the early morning. The woman he loved more dearly than he thought possible had disappeared into thin air.

"I thought I'd find you here."

Blaine turned to see his smiling father, a most unwelcome interruption.

His father put an arm around his shoulders. "I know we haven't seen eye to eye, but I'm ready to make you my partner. I haven't given you enough credit. Why, at your age, I was still sowing wild oats. You are not the average twenty-four-year-old, and I see that now."

Blaine stepped back from his father's embrace. His words sounded hollow—too little and too late.

Mr. Prescott's smile did not reach his eyes. "You're not making this easy. I'm offering an olive branch. Do you have sense enough to take it?"

"You're here only to talk business?"

"What else? Oh, did you think I came to discuss that nasty Chinese affair?" His father stuffed his hands deep into his overcoat pockets. Nothing remained of his smile. "It's over and done. There's nothing more to say."

"It isn't over and done. We will answer for this. The Chinese played an important role in our community. They cleaned our houses, washed our clothes—I doubt Mother knows how to do half of what Ah Lee did for us."

His father squared his shoulders. "I'll not listen to you speak ill of your mother."

"I have the greatest respect for Mother. She is adept at overseeing a household; however, actually performing the gritty tasks? She's always had Ah or another Chinese woman to do them for her."

"That is a subject for another time." Mr. Prescott grasped his arm. "Let's get a cup of coffee. Talk about your future."

"My future?" Blaine shrugged. "My future is well in hand. I'm working at the sawmill. I've invested a small sum, and I'm taking care to see a return on the money." He wanted to add that his future included Ida, but she'd vanished like steam from a kettle. "I'll pass on the coffee, Father. My morning is overbooked as it is."

"Then come for dinner. Your mother would love to see you."

"Who's cooking?"

"Blast it, boy! Are you so shortsighted? Our economy is in shambles. The lumber mills that haven't already closed are barely hanging on. Even Carson has his crew building that ridiculous mansion just to give them something to do. Everything is affected, including the shipping business. Would you see our town falter, or thrive? The truth is, with the Chinese gone, there's more work for the real Californians. Eureka has a chance now."

"You mean white men with a European background have a chance."

"Is that so bad? There's nothing wrong with protecting our own. Even your precious Chinese stuck together in their cesspool of a community."

How could one go to church every Sunday, be recognized as a pillar of the community, and be so prejudiced? Blaine gazed across the water. The fog had lifted, exposing more of Indian Island. Not long ago, the island had been a sacred place for the Wiyot tribe. Twenty-five years prior, in 1860, the tribe had been massacred, the attack reportedly led by Eureka's businessmen, although no charges were brought against anyone. As he gazed at the island, a thought ambushed his mind, one he had never considered. It took his breath momentarily. Then he locked eyes with his father. "Were you involved with the decimation of the Wiyots as well?"

Mr. Prescott turned his back to the island. "Why bring up something that happened more than two decades ago?"

"Were you?"

His father jabbed him with a finger. "I don't answer to you, boy. I've always done what I believed best. I sleep every night with a clear conscience. I'm a God-fearing, honest man, and I'm not going to stand here and be judged by a wet-behind-the-ears know-it-all."

Blaine stepped back. No wonder it had been so easy to purge the Chinese—that had been nothing compared to butchering the Wiyot women and children. Who was this man, anyway?

He couldn't look at him. "Excuse me, Father. I'm expected at a meeting, and I'd rather not be late."

"Where? What meeting can you have that's more important than your future with Prescott and Son Shipping?"

"I'm meeting with Reverend Huntington."

"That Congregationalist minister?"

Blaine nodded.

"Forget him. We're Methodists."

"Give my regards to Mother." Blaine tipped his hat and headed down the pier. He needed to put distance between himself and this man who had become a stranger to him. As he strode away, he ached for the days of his boyhood when his father was his hero. He had admired him—wanted to be just like him.

As he reached the end of the dock, an idea presented itself. Reverend Huntington might know Ida's whereabouts. The morning's meeting had been called to discuss what could be done to bring back the evicted residents. He'd ask if the minister knew anything to help him find the woman he adored.

On their way to Chinatown, he'd stopped to defend an elderly man against ruffians and became separated from them. He didn't know where Qui lived. He should have tried harder to find them. He'd assumed Ida would help the cook until separated at boarding, then return home—the ships had sailed over twenty-four hours ago. He'd looked everywhere he could think—at Mattie's, at Well's Drug Store, along the harbor, at Mrs. Bickel's, all through Chinatown. He'd found Wallace wielding a crowbar—not for looting as he first suspected, but in defense of Qui's rooms and others' businesses. Wallace had no new knowledge about Ida's whereabouts.

Fear gripped his heart. Had she been entangled in the violence? Did she lie injured and helpless somewhere?

Reverend Huntington confirmed he'd seen her in the warehouse with Qui on Saturday. She hadn't attended church Sunday morning.

But then, few had.

CHAPTER 50

Ida waited at the edge of San Francisco's Chinatown, hoping against hope that Qui would find her. Together they'd book return passage to Eureka. Since she had no funds with her, she'd use Mr. Prescott's name to obtain a berth.

An hour passed and then another. The damp air permeated through her clothing, chilling her to the bone. She'd not eaten since Qui shared her lunch as they waited in the warehouse. That was two days ago.

Thirst parched her throat. She slipped down the wall to her haunches. Maybe if she closed her eyes for a few moments, her thinking wouldn't be so muddled.

When she reopened them, both baskets were missing.

Qui had never agreed to her plan to return to Eureka. Ida reluctantly acknowledged her dear cook had disappeared into the labyrinth that made up Chinatown, effectively lost to her—at least for now.

She had to move. Common sense suggested downhill would lead to the port and uphill away from it. Blaine had been mugged at the port, so Ida trudged uphill. Trolleys clattered up and down the steep inclines. Pigeons pecked at crumbs littering the walkways.

"Is that you, Ida?"

She lifted her head at the sound of the familiar voice. Who spoke? Abigail!

She knew someone in San Francisco after all.

For all the good it would do.

Ida tried to force a smile and greet this former troublemaker. The smile didn't come for the flood of tears.

A hand grasped hers. "Oh, my dear, you're frozen. Where is your coat?"

Ida managed to shake her head.

"Come with me." An arm draped around her shoulders as she felt herself hustled along. Abigail talked nonstop, reminding her of Mattie. "I'm guessing Blaine isn't with you, or you wouldn't be in this condition. Why are you here? Did you arrive on the morning ship? Did no one meet you? Surely you didn't sail alone, did you?"

Abigail ushered Ida into her parents' home. A servant offered food as another prepared a bath and provided clean clothes—probably Abigail's.

After Ida had bathed and dressed, the servant showed her into her hostess' room. Abigail rested in a rocking chair near a crib, nursing a baby.

What?

"I can see you didn't know." Abigail laughed. "You should see your face."

"The baby is yours?" Dumb question. Abigail wouldn't be nursing someone else's child. Realizing she stared, Ida averted her eyes. "Chester came back. I'm so happy for you."

Abigail snuggled the baby against her shoulder and patted her gently. "Do the arithmetic, dear Ida. No, Chester and I are not married. I don't even know where he is."

An awkward silence ensued.

Ida perched in a chair near the mother and baby.

It could have been a picture of Esther and her.

"Go ahead, judge me all you want. I really don't care." Abigail kept her eyes on the tiny infant in her arms. "This is the greatest blessing in my life. You can view her as shameful, but you're wrong."

"I'm not judging. Not at all." And there in the room, Ida poured her heart out to the most unlikely person. She told her everything.

Abigail rocked and listened, occasionally wiping a tear from her cheek.

Motherhood looked very good on Abigail.

"May I hold her?" Ida stretched out her arms. "Please."

The sleeping newborn nuzzled against Ida's cheek. "Did you feel as if your life was over?"

"Oh, yes. Out of fear I even asked Blaine to marry me. Did he tell you?"

"No. I knew he escorted you home. He never mentioned anything about—about this." Ida stroked the baby's tiny fist. "What's her name?"

"You know how men name their boy babies after themselves all the time? So I named her Abigail. We call her Abby."

"You have amazing parents."

"It took them a while to adjust. They made me isolate at home until she was born, then they concocted a ridiculous story about her being theirs via adoption. I nixed that right away. She's mine."

"You won't lie to her."

"I probably will at times, but not about her birth."

As Ida gazed at the tiny life in her arms, she found the answers her soul sought. The world continued spinning on its axis, the sun would rise in the morning, the tide ebb and flow. Goldy would fetch a stick, because all was right in his world.

And in hers.

Her heavenly Father had known the truth about her all along. The news that shocked her didn't surprise Him. One reality washed over her and became a part of her soul: Just like this innocent life in her arms, her identity as a child of the one true King continued unaltered. Jesus had paid the price once and for all.

Did anything else really matter?

Wasn't that the message she wanted Qui and Esther and the world to understand?

Blaine boarded the first ship available after receiving the wire from Abigail. During the voyage, thoughts about his employment weighed heavily. He'd never prayed about his future occupation. That he'd join the family business had always been a part of his plan. He'd never considered other options, certainly never asked for God's direction, not like he had concerning a wife.

Why hadn't he? He'd do it now, with an open mind, acknowledging the possibility that his heavenly Father never intended him to partner with Prescott and Son. If that was true, he didn't want it either. To give up a lifelong dream was not easy—unless that dream conflicted with God's plan for his life. To be in harmony with his Creator mattered more than his own ambitions, more than a partnership with his father. The decision had nothing to do with Ida. Even without her in the equation, his path led away from Prescott and Son. He didn't know exactly where yet. He trusted God to lead him.

The knowledge brought a sense of freedom he'd not enjoyed since arriving home from the university. The opportunity at the sawmill had fallen in his lap. If God had something else in mind, he'd be open to whatever that may be.

After he arrived at the Goldberg home, a servant showed him upstairs where Ida rocked a tiny baby, peace and contentment covering her face.

Did a baby cause that?

Ida held a finger to her lips. "Shh."

She continued to whisper. "I'm so glad you came."

"Of course I came. On the first ship headed south. Ida, I was so worried. You just disappeared." In his passion, he'd forgotten to whisper. Abigail took the sleeping baby from Ida and exited.

Ida grasped his hand in hers. "I acted rashly, and I'm sorry I worried you. God protected me. He sent Abigail to save my life."

"Abigail did?" Blaine wrapped Ida in his arms. "Promise me you'll never leave like that again."

She snuggled against his chest. "I promise never to accompany Qui on a ship from Eureka to San Francisco ever again."

He kissed her forehead, his heart swelling with gratitude for her renewed spirit.

And for his.

"Something about you has changed." Ida looked up at him quizzically.

"I can say the same about you."

They linked arms and slowly made their way down the stairs.

Two days later, they arrived in Eureka. That evening, when Blaine escorted Ida into the Dempsey dining room, they found a guest already seated.

Esther. Smiling and making eye contact.

Aunt Ruth beamed. "I believe it's time you two became better acquainted."

Blaine squeezed Ida's hand three times.

It held much more than the promise of a kiss.

AUTHOR'S NOTE

Eureka, California, was the birthplace of my mother and the burial site of her father. Because of her and my grandmother's stories, the area holds a fascination for me, compelling several visits to the coastal town. I was thrilled to find the townspeople and the volunteers at the historical society knowledgeable and eager to share information about their colorful community's past. What a past it is! While *The Angel of Second Street* is a work of fiction, included are historical references gleaned from interviews and documents.

Brothels, including Kitty Farris' Joy Emporium, lined a portion of Second Street, which was off-limits for children and respectable women. Wells Drug Store on F Street catered to the "working women's" needs. Regular medical exams were required for their employment.

The Carson Mansion, completed in 1885 after two years' construction, is the most photographed Victorian house in the United States. The lumber baron William Carson built it during a downturn in the timber industry to employ his otherwise out-of-work laborers.

Reverend Charles Huntington served the Congregational Church on Fourth and G Street. His conversations with Ida and Blaine are fiction, but his speech in front of the hostile crowds at the Centennial Hall is a direct quote.

At that impromptu meeting, the community elected a Committee of Fifteen to order the Chinese to leave town. The committee's members were not unemployed loggers, miners, and railroad workers but a cross section of Eureka's elite and working classes. It included a newspaper editor, an owner of a hardware store, a bookkeeper, an attorney, and a carpenter. From this Committee of Fifteen came the edict to purge not only Eureka of its Chinese but all of Humboldt County.

The Chinaman Wei Lum was one of Reverend Huntington's converts to Christianity. When Wei waited in one of the warehouses to be deported, the minister visited him, bringing him his Bible, an umbrella, and a pair of gloves. His parting words to Wei and the Bible study classmates huddled with him encouraged them to consider the expulsion as a "bearing of the cross."

That Wei Lum even made it to the warehouse can be credited to a Methodist minister. Wanting to say goodbye to the Huntington family, Wei was caught "off route" Saturday morning and dragged to a gallows, which had been erected the previous night. The noose was around Wei's neck when the minister climbed onto the scaffold and shouted to the crowd, "Boys, take that rope off that boy's neck! If you hang him, you'll hang him over my dead body." The men dropped the noose.

Much of the violence in Chinatown, located between F and E on Fourth Street, can be linked to a group originating in San Francisco known as the "Chinese Six Companies." This organization assisted Chinese immigrating to the United States find jobs. It helped with transportation to various work sites, provided medicine, and mitigated disputes—all for a price. Greed divided the "Six," who fought with each other for the profits gleaned from the immigrants they were supposed to assist. Tongs, or highbinders, representing the different clans who made up the Chinese Six would arrive on ships from San Francisco and battle each other for the right to collect dues and fees from the working Chinese men and women in Eureka—and other cities up and down the coast. The violence was real. No one in Eureka's Chinatown was safe.

On Friday, February 6, 1885, at 6:05 in the evening, when City Councilman David Kendall crossed F Street on his way to his office, he was caught in the cross fire of two rival gangs and killed. His death provided the spark that resulted in the purging of Eureka of every Chinese resident. Over 300 Chinese were carried away on two steamships, the *Humboldt* and the *City of Chester*. They left without a fight, but after arriving in San Francisco and relocating to its Chinatown, they pursued legal retribution. Their case was thrown out of court.

No one was ever charged with the massacre of Wiyot women and children on Indian Island in 1860. The tribe had gathered on the sacred island for a celebration. When the men left on a hunting party, leaving the elderly, the women, and the young behind, a group from Eureka, under cover of darkness, sailed across the harbor and attacked the encampment, reportedly leaving no one alive.

Today Eureka is a lively coastal town. Redwood logs ready to export no longer crowd its harbor, nor do sawmills exist along the shoreline. People of every ethnicity live and work in its shops and restaurants. Walking the streets of historic Old Town with its well-preserved buildings and strolling along the old, beautifully kept residential neighborhoods makes one wonder about life and the townspeople of the 1800s. Where might I have fit in? Where would you?

ACKNOWLEDGMENTS

Knowing full well I can do no good thing on my own, I owe any writing success to my heavenly Father and those He has placed in my life: my agent, Tamela Hancock Murray, who believes in me and opens doors not otherwise available; my traveling and research partner for this endeavor, Phyllis Phipps; my husband, Terry, for freeing up time for me to pursue my dream of writing; the constant encouragers in the kitchen at Pleasant Valley Christian Camp where I volunteer, namely Kim, Amy, Angie, Ginger, and Riley; and the members of the Inklings, a talented and supportive writers' group, including Kyle, Heather, Debby, Julie, and Joyce. I am eternally grateful to these beautiful people.

Barbara Tifft Blakey lives in the Pacific Northwest on five wooded acres with Terry, her husband of fifty-plus years. She is best known for her award-winning, literature-inspired, language arts program, *Total Language Plus,* which she created over thirty years ago, and is used by thousands of homeschoolers. Barbara teaches Sunday school and enjoys speaking on various topics to Christian women's groups. She and her husband have four grown children and eight grandchildren. She enjoys camping at the ocean, volunteering in the kitchen at Pleasant Valley Christian Camp near Mt. Rainier, and watching soccer.(Go Seattle Sounders!) During the daylight-challenged winter months, she reads, crochets, bakes, plays with her grandchildren, and plots her next novel.